INTO
THE
GROOVE

INTO THE GROOVE

A Steady Groove Deed

Lawrence Kelter

For the many who did the time but not the crime.

Inspired By Events Surrounding The
Palm Sunday Massacre

Praise for INTO THE GROOVE and Author Lawrence Kelter

"Lawrence Kelter is an exciting new novelist, who reminds me of an early Robert Ludlum."—Nelson DeMille

"That often smudged line between right and wrong is masterfully explored in this novelization of a true event—the infamous 1984 Palm Sunday Massacre in New York City. A man spent 34 years in prison for the crime, but the question still remains—did he do it? Find out the answer."—Steve Berry

"*Into the Groove* is a time machine to a meaner, dirtier New York City, a city of corruption where some of the worst offenders wear badges. Parole Officer Steady Groove's battle for his own brand of justice is one we want to fight with him."—Joseph Finder, *New York Times* bestselling author of *House on Fire*

"You can tell that Lawrence Kelter knows how to craft a murder mystery with twists and turns. Expect the unexpected."—NPR

"A little bit Shaft, a little bit Easy Rawlins, Steadman 'Steady' Groove is one bad-ass, rad dude. Kelter nails the art of blending fact and fiction in this masterful recreation of Brooklyn, circa 1984. Snappy dialogue straight from the era melds right into this atmospheric, emotionally-charged portrayal of a man living in two very different worlds. This is Kelter at his best."—Lynn Chandler Willis, Award-winning author, SEMWA President

Chapter One

December 5, 1983

Feet flying skyward, panic and memories flooded back in the split-second it took for me to hit the ice—the twenty-foot fall from the masthead and the cry of a deckhand screaming, *"Brace,"* as I turned and grasped the scale of the giant sea swell thundering toward me. Fire sizzled through my back and radiated outward like a hundred fuses ignited by a single flame. And then came the darkness, the cold, soothing shadow sliding over me like the quiet following a storm.

Laying face-up on the frozen sidewalk my vision slowly cleared. Above me, I saw the faces of two concerned gents in the process of kneeling next to me on either side.

"You okay, buddy?"

"Can you stand?"

My pride said, "Yes," even before I was able to assess my condition—while the depth charges were still going off in my back.

Each took hold of an arm and helped me to my feet.

"Are you going to be okay?"

"Should we call someone?"

"Been hurt worse," I said. My eyes squeezed shut, I thanked them and hobbled off, my hurt pride one-upping my aching back. I pulled off my gloves and fished for the amber vial of Vicodin I kept in my coat pocket. Shaking two tabs into my mouth I mashed them between my teeth and swallowed. The fog hit me like that giant wave that had knocked me on my ass, the one that boxed me up like frozen mackerel and shipped me home.

I remember Auntie taking one look at my torn up hands and bought me that pair of gloves that I was quick to put back on. "To keep them warm," she said—"help them heal faster." They were soft and felt good on my skin. The small tag that rubbed against my wrist said that they were made out of something called polar fleece, and the packaging said that they were manufactured from recycled soda bottles. For all I knew I might've downed that bottle of cola my gloves were made from.

That's some cycle of life shit.

Can you dig it?

I put my fingertips to my nose and sniffed for the lingering odor of fish that was always present in my mind, a smell I was always aware of, the odor of the sea that neither lemon juice nor a good soap and hot water scrubbing could get rid of. I could almost visualize the smell wafting right through the fluffy Coke-bottle fabric right into my nostrils. The fish smell was always there, the stink of crab and Rock Sole roe, of perch and mackerel. It was in the pores of my skin and in the wells beneath my fingernails, the stink rising to my nose whenever I let down my guard, reminding me of all the trips I'd made out to sea. I could purge it from my flesh but not from my mind. It was always there, trapped, lurking, reminding, and condemning me for not having done more with my life.

And always would.

I hadn't been to sea in many months, and there was no going back—not back to fishing work anyway. That twenty-foot fall onto the deck after ice had fouled the masthead radar was the final nail in that coffin—it killed my seagoing career dead. I'd suffered many injuries aboard *Mjolnir*, the ship that had been so named because like Thor's hammer, it always returned. None of my previous injuries had been game-changers—none that made me wince with every step. The doctors said the pain would improve with time, with exercise and rest. The rest and exercise helped to a degree but not nearly as much as the Vicodin. It was always in my pocket along with my house keys and wallet—my doctor-prescribed buzz in a bottle.

The smell of the sea embarrassed me, announcing to all who I was and where I'd been. I accepted the fact that the stench of the sea would linger until the day I died and would probably follow me into the hereafter. The hood folk knew me as "Steady" Groove, Steady being short for Stedman—the kid who graduated college and went nowhere, fast or otherwise, the first and only member of the Groove tribe with a real shot at becoming someone and just plain shit the bed.

They were right—I had a shot, and yes, I did blow it. Spin it any way you like, it makes no difference.

Bitter cold winds screamed in my face as I walked the blocks to the Brooklyn County office of the Department of Corrections and Community Supervision, the sky gray, the wind damp and howling as it had been out on the Bering Sea in the winter. For most people, all the day was missing was the salty brine of ocean musk. But me...I had that shit covered.

The gloves came off the moment I hit the elevator. They were soft as sponges—I was able to squeeze them into small balls and stuff them into my already crowded pockets. I hadn't been in a municipal elevator in years, and it reminded me of the cabin I'd slept in on the fishing boat, which had been about three meters by four—just barely large enough for four men with our duffle bags stuffed into a nook within the bed compartment. One of the bulbs in the elevator was out, the interior dark and shadowy. The lighting reminded me of the small bulb that illuminated my berth on *Mjolnir*, and my small living space, my only personal space aboard the ship, which was delineated by a curtain that closed around my bunk.

You never knew who you were going to sail with. Every trip was different. We'd pull into port, offload the catch, and restock with fresh water, fuel, and supplies. Some men, those who hungered for money, went right back out to sea. Many of the rookies, the ones who didn't have enough fire in their bellies to earn their keep, got the axe. Good riddance to them—their laziness meant extra work for everyone else, and God knows there was always more than enough to go around. There were always new men eager to sign up. Some who worked their first trip for free to gain experience and prove they had what it took. It was an apprenticeship of sorts.

There was always a different mix of men, hailing from points all over the world—men from Samoa, Mexico, the Philippines, Nigeria, Ethiopia. There were Muslims, atheists, Buddhists, vets, and ex-cons. We were our own little melting pot. Not a hell of a lot of men from the states, though. Most trips, it was just me and Uncle Barney representing for good old Uncle Sam, the college grad wasting his degree at sea and the tired old con man. Some of the men called him Sockeye because, like his scams, he was fishy, and his eyes bulged when he was tense. He was always running little scams, trying to score extra cash and cigarettes from his shipmates. Some of the mates would turn and walk in the other direction when they saw him coming.

Latinos might've hung out with Latinos and Islanders with Islanders, but no matter where any of them came from, there were traits we all had in common. No one was afraid to say anything straight up, and there was no jawing when it was time for work. Respect was earned with the sweat of one's brow and not with bullshit. I figured maybe that was the reason I'd make a good parole officer (that and because the corrections department just happened to be hiring). I had learned the right reasons for respecting a man and that the overly friendly, touchy-feely kiss-ass types were the ones to avoid. As were the toxic ones, the ones who ate away at you like maggots at flesh. You could smell it on them, the hate they cast off—it stunk worse than the damn fish. Once their hate rubbed off on you, you were doomed because that shit never went away.

The smell was in my nose again. Checking for the smallest discernible scent of fish guts or scales, I put my fingers to my nostrils once more before the elevator arrived at the intended floor. I massaged my hands for warmth and was reminded of all the places where spiny barbs from the dorsal fins of rockfish punctured my thick rubber gloves—my hands continuously weeping blood throughout a twelve-hour shift. Those trips made me wish September would come back around pretty damn quick because that was mackerel season, and catching Atka mackerel was the easiest trip by far. Atka wasn't too big or too small and easy to work with, thanks to their shape. We'd process a hundred tons in less than a week and head back to port in a hurry. We'd fill our pockets with green and have few aches and bruises to show for our trouble. It was as much as any fisherman had the right to expect.

Most often, the work was harder, a hell of a lot harder, and from November through February when the catch was crab…life was downright miserable. You were always cold whether you were on deck swinging an eight hundred pound crab pot or with scalding hot water running down your back in the shower. The chill was in your bones, and there was no way to get rid of it. Some filled their lungs with smoke. Others layered sweaters until they could barely move. Some slept with bricks they'd warmed in the oven. Nothing helped. It was just nasty, putrid cold. Some say that hell rages with fire, but I know different.

I identified myself to the receptionist and was asked to take a seat. Right away, my back stiffened faster than quick-setting concrete. I unbuttoned my coat and checked to make sure that the resume I'd stashed in my breast pocket hadn't gotten creased when I fell. I checked, and it still looked crisp—a damn good thing because I'd worked days on getting it just so. I'd typed it at the unemployment office, where finding a Remington with a decent ribbon was a chore and a half. I'd forgotten to make a Xerox and hoped that Mr. Houck, the hiring manager, wouldn't mark it up and would hand it back to me when he was done.

Just in case, right?

Don't all black men get hired on their first interview?

I reviewed my strong suits, those qualities I'd recount to impress Houck and convince him that I was earnest and hard-working, someone who wanted to do a good job—all the crap candidates are told to say on a job interview.

And *I* needed a job badly.

I'd become a true fisherman, and the extended feel of solid ground beneath my boots meant it was time to forget the sea, to relearn the reasons for living, and forget the ones I'd had for hiding. I worked hard on the water and played even harder when on shore leave. There was a lot of booze, a lot of women, and carousing when we put into port. Time ashore was short, and if you were savvy, you learned how to make the most of it. I'd have to unlearn some of those ways, forget them and move on.

And yeah, I saved a little—too little. Believe it or not, they've got banks in the Aleutian Islands. Like roaches, banks are everywhere.

Money talks, don't it?

A pretty little gal I once met on shore leave worked for one of them, Dutch Harbor Savings and Loan. She convinced me to open a passbook account even though I had practically nothing left by the time I was finished blowing off steam and had to head back to sea. Good thing she did, or I'd have had to drag my aching ass back to the Brooklyn from Cold Bay, Alaska, hitching rides every step of the way.

The pills were wearing off, and it felt as if someone was working on my back with a welding torch. I squirmed in my chair and shook the bottle in my pocket—I was always afraid of shaking it and hearing nothing. And the doc only dispensed thirty Vicodin at a time.

"So, you think you've got what it takes to handle parolees?" Houck asked as he took the envelope from my hand, practically tearing the resume in half extracting it. He was stocky with one of those military haircuts. His sleeves were rolled up, and his forearms were the thickness of steam pipes. He scrutinized the resume while I replied. Looked like he was gleaning what he thought he needed to know about the man sitting in front of him. He never once made eye contact.

"I do, Mr. Houck, sir. Yes, sir, As you can see from my resume, I'm not afraid of hard work, and living on a boat, you get to know men."

He finally looked up, eyes wide. "Not in the biblical sense, I hope."

The man has balls. I give him that. Or he's just plain stupid talking shit to a man of my size. Bad back and all, at six-two, two-forty I could've jumped across the desk and twisted his bull neck until it tore. Instead, I replied with a polite, "No, sir."

"Do me a favor, Groove, call me Harry or Mr. Houck. All this yes, sir-no, sir, coming from a black guy like you…it just rubs me the wrong way. This isn't *The Amos and Andy Show*, and as best I know, slavery was abolished in Lincoln's day. So, stop talking to me like I'm some kind of plantation owner. Can you do that?"

Like I said, *the man has balls.* "Yes, s—" I had to clear my throat just so that I wouldn't say the wrong thing again. "Yes."

"That's better." He went back to the resume. "Graduated CUNY with a major in sociology, I see."

"That's right, Harry, and you were right about Lincoln freeing the slaves."

He shook his head. "Four-year degree in the social sciences, and that's the most impressive thing they taught you?"

"No. I minored in English with a concentration in sarcasm."

"Good…*good,*" he said, his expression hovering between holding back a smile and kicking my ass out the door. "I'd much rather hire ball breakers than bureaucrats. You ever been arrested, Groove? Now be straight with me because we run a background check, and it's thorough."

"Should've been—more than once come to think of it, but no, never." There were times, shit, several, when it was a miracle I didn't get arrested. You see, I've done some shit—shit I'm not proud of, stupid shit, the kind I should've been smart enough to stay clear of. But that's what youth is for, right, to screw up and learn?"

Mistakes.

They can cost you.

Running my mouth—I had a feeling one was about to cost me this job.

"Speaking your mind, huh? Tell you what—I like you, Groove. You earned a degree and you're not afraid to get your hands dirty, which is a hell of a lot more than I can say about some of the Ivy League slackers I interviewed today. Why, some of those entitled bastards can hardly fog a mirror. So tell me, why fishing? Why does a man bust his ass to earn a college degree, then turn around and scoop up guppies?"

"*She-it.*"

"Shit?" His eyes grew large. "What happened to Mr. Polite? Feeling a bit relaxed, are we, Groove?"

"I was hoping you wouldn't ask—about the fishing, that is."

"Isn't that the kind of question that gets asked during a job interview? What makes you tick? What did you expect us to talk about, your fondness for peanut butter and banana sandwiches—whether you prefer tits or ass?"

"No. I'll explain. It's just that…it's a long story."

He rolled his head, then stood unexpectedly. "Ah, screw it. I don't have the time to hear your entire life's story. Follow me, Groove. We'll get your background check started. It'll take ten days or so before it comes back, but as long as the only living thing you've gutted is giant tuna, you're hired."

Chapter Two

It's supposed to get warmer as the day goes on—isn't that the usual way? The weather had an attitude problem and wasn't cooperating. The sun wasn't out to warm things up, and the temperature felt as if it was dropping steadily. And the subway car I rode to get home—damn if it didn't feel like I was sitting inside a refrigerator. It was that dead cold that you felt in your bones more than on your skin like I was a side of beef hanging in a meat locker. I stood up and paced the subway car for warmth until it finally dragged its tired old electromechanical ass into the station.

Back on the street, my Coke-bottle gloves weren't standing up to the dampness and cold. Out at sea we wore thick rubber mitts with a pair of woolen gloves underneath, not trendy recycled soda bottle gloves. Now, those mitts and woolies, they kept you warm and dry—they were close to bulletproof.

On the water, there were only a few ways to get warm when you were frozen to the bone, and that was with a belly full of hooch. There was a bar around the corner from where I lived with my auntie. I knew that stepping inside wasn't a smart idea, but the new job offer kind of made me feel full of myself, and I figured I could handle a snort or two with the old crowd. Besides, my back hurt like a bitch, and I figured a belt would amp up the Vicodin.

Now, our hood wasn't exactly an Armani suit kind of place. East New York was the kind of neighborhood where most did dope and died young. Those who were lucky enough and had enough get-up-and-go to break free didn't come back and were smart enough not to look back. Except for me, that is, dumbass Stedman Groove. I came back into town with a few bucks squirreled away but not real money to speak of—if you know what I mean. And Auntie, she offered me free room and board. I'd lived under her roof since before my moms passed away, since before I left for the Bering Sea. She was my second mom, the one who took over for her sister and made it her business that I turned out okay.

And I know she tried her best.

But options in the hood were few.

Hooch wasn't.

The place I was headed for was the epitome of nondescript. It was called Big John's, but there wasn't any overhead signage, and the name painted on the marquee had long ago weathered away. Between the window and a dusty green curtain that obscured the view of the interior watering hole was a grimy neon cocktail glass that flashed the word Bar. Truth was, the place didn't need a sign. Like all those speakeasies of the prohibition era, people knew where to go if they wanted a drink—you didn't need no damn Rand-McNally to get sloppy. And the alchies, they could smell white lightning on the goddamn breeze.

Big John's was like the McDonald's of watering holes. No such thing as credit, you laid down your cash, or you walked. I dropped a five, and it stuck to the bar like a fly to flypaper. Big John peeled the bill off the counter, stuffed it in his trouser pocket, and spilled two fingers of cheap whiskey into a smudged glass without asking what I liked. "Big" John didn't give a rat's what anyone liked—he was only there for the do-re-mi, and if he opened his mouth, you knew a sales pitch was coming because he didn't waste his breath on idle chatter. He had a sawed-off shotgun mounted behind the bar that made him taller than his natural six foot four. Being a beast of a man, though, most times he could handle an altercation with his massive fists and the slapjack tucked away in his back pocket. He probably clocked in close to three hundred and had a four-inch scar on his cheek as evidence that at least once he done more than just talked the talked.

"You look cold, Bait," he said.

"You know I don't like that name." I found it even more distasteful than the smell I couldn't purge from my mind, but Big John had to bust balls because my college degree was turning brown at the corners while I was out at sea harvesting slimy fish.

"Sorry 'bout that, college boy. Listen, I got three fillies upstairs warm you up quick if the poteen don't do the trick." He had a deep voice to go with his barrel chest. If he could sing, I imagine he'd make Barry White sound like a soprano. "One of them just got here from the African continent—damn Amazonian with a set of big-ass pillows, smother a brother to death. You dig me?"

"I dig you, Big John. Right now, though, I've got that *I-talian* disease."

"Don't worry, the girls got plenty of rubbers. Don't mean shit to my hoes if you got the clap."

"*Ha.* Not that kind of disease. *My-funds-are-low.* It's a joke. You never heard that one before?"

"Sounds like one dumb-ass joke to me." He leaned in closer. "You need a TV? RCA—I'll give you a good price. Still in the box. *Thow* in the rabbit ears—no charge."

"Not today, Big John."

He grimaced and muttered, "Lame-ass fish bait motherfucker." Upsell over, he walked off down the bar trolling for an easier mark.

I nursed the whiskey and basked in the chatter that occupied the smoke-filled bar. Now, there was hardly any light to speak of, so you were never completely sure who was in there with ya. There was always lots of talk going on about stuff like folks getting sent away, lazy-ass men who'd rather suck on a crack pipe than take care of their families, women turned to street hoes to support their babies, the po-po rousting innocent folks, and the like. It was standard ghetto chatter, but every once in a while, something special would catch the ear, like good news about a brother or sista done well. My name used to come up in some of those discussions. Don't imagine my name was coming up anymore. I imagine few knew how I turned out, being I was away at sea and all—all those years. They must've figured I just fell off their face of the earth. I was staring at the bottom of an empty glass when someone gave me the shoulder, you know what that is, a friendly arm laid across the back—usually a prelude to being hit up for a twenty spot.

"Steady, *m'man*. Y'all back from the dead? I ain't seen you in a *dog's* age."

I looked over my shoulder into the buttery yellow eyes of D. Wayne Tyrone, then glanced at his arm, which was still resting on my shoulder. He lifted it right quick.

"My man, when'd you get back in the hood?"

"Not that long. Been staying with my auntie like before."

D. Wayne motioned for Big John to pour me another round. "On me, old friend. It's good to see you, Steady. You grow tired of swashbuckling on the high seas?"

"Something like that."

"Too much briny air and boats filled with hairy-ass sailors?"

"Like I said, something like that. Messed up my back—can't do that kind of work anymore."

"*What*, I gotta pull teeth? Why you so tight-mouthed around your old friend, D. Wayne?"

D. Wayne was a schemer, an opportunist, and a con, but looking back, yeah, I guess he'd been some kind of a friend. We were poor kids living in a poor neighborhood, so we ran hustles together back in the day. There was little choice but to do that kind of thing. The good Lord didn't give us ghetto kids too many routes to take. Down the road, though, some of our partnerships had gotten nasty—severe-consequence nasty. One of them went *real* bad, and D. Wayne, he manned up for me. He took the heat if you know what I'm saying—kept me from slammer time. I owed him that for sure.

"How long do you expect me to look over my shoulder at that nasty face of yours? Hop your ass up on the barstool and talk to me man to man."

"That's more like it," he said. He was the runt of the Tyrone litter and had to hoist a leg up high just to get up on the padded stool. We weren't exactly eye-to-eye, me being so much taller than him, but the new angle was a hell of a lot easier on my neck.

"Your new usual?" Big John asked. D. Wayne nodded, and the big man screwed the top off a bottle of rum, dropped two cubes into a tumbler, and filled it to the rim.

"Doc says I'm gonna lose my liver if'n I don't cut back on the hooch, but I figure I ain't gonna live a hundred years no how—might as well enjoy myself. Am I right?"

"I sort of thought that might be coming. You and the booze, you go back, don'tcha?" His face told a story of drug and alcohol abuse, of needles and hittin' the glass. He may have been drinking pirate juice, but his pumping leg and twitching arms said there was a hell of a lot more going on. That poor, miserable liver of his—must've been on its last leg. "The doc gave you good advice. You'd do wise to listen to the man."

"Told me I had to stay off everything, Steady. Doc says my liver is severely *compromised,* and it could take years for it to bounce back. You think I got that kind of time?"

"How 'bout could kick *all* of your habits—shock the ever-loving shit out of everyone."

"Ha! No one will see that coming, I bet. But I ain't exactly Mr. Willpower, you know? And my girl, Vonda, she likes to get high and ride that baloney pony—that some powerful persuasion, Steady, hard as hell to say no to." He picked up the cold tumbler of rum and slugged it down like it was Lipton's Iced Tea. "My hairy yellow eyeballs bothering you? I got some shades I can put on."

"Don't bother me at all. After all, I've been staring at nothing but beady little fish eyes the last three years."

"Good to hear it." He drained the glass and smacked his lips. "Say, Steady, how you fixed? You looking to score some skrilla? I can hook you up, you know—low risk. Me and you—like the old times."

"Thanks, but no, man. I got my eye on some *aboveboard* work. Went on an interview this morning. Looks real promising."

"For real? What kind of job you chasing?"

"Planning on becoming a parole officer."

"A parole officer? *What?* You gonna be a po-po? Is that the best you can do with your fancy-ass *four-year* college degree? What you want to do that for—playing nursemaid to nasty-ass ex-cons and dirty old crack hoes? I figured you for some executive kind of work, you know, running some big-ass business…maybe become one of them mogul entrepreneurs."

"I figure being a PO ain't so bad. Civil servant work, you know? I can do twenty, bang out, and collect a pension until I'm looking at the grass from the bottom up. After all those years crabbing out at sea, I figure I can do a parole officer's twenty standing on my head. What do I have to do besides making sure a bunch of ex-cons keep their noses clean? I've got to pass a Civil Service exam and complete an eight-week training course, but I had enough on the ball to earn a college degree…The boss man says I'm as good as hired as long as I pass a background check."

"Well look at y'all. I'm impressed." He put the glass to his lips, but it was empty. "Smart-ass college boy like yourself, you got all your ducks in a row now, don'tcha? Still, if you find you're running thin between po-po paychecks, you give your old friend D. Wayne a call. This homeboy got some big old plans of his own."

"I've got a clean sheet, thanks to you. I'll never forget that, brother." I put out my fist, and he bumped it with his own.

"Made more sense that way—you was the college student and me…*she-it*, if I dropped out in kindergarten, it wouldn't have been too soon."

"But prison is prison."

He waved his hand dismissively. "Easy peasy. Met some cool brothers on the inside and learned a thing or two along the way. I did my time in the big house while you were doing your thang at sea. Not sure which of us got the short end of the stick—least my back ain't broke like yours. Anyway, you better pray they don't make you *my* po-po. I'll drive your black ass crazy."

Now, I thought, *what are the chances of that?*

Damn.

Chapter Three

Four Months Later

That background check took a hell of a lot longer than Mr. Houck said it was supposed to and that eight-week training course…well, they don't just start up a class because Stedman Groove is ready to move ahead with his life. The days ticked by, a lot of days. Let's just say I'm not wearing the gloves Auntie gave me anymore—although to tell you the truth, I'm not exactly sure where they're at. Back on the ship, all your gear had to fit into one little cubby, so nothing was hard to find. There were too many possibilities at Auntie's place. I had to learn to manage my stuff better, or I'd never be able to find anything.

She'd given me back the room I used to sleep in before I went away. It was going on five years. I used to share the room with my moms. All of her stuff had long been cleaned out, but on warm days I imagined I could smell her perfume in the air. She used to wear a five-and-dime store perfume from Woolworths, and it must've been absorbed by the paint. It distracted me from the fish smell that resided in the space between my eyes, embedded at the very top of the nasal bridge where it couldn't be removed.

I missed my moms. She was no less with me now than when she was alive—working all those hours to help put me through school and paying her end of the apartment expense. My father, he didn't hold up his end of the marriage contract. For better or for worse meant better for him, worse for my moms. He was lazy and selfish. He made no impression on me I cared to remember.

What I knew for sure was that my gun and badge were on the top shelf of the closet in a locked box. Not that I was afraid of Auntie accidentally blowing her head off, but God forbid someone broke in and used it on her—I'd never be able to forgive myself.

Auntie's apartment wasn't big, two bedrooms, a single bath, a living room, a dining room, and a small kitchen. But the aromas that came out of that piddling galley kitchen were out of this world. Being the apartment was so small, I began to salivate every time I opened my bedroom door. Close as I could figure, I was like one of Pavlov's dogs.

Now, Auntie, she had a past. My moms said Auntie had been a chanteuse, a jazz crooner with a velvety voice. And with her looks, she had more beaus than she could shake a stick at—or so the stories went. But she didn't have eyes for any of those flashy suitors, those slick brothers in their peak lapel suits and baggy pants. She ended up marrying the nightclub landlord, a Jewish man named Meyer Cohen, who always misbuttoned his shirt and had gravy stains on his collar after finishing a meal. They were together almost twenty years before the mob punched Meyer's ticket for skimming off the top, bottom, and middle. Turned out that old Meyer had sticky fingers, and when I say sticky, I mean epoxy—like a metal-to-metal weld.

Auntie could cook any number of delicacies, both southern and Eastern European. Until I sat down at the table, I never knew if she had prepared ham hocks or chopped liver. But like Pavlov's mutt, I never complained. She had a little Swiss dinner bell and whenever she rang it…

Auntie was pushing sixty-five, but she hadn't put on weight like most of the women her age, and she moved around like a younger person, her back straight, her gait fluid. Despite how good her cooking was, she didn't have much of an appetite. She'd take a few bites of this and a couple of that and was done. She liked her wine, though, and we always had gallons of jug wine handy at dinnertime.

"You excited about starting the new job?" she asked as she placed a mound of sliced brisket on the table. Now, brisket can be Jewish or southern, and it wasn't until she brought out the sides that I knew which she was aiming for.

That night it was hush puppies, yams, and okra, enough for a family of six.

"More nervous than excited, Auntie." I was overwhelmed by the feast she'd just placed in front of me and answered without looking up. "Who's going to eat all of this?"

"You are, Steady—and I'll give you brisket on a Kaiser roll to take for your lunch tomorrow. Don't stand on ceremony, hon—dig in."

Auntie didn't say grace, didn't believe in it. And she'd stopped going to church after burying Meyer. She fished a gallon of red wine from under the dining room table and poured a full glass for both of us. Now, most women her age wouldn't have been able to handle that big jug, but she maneuvered it with ease. We toasted, and she began to drink up. My plate was full and hers, completely empty.

"That reminds me—" I reached for my wallet, but she shut me down before I could get it out of my pocket.

"Now what have I told you, Steady. You save your money for now. Between social security and my little off-the-books job, I take home more than I can spend. A fine, eligible employed man like you is going to meet a nice girl one day, and when you do…you'll need all you can save to start a family. Besides, you already paid for the wine." She flashed a smile and took a big gulp.

"I don't like being a leech, Auntie. You've got to let me contribute every once in a while."

"Honey, your company is payment enough. I was going nuts in this empty apartment." She finally placed a slice of brisket on her plate along with a spoonful of okra and a solitary hush puppy. "I like watching you eat—does my heart good to see you enjoy the food I make." She rotated the wine bottle until she could read the label. "Carlo Rossi Paisano Red—you figure this here's Italian wine?"

"You'd think so, but it says, 'Product of California' on the label."

"Maybe they brought those grapevines over from Italy. You think? I tell you what, though, sure is delicious."

The dining room wallpaper was white with a gold-flocked pattern on it. Far back as I can remember, it had always been that way. I figure it reminded her of the times she'd had with her late husband and didn't want to put an end to her memories. She had one of those menorahs in the closet, and she lit the candles every year just before Christmas time. She picked up that hush puppy and nibbled on it with the glass of wine in her other hand. "You heard from your Uncle Barney lately? He still out on the ship?"

"No, I haven't heard from him, but I reckon he's still out to sea. That's where I'd be if I didn't take that fall. Even if he's planning on hanging it up, I'm sure he'll sign on through the fall. That's mackerel season—easy money and Unc, he sure likes that easy money. You know what they called him on the boat, don'tcha?"

"Uh-uh."

"Sockeye."

"Sockeye? Why, do they think he looks like a fish?"

"Maybe he smells like one."

"Oh, gracious. Really?"

"No, I'm just kidding, but he sure does just love 'em? When they're running, he can eat an entire fish in one sitting."

"Sounds like a lot of fish to me. I love fish too, but that much…? I think I'd hurl."

"The small ones run five pounds on the hook—probably two feet tip-to-tail."

I dug in for seconds and told her that the nickname came more from the way his eyes bulged when he was on the wrong end of a poker hand than from his hearty appetite. It didn't surprise her one little bit. After all, she knew the man way better than I did.

"But he eats the whole dang thing?"

"All the eating parts."

She laughed so hard she had to cover her mouth to keep from losing that bullet-sized hushpuppy. "I do love having you here, Steady. Things just ain't been the same since my baby sister passed on. And to watch you eat…" She smiled with such deep satisfaction that I got choked up.

"You keep cooking like this, and you'll have to watch me eat myself into a pair of stretch pants, Auntie. Your cooking is way too good."

"Eat up. You're going to need all your strength for your first official day on the job tomorrow. Besides, Steady, you don't have an ounce of fat on you."

"Yeah, but I'm not tossing around crab pots anymore. All this fine food is bound to take a toll."

Her glass was empty. "You think it's all right if I help myself to a little more of this delicious Italian wine?"

"Not until you eat what's on your plate."

"Now listen here—who's the senior and who's the junior in this household? I suppose next you're gonna tell me no dessert until I eat all of my vegetables."

"You *could* use a little meat on your bones, Auntie."

"Praise Jesus, I have never had a problem with my weight." She toasted herself and took another long sip. "Say, I ever tell you about the time that Uncle…Sockeye." She snorted. "My word, thinking about it, that name does fit him to a tee. He does have a fishy look about him with those thick lips of his and those bulging eyes. If I didn't know better, I'd think the man might have a thyroid condition." She laughed. "God help me, that was a mean thing to say."

"What were you going to tell me—about Unc, that is?"

"One time, back in the day, that senseless uncle of yours tried to sell brownies outside one of George Clinton's Funkadelic concerts."

"Brownies?"

"Don't be so naïve, Steady. Marijuana brownies. And he sold out, every last one of 'em. Only problem was he didn't have the money to buy the chronic to bake into the brownies, so he used McCormick's parsley seasoning, jars and jars of parsley seasoning—gave half the audience the galloping trots."

"*What*? No, he didn't."

"The fool sure did. People running from the building like there was a four-alarm fire. Folks got so mad, I thought they were going to murder the chump. Not the first of his foolhardy cons that went sideways. If I had a dollar for every bad idea that man has had…"

The doorbell rang.

"Now, who could that be?" she asked. "Can't be the landlord—rent's not due for another week."

I wiped my mouth and pointed to her food. "I'll get it, Auntie. You eat what's on your plate."

"Yes, *daddy*. I'll be a good little girl."

The doorbell rang again before I could reach the door. "Hold your horses, would ya?" I flipped the deadbolt and yanked the door open. "Well, I'll be damned."

"Who is it?" she hollered.

I didn't know how to break the news to her, and it took me a moment to hunt for the words. "It's someone selling parsley brownies door-to-door. What do you think, Auntie—should I let the fool in?"

Chapter Four

"Would you believe the luck—I done developed a doggone fish allergy." Sockeye wasted no time filling his glass with that California Italian wine Auntie was enjoying so much.

"That doesn't make any sense at all. After all the fish I've seen you eat?"

"It's not the fish *I* eat, Steady. It's the tiny fish the bigger fish eat, small fry, krill, and krill is everywhere."

"What's krill?" Auntie asked. "Ain't never seem it in the supermarket."

"Tiny little things," Sockeye began as he delineated the tip of his thumbnail, "About yea big. Almost everything in the sea eats 'em, all the way from salmon to big-ass whales."

"How'd they find out?" I asked.

"How'd they find out? I'll tell ya how they found out—I done stopped breathing and right in the middle of pulling up full crab pots, too. I just fell down dead on the deck. They had to carry me below to the infirmary. Took jabs from two EpiPens and a tank of oxygen before I started breathing half-right—scared the ever-loving shit out of this negro."

"Just like that, huh?"

"Air rescue had to chopper my ass to the mainland. The doc over there said they been seeing cases here and there—some kind of mutation in the species, he said."

"A mutation?"

Sockeye had already drained his glass. He hoisted a now significantly lighter jug and refilled it. "That's what the man said. Told me not to eat fish no more. Now I ask you, how in the hell do you work on a fishing boat if you can't eat no damn fish?" His eyes bulged, and I couldn't help but laugh on the inside.

Auntie placed her hand on his. "Worse things than not being able to eat fish, Barney. You're not allergic to good downhome brisket and sides, are you?"

He smiled robustly. "Sure as hell not, my dear. I've got to nurse myself back to health, now don't I, Carrie Mae?"

"You sure do. I'll get you a plate."

There was something in Auntie's manner that just wasn't right. She was a kind and giving person, and especially with family…but there was something insincere about the way she spoke to Barney, condescending or something. I'm not sure if she was aware of the way she was acting, but it was there, plain as day as far as I was concerned.

Barney watched her walk toward the kitchen. "Ain't nothing in the world like a beautiful woman, Steady. My big sister, she takes the cake—pretty on the inside and out. Still got a flat little belly like when she was a young girl. I'm surprised she never picked up with someone after the Italian boys put the smackdown on old Meyer Cohen."

"She took that pretty hard—walked around like she was half-dead for a long time."

"Still, we all got needs, am I right?"

"You're right, she has been lonely. She says it all the time. I don't think she's looking for that. She had my moms and me for company until…" A lump formed in my throat as I remembered those evenings with the three of us sitting around the table. "Now I'm here. I guess that's enough for her."

"Think she'll let me sleep on the couch tonight? I hit town and came straight here."

"*You* ain't got anywhere else to go?"

"Brooklyn-Queens Expressway if'n I'm lucky enough to find an empty refrigerator box—the fishing company's insurance paid for most of my hospital stay but not all of it and with getting back home…done just about wiped out all I have."

"I can lend you a little. I'm starting a new job in the morning."

"Say what? Look at you, young nephew. Doing what?"

"I just finished my training—I'm officially a parole officer."

"Well look at y'all," he said, beaming. "Wasted no time getting back on your feet. How's your messed up back, by the way?"

"Good days and bad. I got a scrip for Vicodin for when it hurts. It's warm now, so I can live with it mostly. Come February, though— the damn thing hurts like a bastard."

"Ain't nothing they can do for it?"

"Only a big complicated surgery. They've got to fuse the vertebrae. At best, I'd be six months on my ass—at worst, a cripple. I'll take my chances with the Vicodin."

Auntie came back with a dinner plate and utensils. She eyed the mostly empty jug of wine. "I'm guessing you won't be needing a water glass," she said and set the plate down in front of him. "Fill your belly, Barney. Eat up."

"Don't mind if I do." He went to work straight away. "Sure is good to see you, Carrie Mae." He sliced into the brisket and stuffed it in his mouth, his cheekbones rising. "Now, that's what I'm talking about. Beef. You know how long it's been since I've had me some meat like this? *Yum-yum*—I can eat a whole damn platter of this meat."

"Does the heart good," Auntie said.

"Actually…Unc was kind of hoping you'd let him stay on the couch tonight."

"Of course. Where are my manners? The couch is yours, Barney—I'll fix it up nice and comfy."

Absence might make the heart grow fonder, but it definitely made Auntie's memory fade. She must've plain forgot how much trouble her brother had always been. He was always cheating, and borrowing, then lying to cover it up. As I sat and watched him wolf down her brisket, another memory rose up. The more time I gave it to develop, the more it surprised me that she'd extend him even the smallest courtesy. Because the last time she saw him, he'd done something far worse than skipping out on some little old debts.

Chapter Five

Four Years Earlier

Barney Booker stood only five-foot-eight, but he was feeling a might taller with a Smith & Wesson secure in his pocket. It didn't matter that the cylinders were empty—It was a prop and was only there for show. All he needed to complete his preparations was a ski mask, and he knew just where to get one.

He cussed when he saw that the elevator was out but had significant spring in his step as he attacked the eleven floors of stairs to Curtis Matthew's apartment.

The apartment building stairwell was filled with graffiti painted over the cinderblock foundation. An elaborate mural on the eighth floor depicted Mayor Ed Irving getting nailed from behind by a brother smoking a joint. He paused for a moment to admire the artist's handiwork before pressing on. Crystal meth still pumping through his veins, he hit the exit door with both hands extended and breezed into the hallway.

Hammering on the door with the side of his fist he created enough clamor to draw the stink eye from a neighbor who had just come out into the hallway before Matthews could answer the door.

"What you looking at?" Barney asked, narrowing his eyes at the neighbor. "Brother got to take a wicked shit."

"You don't live here, and the elevator's out," the neighbor said. "You mean to tell me you ran up eleven flights of stairs to drop a load? Use the toilet, my ass." The man turned around and went back into his apartment.

Barney returned to knocking on the door. "Curtis, you slow-moving motherfucker, open the damn door." A few moments passed before he heard the deadbolt turn. "About damn time." He pushed past him without being invited in.

"Don't stand on ceremony or nothing—make yourself at home." Curtis secured the door while Barney breezed through the apartment into the kitchen and sat down at the kitchen table, a small soda fountain-style table with chrome sides and a Formica top. A cigarette smoldered in an ashtray that had the red Miller High Life emblem printed on the bottom. A metal can of beans sat cooking atop a gas burner on the cooktop. Nearby was the paper label that had been torn from the can. I read Bush's Best Southern Style White Beans.

"Smells good," Barney said.

Curtis moseyed into the kitchen. "If I knew you were coming, I'd have ordered lobster for two. What the hell you doing barging into my place like you're first kin?"

"Didn't come for the food," Barney said. "I come for your mask."

"The hell you talking about? It ain't Halloween."

"I don't want a damn Halloween mask. You got a ski mask, don't you? I know I seen you wear one."

"What? In *June*?" A few seconds ticked by before Curtis put two and two together. "Tell me you're not going to rip off a damn convenience store? Last time you tried, you left with a load of buckshot in your hind parts. You're lucky that Hindu store owner didn't have a 12-gauge slug in the chamber, or he would've paralyzed your lame ass, permanent."

"Just get the damn mask. I'm not gonna hit no convenience store." He pulled the Smith & Wesson out of his pocket and laid it on the kitchen table. "Gonna take charge this time—leave nothing to chance."

Curtis picked up the gun and released the cylinder. Holding the gun to the light, he spun the dial. "Just what I thought—no bullets. Ha. Okay, man, I'll get you the mask. Just don't bring it back. I don't care what you do with it, just make sure I never see it again." He walked to the stove, fanned the aroma toward his nose, and killed the flame under the can of beans.

Curtis' equivalency schoolbooks were on the table. Barney grabbed a stub pencil and wrote on a slip of paper he found at arm's distance: *All your cash or die!* He stuffed the note into his pocket along with the gun, then turned in his chair, eager to get his hands on the mask.

* * *

Barney spent fifteen minutes leaning against one of those hideous square Volvos doing his best to look inconspicuous. The storefront he was watching was made of glass and aluminum with a store-wide overhead housing for a pull-down security gate with the ad Checks Cashed in yellow paint against a green background.

It was Wednesday, and as far as Barney could figure, no one got paid on a Wednesday—traffic was supposed to be light.

"Why all these people cashing checks?" he muttered. A silver-haired man came out of the store and untied his dog from a street sign where it had been leashed. A moment later, an elderly couple provided the spark that allowed him to put it all together. "Damn Social Security checks must've come in the mail." The aged couple was in the store for quite a while. A second couple followed right behind them, then another. It was a full hour before the store was empty of customers.

He pulled the jet-black balaclava out of his pocket and pulled it over his head. Only his eyes were visible through the two round cutouts. Gun in hand, he charged into the store, pointed the gun at the female clerk behind the counter, and slapped his handwritten note down in front of her.

"*Got the message?*" he said and slapped the counter with his gun. "Make it quick."

She began to shake but quickly began to pull bills out of her drawer and handed them over.

He stuffed the bills into his jacket pockets, then fled at the sound of a chambering pump shotgun coming from the back room. He ran down the block and around the corner, putting distance between him and the robbery.

He yanked off the mask and discarded it along the way, not slowing to a normal pace until he was a full three avenue blocks away, just in advance of a pair of police cruisers whizzing past him in the opposite direction.

Ducking into a local bar for a cold one, he had planned to stay a short time, but it was almost two hours before he made it home. He was approaching his tenement building when Carrie Mae grabbed him by the arm and pulled him into the tunnel that led to the rear courtyard.

"Barney Booker, where the hell have you been?"

He was sloppy drunk and didn't pick up on her furious mood. Or perhaps he was simply too drunk to react appropriately. "None of your damn business."

"I damn well hope you weren't at the check cashing store on New Lots and Penn with a mask and a gun."

His temples began to throb, and his vision blurred.

"Barney, you dense son of a bitch, look me in the eye and tell me you didn't just stick up that store."

He rubbed his temples. "Why, the police been here?"

"No, you damn fool. Worse, a lot worse."

"The hell you mean, worse?"

"You wrote the damn stickup note on the back of Curtis' paystub. The police arrested him. His brother, Antonio, was here with his boys. You know Antonio, the ex-con with a scarred-up back that looks like a map of the Jersey Turnpike. That man is going to kill your ass dead, and I ain't fooling. You better get the hell out of town, pronto."

He came off the meth high at just the wrong time. Between the meth and the beer, he was unable to string two lucid thoughts together. A tear ran down his cheek. "Where I gonna go, little sis?"

"I've been thinking about it since the moment Antonio left, and I've only come up with one idea. Your nephew, Steady, is flying out for the west coast tonight. You heard he intends to sign on a fishing boat, right?"

Barney nodded with uncertainty, and she thumped in the forehead with the heel of her hand. "You better clear your head, fool. How much money you get?"

He reached into his pockets and showed her the handfuls of crumpled cash.

"Looks like plenty."

"What you mean, plenty?"

"You get in a cab to the airport and find Steady. He's taking American Airlines to Washington state, then a connecting flight to Anchorage." She handed him a scrap of paper. This here is his itinerary. You pedal my nephew some mumbo-jumbo about always wanting to be a fisherman and pray he don't see through your lame-ass bullshit."

"I'm going to what?"

"You get on that plane and don't look back. Don't let Antonio find you, hear me?"

He nodded, looking ashamed and confused.

"You understand what I'm telling you, right?"

He nodded again.

She gave him a hug, then walked off. "Damn fool," she muttered. "Still is and always been."

Chapter Six

Auntie told me I looked sharp in the suit I had picked out for my first official day as a parole officer. There was a two-for-one sale at Syms—I got a navy and a gray, ties, loafers, and some white button-downs. I'd gotten a haircut, and a hot towel shave on Sunday morning and was still feeling neat.

I wasn't feeling the pain in my back when I came off the elevator for my first day of work, fifteen minutes early. In my mind, if a man wasn't early, he was late, and I wasn't going to be late on my first damn day.

The receptionist was the same woman I'd met the day of my interview. It seemed as if she was expecting me and greeted me with a warm smile. I figured it was her way of welcoming all the recruits. Her name had stuck like glue, Sandra, Sandra McQueen. She was tall and athletic, with light brown hair she wore in a ponytail. When she came out from behind the desk I noticed she was wearing the same plaid skirt she wore the first time we'd met. I didn't think of it in terms of her not having money for more of a wardrobe. It was more like a *hot damn, Sandra looks fine in that skirt*. I was guarded and didn't allow her to catch me staring at her figure.

"I have a few forms for you to sign, Mr. Grove. That's a great name, by the way, Groove. It's so hip, so...*now*."

"My daddy changed the family name after he married my moms. Used to be Graves, but my moms wouldn't have it. 'I didn't want to go through life with a name like Graves? It's like saying death,' she used to tell me. Her name was Kitty. Can you imagine folks calling you Kitty Graves? Sounds like a character from that new Stephen King book."

"Which one is that?"

"*Pet Sematary.*"

That seemed to have rubbed her the right way, and I got a look at her pretty smile.

"My daddy liked playing vinyl so much he changed our family name to Groove. If nothing else, I'm indebted to him for that. Steady Graves—that *really* blows."

"I guess there's a story there. Maybe you'll tell me one day."

"Yeah," The notion made me smile on the inside, "maybe I will."

"Come with me, Mr. Groove. I'll show you which office is yours."

Damn! I got an office? No shit. "You can call me Steady if you want to. All my friends do."

"Steady…" She seemed to let that roll around in her head. "I like that. Okay, Steady. And you can call me Sandy."

"Because all your friends do?"

"No, *everyone* does—except my mother. She prefers Sandra. She named me for Sandra Dee, her favorite movie star. I guess she likes the way the name Sandra sounds."

Maybe Sandy was strapped for cash because that plaid skirt was tight in all the right places, like maybe she'd worn it for her sweet sixteen and had grown out of it. Following along, though, I wasn't complaining.

My new office didn't do much for the eye, just a metal-sided desk, some battered filing cabinets, and scruffy-looking chairs. It had a double window, though, with a nice view of the Brooklyn Bridge.

"Some of the more senior guys wanted your office when Mr. Kennedy retired because of the double window, but Mr. Houck wouldn't have it. He doesn't play favorites like that. When they asked him, he said *and* I quote, 'Sit your asses back down and go back to work.'" She laughed. "Good old Mr. Houck—he has his moments."

"I like any white man who offers a black man a job." I walked around to the business side of the desk and sat down. That worn-out old chair accommodated my posterior like custom-made orthopedic shoes fit tired old feet. There was a painting of tall ships on the wall in front of me. I guess the sea was coming with me wherever I went. I'd never get the smell of the ocean out of my head.

Sandy flipped open a folder and handed me a pen. "Can you sign these for me, Steady? Mr. Houck will want all this paperwork out of the way before he gets in." She covered her mouth. "He hates paperwork. Remember that if you want to stay on his good side—hand him everything ready for signature. He sees you've left blank spaces, and you're dead meat."

"Does he got arthritis or something?"

She shrugged. "He just hates it, is all."

"I'll make a note of that."

I had just finished signing the forms Sandy needed when Houck bristled down the corridor, newspaper under his arm, briefcase in hand, and a brown paper bag clenched in his teeth. At first, I thought he hadn't noticed me or that I didn't rate saying good morning to, but I was wrong. He must've doubled back because he stuck his head in the door and pulled the brown paper bag from his mouth. "Morning, Sandy. You have Mr. Groove all settled in?"

"Yes, Mr. Houck. We just finished the induction paperwork."

"Great. Steady, with me," he said. "I'll show you where the coffee lives. You're a coffee drinker, aren't you?"

"Yes sir, I sure—"

"Hey, what I tell you about calling me sir?"

I don't know if it showed, but I could feel a smile warm my face. "I'd love some coffee, Harry."

"Good. No money in the budget for teabags. Come to think of it, there's no money in the budget for anything except number two pencils and toilet paper. We walk low bridge here, Steady, but the paychecks come regular, and I'm good with that. How about you?"

"I am."

He took off, and Sandy gestured for me to follow him. "He's a force of nature, Steady. Better hurry and catch up."

"Why, he doesn't like to be kept waiting either?"

"Almost as much as he hates paperwork." Her eyes grew large, and I flew out of the office.

There was no sign of him when I hit the corridor, so I headed toward his office just as he blew out, his hands now unencumbered.

"You like Maxwell House?"

"Sure."

"Me too. Too bad we don't have any."

He dropped his newspaper on the counter. The headline in the Post read They Don't Care with a photo of the Reverend Malcolm Pointer addressing a mob. I'd no idea where the man had come from. He seemed to have materialized out of thin air, a community activist inciting the locals to outrage over NYPD's lack of progress on the Palm Sunday Massacre, the mass murder of eleven women and children. To date, the police had no solid leads.

"This Pointer guy—he's a bad penny," Houck said. "Do you honestly believe the police don't want to find the doer of eleven women and little kids? One of the victims was with child. Everyone's screaming for the mayor's head. And if you ask me, that good for nothing police commissioner, Ben Canton is about to get his worthless ass booted out the door. Trust me, NYPD is looking long and hard for these perps. What I want to know is why? Eleven dead women and kids…for what? Meanwhile, this blowhard, Pointer, has everyone up in arms, ranting and raving like a lunatic about police apathy and racial injustice. He's the last thing this city needs. Got any thoughts on this fraud?"

"Where'd Pointer come from? I never heard a thing about him before last week."

"Crawled out from under a rock if you ask me. You'll see things the way I do someday, Steady, and I pity you when you do because I'm as cynical s they come. These people, like Pointer, they're all just lying low until they sense the opportunity, then they grab a pulpit and start hollering at the top of their lungs. Problem is, dumb-ass people listen to them."

It appeared there was some dark sludge simmering in the coffee pot.

"See this? You don't want to drink this. It'll eat a hole in your gut inside of six months."

He poured it in the sink. "I'll show you how it's done." He rinsed the pot, then filled it from the tap and poured it into the coffee machine. He threw out the old coffee filter and replaced it with a clean one before yanking a vacuum-sealed bag out of a cardboard case. The name stenciled on the bag read: Apollo Brothers – Finest Ground Coffee. He tore the bag open and poured it in.

"This stuff tastes like it's been recycled, but the first half of the pot won't rot your teeth."

He flipped the switch, and the machine began to brew. I heard small amounts of water sizzling.

"That's it." He tapped his watch. "Make sure you're back in ten minutes because if someone hits the coffee pot before you get back, you're shit out of luck. And what does that mean?"

"I'll be peeing out my asshole inside of six months' time."

"Good, I see you're a listener. Come with me."

I should've bought a pair of sneakers instead of the loafers because Mr. Houck, he sprinted like Jesse Owens. He was in his chair and already behind his desk by the time I was through the door. He tossed a file across his desk to me.

"I'm starting you off with a slow roller, Steady. Take that file, get up to speed, and have the parolee in for a scheduled visit. Get a feel for the work, and I'll assign you another couple of files tomorrow. If all goes to plan, you'll be carrying a full load by the end of the week. We solid?"

"Solid as a rock, Harry."

"You're going to work out fine, Steady." He looked at his watch. "T-minus seven minutes. Don't forget the coffee."

"I'll bring you a cup."

"Don't be a kiss-ass. Now get out of here and do me proud."

I saluted him and left. I don't know why I did that. I guess there was just something about the man that drew my respect. It was as good a salutation as any, I guess.

The truth be told, I forgot all about the coffee when an intense spasm in my back flared up and traveled down to my ass. It felt as if the circus strong man had brought a sledgehammer down on one of those ring the bell, high striker games they have at all the fairs and carnivals.

The name on file Houck had handed me read Tyrone, Dennis Wayne.

Chapter Seven

I read D. Wayne's file from end to end. It was a big fat folder, pages and pages of records and, a rap sheet that read like Who's Who of ghetto elite. I read some of it twice. He'd done a lot of shit I never knew about and was kind of glad I hadn't. Still, you can only spend so much time rehashing the same material before the boss realizes you're just killing time.

It was coming up on eleven when Houck walked by again. I'd seen him flash by at least three times since I left his office. The man was a blur—it almost seemed as if his feet never touched the ground. And on the last pass, he gave me a stink-wise glance that said, "Get on it, rookie."

I tried D. Wayne at the phone number listed in the file—three attempts—no answering machine, nothing. Now, D might've been anywhere, doing anything. He hadn't missed a previous check-in so he had the right to be unavailable for an impromptu phone call but knowing him as I did… smart money said he was doing dirty, drugs, money, what have you. How'd I know? Because, knowing the man as I did, I knew how he passed the time, and it wasn't in bible study.

Sandy walked by, her ponytail swinging back and forth. She must've sized me up because she walked in, gripping a stack of heavy folders in her arms, folders I'm sure she wanted to dump on her desk. She looked back to make sure no one was around. "It's a test," she whispered. "He gives everyone just one file on their first day. He wants to see if you've got initiative. He calls it 'moxie.'"

"What do you mean?"

"How often do you think parolees answer the phone? If you get lucky, a family member or a paramour will pick up, but if they live alone..."

"They didn't say anything about that in training."

"Well, what did they say?"

"A lot of stuff about statutes, laws, and procedures—code of conduct and such." I picked up my training manual. "The stuff in this telephone book."

"For eight weeks?"

Eight *long* weeks—five days a week—eight hours a day." I cocked a pretend gun and fired a round at my temple. "It's a good thing they didn't issue the guns until the very end."

She checked the corridor again before continuing. "Houck wants to see if you'll sit on your ass until five o'clock or if you've got the gumption to go out and pay your parolee a visit."

"Do most pass?"

"It's about fifty-fifty, but if you're out of here in the next few minutes, it'll be the earliest anyone's ever taken it upon themselves to leave the office. *Or,* you can sit there with a thumb up your ass until you're ready to eat your newly issued sidearm." She raised her eyebrows. "What's it gonna be, Mr. Groove?"

* * *

Until I read his name on the folder, I'd completely forgotten that D. Wayne's real name was Dennis, a name he just outright hated. As mentioned, my street thug friend was the runt of the Tyrone brood, and he used to get his ass kicked regular—not only by street hooligans but by his bigger brothers as well. The man was a virtual punching bag. He disappeared one summer, and when he returned, he had sprouted a couple of inches and began strutting street style. He announced to the world that he was now D. Wayne. That and a quick move with a switchblade curtailed his ass-kickings significantly. It was as if he went away a caterpillar and emerged a butterfly or, in his case, a skuzzy old moth, the kind that chews holes in your sweaters and leaves nasty old powder from its wings on everything it touches. Most folks are grossed out by caterpillars. But a moth, even a scuzzy moth like D. Wayne can take to the air, and flying gave that man some much-needed confidence.

Now, a group of butterflies is called a kaleidoscope. Ain't that rich, a kaleidoscope? The name brings to mind images of brilliant sunshine and vivid colors. Our ghetto, on the other hand, didn't look anything like a kaleidoscope. The entire area we lived in looked drab and murky, as if a swarm of moths had dusted the buildings and streets with that dreary gray stuff. The sun never shined on our hood unless it was intense enough to give a brother heat stroke.

I got off at the same subway stop I took to go to and from work. I had D. Wayne's address, which was only half a mile from my auntie's place, a six-story walkup in between two condemned apartment houses. A police cruiser was in front of his building when I arrived. Now, in this neighborhood, a patrol car could've been there for anyone and just about anything. The precinct would've been smart to leave a few cars there permanently. But with all roads leading to D. Wayne…a rumble started up in my gut like a V-8 on watered-down gas. Dollars to donuts it wasn't the three cups of office pigswill I had downed.

It looked like those moths had visited the inside the apartment house as well. I saw spider webs and dust bunnies that were large enough to trap a fully-grown Rottweiler, roaches, syringes, and discarded Coney Island whitefish. I vaulted a junkie lying in front of the staircase and began hot-footing it up the stairs thinking I should've chewed a Vicodin before I'd begun. I heard the sound of someone banging on a door. I couldn't tell how many flights above me the noise was coming from. Having forgotten D. Wayne's apartment number, I was thinking two and praying it wasn't four. I've learned to live with pain, but that didn't make me a glutton for punishment. I could've stopped, pulled the amber vial out of my pocket, and let some buzz out of the bottle, but it seemed as if I was charging head-first into an altercation which made dropping Vicodin seem like a bad idea.

"Parole officer," I announced, holding my badge for the two cops to see. I drew a quick pair of unimpressed glances just as the apartment door opened.

A black woman flopped against the doorjamb, half-undressed and by half-undressed I mean you could see pretty near everything—both titties and half her cooch was sticking out of a robe that was hanging open. She was stoned, eyes squinting, head twitching stoned—she had that far off look like she was focusing on an object on a distant shore.

"You called 911?" One of the officers said. He was turned toward me so I could read his nametag: Mulligan.

She turned her head slowly until she was looking in the cop's general direction. "Motherfucker raped me."

"You were raped, ma'am?" Mulligan asked.

"That's what I said, didn't I? *M'i* talking motherfucking Swahili?"

Mulligan's partner rolled his eyes. "Who raped you, ma'am?"

"That chump, D. Wayne *Tyrone* raped me."

"And who's that?" Mulligan asked.

"He's my boyfriend."

"You're *boyfriend* raped you?"

"Uh-huh." She put a stogie to her lips and sucked until it burned down to the filter.

"You didn't provide consent?" Mulligan asked.

I could see that she was going, going…gone, completely unresponsive.

"Ma'am?" the second cop said, then more loudly, "*Ma'am?*"

Her eyes cracked open for a second, then closed. "Didn't provide noffin'."

I watched her eyes close, then flicked open for a moment. *Three, two, one… there she goes.*

"Do you need an ambulance?" the cop asked.

"Call a bus," Mulligan said, "before she codes on us." The cop pulled his radio and moved off.

"Ma'am? MA'AM," Mulligan shouted.

She shuddered. Her eyes flitted open. *"Dafuq?"*

"Where's your boyfriend now?"

"He walked out just when you walked in. You didn't see the little playuh?"

"Bus is on the way," the second cop said. I could now see that his nametag read Messina.

"You stay with her," Mulligan said. "The perp didn't get past us on the way in. There's a chance he's on the roof." He turned to me. "You, Parole Officer, this Tyrone guy, you know him?"

I nodded.

"What's the likelihood he's armed?"

"Chicken got lips, don't they?"

"*Shit.*" He drew his gun. "You come with me."

It was another two flights to the roof, but at least I'd had a few minutes of rest in between. The rooftop door was unlatched, and I saw D. Wayne clear as day against that gray, moth-powdered sky the minute I pushed it open. He was at the ledge looking over at the adjacent rooftop. A desperate man might've been trying to assess if he could make the jump to the next roof to make his getaway. But knowing D. Wayne, he was probably staring off in a stupor. His hoe was mashed on junk. Even money said D. Wayne was as well. If he had meth in his veins, he would've soared across to the next rooftop like an eagle, but on heroin…The two rooftops weren't all that far apart, but to him, the other side must've seemed a million miles away.

"Call to him," Mulligan said. "Get him to lie down on the roof."

"D. Wayne," I said. "What's up, m'man?"

Turning around, he squinted worse than his ol' lady had. I think he must've recognized my voice because he sure didn't seem to know my face. "That you, Steady?" It looked like he was about to nod off. "The hell you doing with that po-po?"

"D. Wayne, lay down and kiss the rooftop."

"Why you want me to do dat?"

"Because this po-po got a gun pointed at you. Don't give the man a reason to put your stoned ass down."

Chapter Eight

Sandy stood up the moment I got off the elevator, showing more eyeball than a cartoon character with its finger jammed into an electric socket. She gave me a double thumbs-up. "Houck knows everything," she said in a low voice, "and he's impressed, *really* impressed."

The wall clock behind her pointed to 4:00 p.m. Apparently, I'd accomplished a supernatural feat on my first day. But on the inside, that gas-starved V-8 was still wheezing and sputtering. I wasn't happy to see D. Wayne in cuffs. Even if his paramour did drop the rape charge, I'd still have to slam him on violation of parole. When I left the scene, Michael Mulligan, the cop who'd made the arrest, told me that D. Wayne was on his way to central booking. From there, he'd be arraigned and likely denied bail because of his imminently withdrawn parole status. If that happened, he'd be sent to Shawangunk Correctional, the North-American equivalent of the black hole of Calcutta. He'd be beaten, abused, and God only knows what else. Inmates would knock him down just to see if he could get back up—and all because he probably snatched his ol' lady's last bag of smack. I'm not dismissing her rape allegation out of hand but in the condition in which we'd found D. Wayne...I doubt he could raise a pup tent, let alone timber.

"So Houck's happy?" I asked.

"You made him look good. That doesn't happen a lot. He got a pat on the back from his boss."

"Good time to ask for a raise?"

Straight deadpan. "What's a raise?"

"We ought to celebrate."

"How?"

"Cold ones after work?"

"You don't waste any time, do you, Steady?"

"You told me to show initiative. It worked the first time."

"All right, beers—but *just* beers. I don't want to get a reputation."

"Is that Stedman Groove I hear?" I heard Houck's voice booming in the corridor, drawing closer. It was a left turn into the reception area—he came around the corner like he was on rails. "Rookie all-star," he boomed and laid a hand on my shoulder heavy enough to cause joint dislocation. He must've gotten his sidewalls shaved during lunch. I could see where the razor had nicked him just above the ear. "Beers after work?" he asked.

Over his shoulder, I could see Sandy shrug. "Sure, Harry, that'd be great," I said.

He flashed a keyboard's worth of ivory. "Good. Sandy, you come too. The Bull's Bollocks at six." He gave me the finger gun and the cheek trigger sound before disappearing, but I could hear his voice carrying back, "Good day. A good, good day."

"Sorry," I began, "not exactly the celebration I had in mind."

"Houck's the best cock-blocker in the entire Department of Corrections. Look at it this way—at least the beers are on him."

* * *

The Bull's Bollocks looked to be a parole officer bar. I saw faces I'd seen around the office but hadn't yet been introduced to, and officers of varying designations I was unfamiliar with. Houck was next to me. His appearances drew acknowledgments from his peers—glasses were raised, and thumbs elevated." The boss made the rounds, shaking hands and introducing me to the guys before we settled into a booth.

"Sandy will be here in a few," he said. "I asked her to fax some docs before she left. "You hit it out of the park on your first day, Groove, but before we get into shop talk…"

"Yes?"

"Are you planning to make a move on Sandy?"

"What?" The fucker had me dead to rights. "No. Why would you say?"

"Yes, you are. It's all right. You can admit it."

"Mr. Houck…Harry, I'm telling you—"

"You come within twenty feet of that pretty young thing, and I'll cut your balls off."

My jaw dropped.

"Ha! You should see your face—classic."

"I'm sorry, boss…Harry, I'm having trouble reading you. Are you telling me to keep my hands off or to dive right in?"

"Look, she's a nice, single girl, and the other *mooks* in the office are married. They shouldn't be swinging their dicks in her general direction, but they do all the same, and I don't like it. Most POs are sleazebags, and they wouldn't think twice about screwing her. Are you a sleazebag, Groove?"

"No sleazier than most."

"At least you're honest. I heard you ask her out for beers, and I heard her accept on the spot. You're consenting adults. I just figured I'd better lay out the ground rules."

"And you don't have a problem with me swinging my black dick around her?"

"You know what they say, Steady…we're all the same in the dark. If it's okay with her, it's okay with me. Just keep it on the down-low. I don't want any guff from the office horny toads. Last thing I need is Sandy getting embarrassed and quitting. She's the best administrative assistant I've ever had. You hear me?"

"Heard."

We fist-bumped just as Sandra approached the table. "What are you two so happy about?" she asked.

"Man talk," Houck said.

"I hope you weren't talking about me."

"Not in a million years. Now have a seat, darling. Harry Houck needs a drink."

The man liked his beer. He drank enough to fill the bladders of a dozen ordinary men without so much as making a move for the head. He wasn't sloppy wasted either, just happy, a side of him I didn't expect to see so soon in my new career.

"So, Steady," he began, "Officer Do-Over said you handled yourself well."

I guess he is drunk. "Officer *Do-Over*?"

"Yeah, Mulligan. Get it?"

"Don't suppose I do, Harry."

"I guess you don't play golf."

"Roller hockey's the closest I ever come. That count?"

"Never mind. Anyway, great job today. Most rookies sit around all day until they've got spiderwebs growing on their keisters. You took the initiative to go out and track down your man. You walked into a dicey situation and kept your calm." He drained his glass. "Can't wait to see what you do tomorrow. I may ask you to track down Jesus Christ. I'm told he blew parole about two thousand years ago and hasn't been seen since. We just got a tip that he was spotted around the East River…walking across the water."

We laughed at his silliness more than at the joke.

"One last round," he said and moved off toward the bar.

"That man *is* thirsty. How many have you had?" I asked.

"Three," Sandy said. "You?"

"Same, or roughly one for every three the boss sucked down. You think he'll get home all right?"

"I'll walk him to the subway. He's got about thirty stops to sleep it off."

"Where's that?"

"Sheepshead Bay."

"That is one hellacious commute. He does that five days a week?"

"Six when he comes in on Saturday morning to clean up his desk."

"If I were him, I'd asked to be reassigned."

"Good thing he never has, or you might still be pounding the pavement instead of working here."

"How about you? Where do you live, Bayonne?"

"Hell no. I'm a Brooklyn girl—went to Canarsie High School. I'm all of two subway stops."

She was far from sloshed, but her eyes were a little glassy, her focus wandering here and there. "Fine woman like you. I'd hate to see you taken advantage of in the state you're in. Maybe you ought to allow me to see you home."

"Maybe you should, Steady. I know you'd never forgive yourself if I fell into harm's way."

I saw Houck navigating his way back to the table, hands empty.

"Changed my mind. I settled up," he said. "I'm gonna hit the can, and then one of you sober bastards needs to put me on the F train."

Chapter Nine

I got back to Auntie's about seven in the morning, barely in time to shower and change my clothes. She was already up, pushing a Hoover in front of the couch. I hadn't gotten a ton of sleep, and when I opened the door, it sounded like I had just entered the engine compartment of a 747 during takeoff.

She shut the vacuum, put her hands on her hips, and scolded me with a stare. "You dirty stay-out. Where the hell have you been, Steadman Groove?"

"Went out for beers after work. You know, like a college hazing because—"

Auntie squared her shoulders and gave me a soft hand across the face. "I asked where you were, Steady."

"One of my coworkers lives nearby, I stayed with—"

Auntie knew how to handle her men. She hauled off and gave me another. "Now, Stedman Groove, unless you want more of this…"

Another? Yes, please. I was groggy anyway—needed a quick pick-me-up.

"Does your coworker have a name to go with that love bite on your neck?"

"Sandy."

"Sandy as in Sandra? Not Sandy as in Sandy Koufax, I hope."

"Auntie, when did I ever give you cause to think I bounced that way? Sandy as in Sandra Dee—that's who she was named after."

"And you actually do work with this woman?"

"Yes, Auntie—she's the office administrator."

"Lord have mercy, Steady Grove is back in town. Mothers better hide your daughters." She threw her arms in the air and wheeled around. "I'll put up a pot of coffee. Take a shower, Steady—you look like something the damn cat dragged in."

* * *

Thirty minutes later, I was sitting at the table gulping steamin' joe while Auntie buttered toast to go along with bacon and eggs she had whipped up. "I already know about your evening," she said. "How'd your first day in the office go?" She placed the last slice of toast on my plate and slid it in front of me.

I put down the coffee. "That looks great, Auntie. Thanks."

She tapped her toe impatiently like a movie star waiting on a proposal of marriage—had it down cold. "*I'm* waiting."

"Good and bad, Auntie. You remember my old friend, Dennis Tyrone?"

"The little hooligan used to sell his grand pappy's back pain medication?"

"So, you do remember."

"I can't prove it, but I'm certain that little thief took money out of my pocketbook once or twice. He was smart about it, though. He took a five here and ten there—made me wonder if I remembered what I had. I had to start locking my bag in the closet when you brought him over. There's a transistor radio I ain't seen in years either. Had to go get a new one, and it doesn't play half as well as the one it replaced."

"Well, the little thief now calls himself D. Wayne, and he's got a record as long as Seabiscuit's. Wouldn't you know it? He's the first parolee they assigned to me. Day one, right out of the damn gate, I went over to his place and found two policemen looking for the fool."

"What's that scrawny little shrimp done now?"

"He's living with some low-class floozy. They were both stoned out of their minds on smack. She claims he raped her. Now he's in jeopardy of having his parole revoked."

"Doesn't he have to stand trial before they can do that?"

"And he will unless this woman drops the charges. He was under the influence, and there are eight benchmarks a parolee has to meet to stay out of the joint. Number five is: *avoid using, administering, or possessing any* controlled substances. Thank God they didn't find any drugs when they searched his place. They were so wasted, all the H must've already been in their veins."

"How'd you end up responsible for a loser like Dennis Tyrone? Just lucky?"

"Guess I'm just star-crossed with the damn clown."

"Why didn't you just tell your supervisor and get Dennis reassigned to a different parole officer?"

"Now, how would that have looked? My status is probationary, and right off the bat, I admit to having a relationship with a former convicted felon. Maybe I ought to just fess up and tell the man the real reason I went off to Alaska was because D. Wayne did the time for a crime I was involved in." No sooner had the words come out of my mouth than I realized how harshly Auntie would be stung by the truth.

"I thought you were a bystander in that thing? I didn't know—"

"All depends on how you spin it, Auntie. Bottom line, I did three years at sea, and he did three years in the joint."

"So that's why you ran off in such a hurry. 'The sea's calling me,' you said. That was just bullshit, Steady? You lied to me?"

"Had to do what I had to do. They had D. Wayne and he was going away anyways. What point was there in me going down with him?"

"Hmmm." She shook her head and gave me a look of disappointment. I had a feeling about what was coming next.

She snatched that plate of food and dumped it in the trash. "You get one pass, Steady. Next time you lie to me, you go the way of your uncle, out the door on your motherfucking ass." She snatched my coffee cup and showed me the back of her hand—this time, it wasn't so soft. "Go to work, Steady. I can't look at y'all right now."

Chapter Ten

Auntie was fond of saying, "When one door closes, another opens." Thank God Sandy opened her door to me because Auntie made it clear that I was persona non grata for the near term and that maybe (maybe as in pack your things) I should start looking for another place to stay. She's already shown Uncle Barney the door—he'd gotten one night on the couch, then kicked to the curb. Can't say I blame her—her brother was a living, breathing liability, an accident looking for a place to happen. Antonio used to visit her regularly after Barney blew town. I can't imagine that was easy for her. I'd seen Antonio around the hood, and that man was a beast, a take no prisoners, rip-off-your-head beast. It was a credit to her that she had the wherewithal to handle a cold-blooded killer like him.

Sandy and I were careful not to be seen together at or near work. She was impersonal between the hours of nine and five. She never flirted in the office. There were no girlish giggles or longing stares—no secret caresses at the copy machine. She was all business, and I wisely followed suit. We'd leave at different times and meet up far away from the office before heading back to her apartment.

All that restraint she showed in the office broke down in one smoldering heap the moment we disappeared behind closed doors. The gal was bona fide man-eating machine—hungry, passionate, close to insatiable. Some of it was the woman she was, and some of it might've been me. I wasn't kidding myself. She was feeling insecure and likely valued having a man in the house. The whole city was in a state of shock because of the eleven Puerto Rican women and children that had been gunned down in what the papers described as the biggest mass murder in the city's history. It affected every man, woman, and child old enough to understand the brutality of the crime. We were one and all, rocked to our cores. The atrocity was the headline of every newspaper and the feature story on every evening news report.

Mayor Ed Irving and Police Commissioner Benjamin Canton held daily press conferences on the Palm Sunday Massacre and took lots of shit for their trouble. It was now several weeks, and no arrests had been made. Racial tension was high. Community spokespeople were saying the police were dragging their feet because the victims were ghetto Puerto Ricans that no one cared about.

We were all walking an emotional powerline. For Sandy and me, that meant intense hot, sweaty sex. Now, I'm not saying we didn't have some mighty fine chemistry because we did, pools of it. But the mass murder thing…it took our game up to the next level and beyond. We were like the Knicks when they cleaned Bob Cousy's clock by scoring six points in sixteen seconds to defeat Cousy, Oscar Robertson, and the Royals after the Knicks had taken seventeen games in a row. I was only a kid then, but I still think it was one of the greatest moments in professional sports, one I know I won't ever forget.

In a sense, I wasn't just Sandy's lover. I was her security blanket, and she wrapped herself up in me head to toe, unwrapping me only when push came to shove, and she was forced to leave her apartment to earn a living, eight hours a day, Monday through Friday.

I made a habit of stopping for breakfast before heading on into work. Sandy hit the office just after eight, and I trailed by half an hour or so. She got in before Houck so that he could witness the separation in hour arrival times. Not that he cared because we already knew he didn't, but it gave him ammunition to use in case someone made an allegation about Sandy and me shitting where we ate. Yeah, it was a thinly veiled sham, but it was holding up so far.

Houck was standing alongside her at the reception counter when I walked in, their heads snapping the moment I came off the elevator.

"About time, Sleeping Beauty," Houck said. "Turn around and head right over to the Seven-five."

"What's going on?"

"Dennis Tyrone's arresting officer phoned ten minutes ago," Sandy said.

"Officer Do Over?"

"You catch on fast," Houck said. Tyrone's live-in made a surprise appearance at the precinct this morning. Mulligan is holding her until you arrive." He flashed white eyes. "What, still here? Make haste, rookie. When duty calls…you know?"

Sandy smirked, and that was okay. It didn't hint at our relationship. I wheeled around and got back into the elevator.

Five minutes and a layer of shoe leather later, I arrived at the 75th Precinct. I'd been reading the newspapers since returning to Brooklyn, and the 75th Precinct was written about often. The precinct covered East New York, which had become a crack war nightmare with gangs hunting gangs, civilians, and police getting gunned down in the street. There were allegations of crooked cops taking big scores of money from drug dealers and doing pay-for-hire murders for crack bosses. Some were calling East New York the murder capital of the world. It was a goddamn dangerous place to live—carrying a sidearm sure didn't bother me none.

Mulligan was waiting for me with Detective Second Grade Cal Detti. Detti was in an expensive suit and had one of those hundred-dollar Jerry Lewis razor haircuts. It smelled as if he bathed in some kind of cloying cologne. Had a spit shine on his shoes polished glossy enough to blind a brother. I didn't realize detectives earned so much money.

"What's going on, Officer Mulligan?" I asked.

"Thanks for coming down," he said. "A Miss Vonda Gale—"

That was all he got out before Detti cut him off at the knees. "Parole Officer, Miss Dark, Naked and Semi-conscious paid us a surprise visit regarding your parolee, Dennis Tyrone. Officer Mulligan wisely placed her in an interrogation room where she's currently *sweating* it out. You know what I mean by sweating?"

"Uh-huh."

"Dollars to donuts she woke up and realized that she couldn't continue to mainline without her paramour supplying her with drugs. We figured this might affect his parole status and so…"

"You called me. Appreciate ya."

He shot his cuffs and slicked back his hair. "Ready?" He made for the door without waiting to see if we were following.

Detti was right on the money. The woman who'd been asleep on her feet the first time I met her was now shaking like she was hooked up to a Vic Tanny vibrating machine and sweating like the humidity was one hundred percent plus. You could see on her face that she was in pain, gut-wrenching pain. It hurt me just to look at her. The room smelled as if she had puked. I scanned the floor and saw a splash of bile on the outside of the trash pail.

Detti put his spit-shined wingtip on a chair and looked Gale dead in the eye. "What's on your mind, sweetheart?" He pulled out a pack of Beech-Nut gum and pushed a stick past his lips.

Her teeth were chattering so badly she could badly speak. "You gotta let him out."

"Let who out," Detti said, indifferent to her distress as he examined his manicure.

"My husband, D-D. Wayne Tyrone."

"Your husband? Our records indicate no such relationship." He seemed to enjoy stringing her along. "When did you two lovely kids tie the knot?" he grinned at her, taunting her.

"He's my boo, my live-in man. We been together, you know? Long time."

"No, I *don't* know. I hate to sound unsympathetic but you do remember that you had us arrest Mr. Tyrone with the charge of rape. That's a serious crime. If convicted he could go away for twenty years. You were good with that, remember?"

Don't play her like that, you callous motherfucker. Okay, the woman's a lying no-integrity junkie, but that didn't give Detti the right to toy with her. I bet he was the kind of kid that pulled the wings off butterflies. "Can we move this along, Detective?"

Detti shot a glance that could sever flesh. Reading between the lines he was saying, "How fucking dare you?" That was the only response he offered.

"So you want us to drop the charge against Mr. Tyrone, is that right? Am I understanding you correctly?" Detti asked.

"Ye-ye-yes. How soon can you let D out?"

"Before we get to the when, how about we discuss the why? Why'd you say you were raped?"

"Hell, Officer, can't I just change my damn mind?"

"It's Detective, not Officer, and it sounds like you just did. By making a false accusation, lying to an officer of the law the way you did, you could be subject to—"

Mulligan was a big dude, maybe a refrigerator span across the shoulders. I could see he'd lost his patience. "Detti, is this necessary? Don't you have bigger goddamn fish to fry?"

Someone had murdered eleven women and children, and the hotshot detective had nothing better to do than break a junkie's shoes. *How about you take care of business, man—real business.*

"I can take it from here," Mulligan said. He squared his shoulders and looked Detti in the eye. "Unless you've got a problem with that."

Detti gave Mulligan the same indignant stare he'd given me earlier. Then Detective High and Mighty abruptly took his foot off the chair and walked out.

"Thank God," I whispered in Mulligan's ear. "What a big bag of wind."

* * *

Despite having been arrested for being under the influence, D. Wayne had no previous parole violations on record. Whatever dark deeds he had committed somehow managed to fly under the radar. And with the prisons being as overcrowded as they were…He was released on Friday afternoon, which gave him the time needed to rob, burgle, and score all the street drugs his faltering little body could process.

Poor Vonda, her rock star drug daddy was arrested and back in Central Booking by Sunday night.

Chapter Eleven

It didn't take a ton of investigative know-how to find out what kind of shit D. Wayne was involved in. The entire court building was buzzing when I arrived there on Monday morning to see what new travesty my parolee had committed. An arrest had been made in the Palm Sunday Massacre case. A street urchin by the name of Dennis Wayne Tyrone had pulled the trigger and murdered eleven women and children, sparing just one young girl who hid during the assault and managed to stay out of harm's way.

Now, no one was nominating D. Wayne for the Nobel Peace Prize. Shit, with his record, he didn't qualify for work at the local post office. Still, no way in hell did I figure him for a mass murderer. That went well beyond his MO of scoring just enough cash to put a needle in his arm. *No way did he'd do it.* I was convinced before I heard the reading of the charges.

I was in court when he was arraigned, standing alongside his court-appointed lawyer as the long list of charges was read, and he was led away. He looked bad, beaten to pulp kind of bad. It's sometimes hard to see bruises on black skin if you're not right up close, but I knew they were there. The arresting officers must've beaten the ever-loving crap out of him. As if that wasn't bad enough, it looked like he was going through withdrawal at the same time, shaking and sweating. He was a ghastly sight to behold.

What a goddamn mess.

Gen pop would've been a death sentence for a man who slaughtered close to a dozen women and kids, so they put him in solitary. A man who murdered women and children…he wouldn't live long enough to stand trial.

The inmates would carve a man like that into little pieces, and honestly—a guilty man would deserve every bit of it.

Now there isn't a hell of a lot an attorney can say during the arraignment other than to fight to have his client released on bail and a legal aid attorney with basic skills at best…but this sorry SOB…his name was Timothy Muckler, and he barely opened his mouth. I don't know if he was dumb, tired, or just didn't give a rat's ass. Regardless, the man seemed like he couldn't care less. Maybe I was expecting too much. I mean, considering the gravity of the charges, life imprisonment seemed like a sure bet. Look, I know D. Wayne wasn't getting out of there, but Muckler, he didn't even try. It was as if he'd been told, "No one wants to stand up for this slug, but legally, someone has to. So, go through the motions, then go home to your family."

* * *

I was back in the office before noon, just in time for Houck's Monday staff meeting. The conference room was packed, every seat around the table taken, folding chairs set up for those who'd walked in late. The room went silent when I walked in, then I was assaulted by thunderous applause, whoops, and jeers. "You sure know how to pick 'em, rookie." "Better you than me, rookie."

"You're famous," Houck said. "Maybe you'll get one of those true-crime TV shows."

They weren't mocking me. It was the calamity of the situation that they were making fun of, the fledgling parole officer and the psycho mass murderer.

Fuck me!

"Relax," Houck said. "This slimeball, Tyrone, is off your plate. Wipe the filth off your hands, grab a cup of coffee, and find a seat. It's time to move on."

All these parolees, they're just names and faces. The pervading mentality was, move 'em in and move 'em out. If they can't stay out of trouble, then put them back where they belong. "You're not a babysitter, and you're not Mother Teresa," is what I was told in training. "Don't hold their hands. Don't get attached. Almost fifty percent are back behind bars within a year. Eight out of ten are arrested at least once within their first two years post-release."

We're not supposed to be miracle workers. God knows, no one would say I'd failed D. Wayne, but deep in my gut, that old gasoline engine chugged to life and was sputtering away. Something felt terribly wrong.

Chapter Twelve

Auntie invited me to dinner the day D. Wayne was rearrested. I don't know if she was over being mad at me or if it was the deathbed promise she'd made to my mama to take care of me that gave rise to the invitation. Either way, I figured it was time to mend fences, at least whitewash 'em with a personal appearance. I kind of wanted to bring Sandy along with me, but we'd only been together a short time, and I didn't want to jump the gun.

My moms died young—a single mother like her needed money way too much to take time off from work to see the doctor. She ignored her symptoms, and well, cancer don't wait until you're ready to treat it. From the time she went into the hospital with a blockage in her colon to the day she failed was barely six months. It was about then that I learned the word metastasis. It meant the cancer had spread—from the colon to her liver, lungs, and brain. Almost killed me to see the way her body broke down—then her mind. She didn't recognize me at the end. And the last week, lying in bed, she was breathing but doing little else. I sat there wondering how many breaths she had left. I was determined to not miss a single one.

Auntie looked after me full-time after my moms had passed. We grieved together and leaned on one another to get by.

If she was asking me back to make a truce...no doubt I was coming.

I guess she was thinking of her beloved Meyer when she decided on the dinner menu: stuffed cabbage, baked potato, and salad. It was hearty food that tasted great and satisfied the hunger.

"So what happened to Uncle Barney? He was gone before I got home from my first day of work."

"It was time for him to move on is what." I could see she was enjoying her dinner. It was good to see she wasn't picking at her food like a bird. "I think it's the sauce I like so much. It's the vinegar that gives the cabbage that distinctive flavor, you know? The recipe has been in Meyer's family for generations."

"That some sleight of hand to distract me from the question I asked?"

She put down her fork and looked up, her cheeks sucked in and unhappy. "Did you have to go and ruin my nice dinner? Here I am, eating with gusto, and you throw my dumbass brother into the mix."

"Sorry, but you were avoiding the question."

"Fine." She picked up a paper napkin and blotted her lips. "Your uncle and me…there's some bad blood between us. By now, I'm sure you know why he just happened to show up at the airport when you were on your way to Alaska, don'tcha, Steady?"

"Yeah, he gave some bullshit story about the call of nature and always wanting to be a fisherman. I saw through it the moment the lie came out of his mouth and realized he must've been on the lam from something again. I tried to get the truth from him, but he never fessed up. One day he slipped, though—too much to drink, and he started to bellyache about how he messed up and how you made him leave town to save his life. He asked me if I thought you might ever forgive him."

"Ain't decided yet. You saw—I took him in and served him a good meal, but I'm not ready to shoulder the responsibility of playing nursemaid to Barney Booker. God knows I still love my big brother, but sometimes the man is more trouble than he's worth. The worst part is that he doesn't mean to hurt anyone. The fool just can't help himself." She ate a small bit of potato. "That's why I've got to be careful about letting him back into my life. Trouble follows that man, and unless I'm a fool, I believe it's still following him. I just can't have him under my roof. Can we leave it at that? Trust me, that man is like a bad penny—he'll surely turn up."

I frowned. I knew it wasn't the way she wanted it but more the way it had to be. "For now."

"I don't suppose I have to worry about that no good Dennis Wayne Tyrone influencing you anymore being as he's now public enemy number one." She picked up her knife and fork and sliced into the stuffed cabbage. "Really distinguished himself that chump friend of yours. Eleven women and children—why didn't he just wipe out an orphanage?"

"He hasn't been tried and convicted yet, Auntie. You shouldn't jump to conclusions. D. Wayne may be a thug and a junkie, but I don't see him gunning down houseful of women and their babies."

"And crazy fools do crazy shit, especially when they want to put a needle in their arm so bad nothing else matters. You're not defending him, are you?"

"I don't know—from day one, the police were looking for two shooters on account none of the victims tried to escape, and neither of the two murder weapons held enough rounds to do all the killing."

"How the police know there were two weapons? I read they didn't find the murder weapon."

"Ballistics, Auntie, they can look at the slugs and tell what kind of gun it was fired from. Those women and children were sitting in the living room, ready to have snacks after returning from church services. I don't know about you, but someone starts firing a gun in my house, the last thing I'm going to do is sit still and wait for my brains to be blown out. Ten of them got bullets in their heads."

"You forgot one of those women was pregnant. Poor baby she was carrying never got the chance to draw its first breath." She dropped her utensil with a clatter. "What kind of dinner conversation is this? Tell me about the young lady you're spending time with, this movie star, Sandra Dee."

She was named for Sandra Dee, but that's not her name. It's Sandra McQueen."

"McQueen, huh? Only McQueen I know is Steve McQueen. You dating a white girl?"

"White as the driven snow, Auntie. She don't care about the color of my skin."

"Didn't say she did." I could see she was poking around in her mouth, then she put a napkin to her lips. "Hate it when there's a piece of gristle in the chopped meat. Think I may have to try a new butcher. You get any gristle in your food?"

"Not yet, Auntie."

"Good. I've got more in the kitchen if'n you want seconds."

"It's delicious, but I'm getting pretty full."

"Tell me about this gal of yours. You met at work, right?"

"That's right. She's got a good heart—helped me outright from the start."

"Helped you out how?"

"You know, advice about the boss and such. She helped me get off on the right foot. Smart girl...caring."

She laughed. "You sure it wasn't her backside you took a liking to? I remember some of your old girlfriends, Steady. Seem to recall you were more interested in boobs and plump butt than gray matter. There was one gal I remember—had a backside big enough to serve lemonade. What was her name?"

I could feel my face become flush. "Joyce, Joyce Cook. You're right about her. She had a real piece back there." I pushed my plate away. The conversation made me think of Joyce and it made my cheekbones rise. "That girl used to leave the room for days. It was like watching a locomotive pulling out of the station—real slow like if you know what I mean?"

"If you're talking about her ample caboose, then yes, I sure as hell do know what you mean."

"I can't eat another bite," I said. "Anyway, Sandy's not like Joyce."

"Why, she got a normal backside?" I could see her holding back a smile as she sipped wine. "She doesn't have one of those flat behinds, does she, the kind what won't hold up a pair of pants?"

"*Auntie*, she's got a nice rear end...but nothing like Joyce had."

"You should've brought your new young woman to dinner.

"I didn't think you were ready for that. Last time I sat down at your table, you threw my breakfast in the trash and told me to get the hell out of the house."

"And you got off *easy*," she said firmly. "Now help me clear the table. I'll show you what I made for dessert."

Chapter Thirteen

Three Weeks Later

Both Sandy and Auntie told me I was crazy, and maybe I was, but I couldn't get over D. Wayne getting arrested for the Palm Sunday Massacre. Guilt comes in all shapes, sizes, and colors. Although I had nothing to do with D. Wayne's arrest, I kept waking up in the middle of the night thinking about the little runt getting his ass beat to hell in prison. Could've been because he'd already done three years solo for something I had plenty to do with. Maybe it was the look of helplessness and confusion on his face when he was led from the courtroom after the arraignment.

NYPD kept trotting Detti out in front of the press. The arrogant SOB was being touted as the genius detective who broke the case, the man who outsmarted the monstrous mass murderer, the evil fiend who killed a houseful of women and kids.

I guess it didn't much matter why because I found my feet marching me into the penitentiary as if they had a mind of their own. He'd called me at the office and asked to see me.

I mentioned it to Houck to see if he had a problem with me visiting with D. Wayne, and he told me, "Over my dead body."

So, I waited for Saturday and went on my own time.

A blind man walking through the door would've known where he was. The assault on the senses was startling. The stench of sweat and piss and institutional cleaner choked me like a long finger down the throat. I felt as if I had to stay on guard, at the ready to choke back vomit at a moment's notice. The noise level was intolerable—the constant clatter and shouting, half-insane inmates muttering and murmuring incessantly—cries for help, grunts, and groans. It clawed through my ear canals inching toward my brain.

There was one prison guard in front of me and one at my back. Even so, not for one second did I feel as if I was safe. I wished my sidearm was in its holster and not stashed away in my bedroom closet.

D. Wayne already served a three-year sentence.

And I hadn't.

The poor bastard, I thought, *this is where he'll spend the rest of his life.*

D. Wayne looked much worse for wear. He must've been getting far more than his share of ass whoopings, body shots you wouldn't notice with his prison uniform on.

He must not have been in his right mind. I could see it in his eyes the minute I sat down at the table across from him. His eyes wandered constantly, searching here and there aimlessly, up on the ceiling and down on the floor then off to the sides, places there was nothing to see.

He started off talking shit, fragmented undecipherable shit, half-comments about the day of the week, and the time of day. It sounded to me as if he was trying to stay in touch with his mind, holding onto his sanity by the slimmest of threads. It took a while until he began to make even the smallest amount of sense.

"It's the drugs, Steady, the motherfucking drugs."

"Methadone?"

"Na, man, I don't know what it is the man's putting in me, but it ain't none of *dat.* I don't know up from down, or my ass from my damn elbow. Methadone don't do none of *dat,* do it?"

"I don't think so, D. Wayne. You talk to the doc about it?"

"Who do you think's giving me the shit? They messing with my mind, Steady. You got to get me out of here, way the hell out."

What in the name of the Lord is he talking about? How am I supposed to do that? "My job was to keep you from going back into the joint, not getting you out. And I would've done anything I could to keep you a free man, but the cold-blooded murder of eleven women and kids—m'man, that's a bridge too far."

"The hell's that supposed to mean? You're my damn parole officer, ain't ya?"

"I was, man. That all ended when they slammed the cuffs on you and charged you with eleven counts of murder."

"You sayin' you can't do nothing?"

"D. Wayne, I'm not sure you understand what's going on here, what you've been accused of. With the charges against you, the good Lord Jesus Christ couldn't get you out of here."

He gripped his head with both hands, then slammed his forehead with the heel of his hand. "Told you, it's the shit they got me on. I can't put two thoughts together to make sense." He looked at me, squinting. "You don't want to help me after all what I done for you? You cold like that, Steady?" He spat on the floor. "Never figured you for such."

He was right about that—I sure did owe the man. Not that sending me away would've kept him out of prison, but he'd done right by me. The man kept his goddamn mouth shut.

"I kept your ass out of jail," he said. "I did three years at Shawangunk, and you went off with your fishing pole like you was Tom-fucking-Sawyer. You figure that's fair? I could've cut a deal, Steady—your ass for mine."

I didn't believe that last bit for a second, but it didn't ease my conscience any. Giving me up might've bought him a reduced sentence. Maybe, maybe not.

"How am I supposed to help you? I'm a rookie parole officer. You're talking like I'm some kind of high-powered attorney."

"Don't mean shit to me. Work with what you got."

"You're saying you're innocent, right? Well, give me something to go on. I'll go to bat for you. Help me prove it. Where were you? What were you doing? With whom? Details man—spit 'em out."

"I already told everything to the police and that dumbass lawyer of mine. I think the fool's on the same shit they're giving me and can't think straight for himself. I need a Perry Mason motherfucker, not that legal aid asswipe."

I flipped open a notepad and wet the tip of my pencil with my tongue. "You want my help? You help me first. Tell me everything, top to bottom, the where, when, why, and motherfucking how. I'll do all I can, but D. Wayne, I'm not a magician."

I put the end of the pencil on the pad, and that's when the son of a bitch guard yelled, "Times up."

I could see desperation take over D. Wayne's face as the guard made his way over. "Talk to that bulldog cop. He saw me—same time they said I *kilt* that damn family. You ask the man. He'll tell you."

"Bulldog cop? Who are you talking about, D. Wayne? Give me a name."

The guard took D. Wayne by the arm and was leading him away.

"Can't remember his damn name."

The guard unlocked the door and was leading him through to the cellblock when he called out. "The motherfucker was on the roof with y'all."

D. Wayne disappeared, and a name popped into my head, Officer Do-Over...Mike Mulligan.

Chapter Fourteen

I was surprised to see Houck out in the corridor meandering toward my office with Officer Mike Mulligan in tow. Both had coffee mugs in hand. Neither seemed to be talking shop. Houck courteously knocked on the open door. "You've got a visitor," he said with a casual lilt in his voice. "Officer 'Second Chance' Mike Mulligan is here at your request, PO Groove."

"Second Chance?" I asked with a curious expression.

"You're not quick on the metaphors, are you, Groove? Mulligan, do-over… second chance—is any of this beginning to click?"

"Happy Harry Houck," Mulligan began, "if you're ever in need of someone to make a foursome, call someone else…anyone else. He's got a handicap like a three-legged horse." He fired off a playful jab that must've smarted because Houck winced.

"And if your team is trying to stay under par…" Houck made a choking gesture. "Anyway, he's here to see you, Groove." He checked his watch. "When's off duty for you, Mike? Wanna grab a cold one?"

Mulligan checked the time. "I might could make that work. I'll have to ditch the uniform first. Can't take the chance being seen with a forty-ounce draft in my hand."

"Got a change of clothes in your cruiser?"

Mulligan nodded.

"Splendid." Houck saluted Mulligan and walked out.

"You wanted to see me?" Mulligan pulled up a chair and sat down. "What's up?"

"I appreciate you taking the time, Officer."

"No problem. What's this got to do with?"

"One former rehabilitated offender now growing ass-barnacles at the men's house of detention—Dennis Wayne Tyrone."

Mulligan straightened his back and cracked his neck. "This Tyrone character…he's getting to be a pain in my ever-loving ass."

"Why's that?"

Mulligan glanced over his shoulder, then stood and closed the door. "I'm not sure what I should and shouldn't say. Your former parolee, he stinks like rancid shit."

"You don't mean literally, right?"

"No, Groove, *not* literally. I mean he's radioactive—like exposure will cause your career to disintegrate."

"I went to see Tyrone over the weekend. He told me that you're his alibi. He said you saw him about the time the mass murder allegedly occurred." Mulligan squirmed in his chair. "Missed an appointment with your chiropractor or something? Your shorts too tight?"

He seemed uneasy and looked back at the door again. "Yeah." He wet his lips with his tongue, looked at the coffee mug, and must've decided dry lips were a better choice. "I saw him. I was in my cruiser when, low and behold, I spot this cherry Monte Carlo SS. I'm a bit of a buff, so I slowed down to check it out, and the car is spectacular—end to end. I mean it was polished up shinier than a new dime in a goat's ass. Then I see there's someone in the car, so I roll down the window to compliment the gent. Brother looks up. It's Tyrone, boosting the radio."

"But you didn't arrest him. You couldn't have because—"

"Correct. I did not. We looked at each other. I knew him, and he knew me. I mean, I could tell he recognized me, and not just the badge." Mulligan must've changed his mind because he sipped the hot coffee, then wrinkled his nose. "I knew another arrest would put him back in the joint, so I decided to look the other way. Besides, by the time I'd have gotten out of the car…" He waved his hand dismissively. "I wasn't gonna run a marathon through East New York over an aftermarket car radio."

"So, you gave him a pass."

"I did. I gave him a pass."

"And that was approximately the time the coroner said the murders took place?"

"It was, and I know it was because I'd just spent my coffee break jawing with some of the boys over at Ladder Company 225. I'm real careful about that kind of thing because I don't need some jerkoff calling community affairs reporting me for being a goldbrick. I keep a constant watch of the time, and I checked just before pulling away, just before calling in I was back on duty. A few blocks away, I take a right on Fountain Avenue, and there he was, seconds later."

I took a leap of faith. "You no doubt reported it?"

"I did indeed. I told my sergeant right after the details of Tyrone's arrest got out. I told him three times over the course of two weeks."

"And…?"

"And nothing. 'Hey, Sarge, anything come of me telling you about Tyrone?' Nothing. 'Hey, Sarge, anything come of me telling you about Tyrone?' Nothing again. The last time he told me to forget it. He said he pushed it up the ladder as far as he could, and there was nothing else he could do about it. He told me, and I quote, 'Drop it!' Just like that, 'Drop it!'"

"And did you?"

"No, I gave him shit over it, and he retaliated."

"What do you mean?"

"The son of a bitch wrote me up on a few bullshit charges, things no one gets written up for. He was firing shots across my bow, you know?"

"What did he write you up for?"

"Having a brew in the break room after my tour, sloppy uniform, shit like that. For the love of Pete, the Seven-Five is like the Who's Who of slimy crooked cops and he comes after me for this petty bullshit. Everyone has a beer now and then. And if he wanted to be a standup guy, he could've given me a verbal, and it would've ended right then and there. But the fucker didn't. He put it right into the system."

I could see that he was getting riled up thinking about it.

"Trust me, nothing like this would've happened if that douchebag Detti wasn't involved. I'm sure he's the one who strong-armed the sarge to write me up. He's been giving me the stink eye ever since I broke his shoes for taking that black chick to task in front of us. Big dick macho detective—he does shit like that because he can."

"Sounds like a great guy."

"Oh, he surely isn't. I could fill your head with all kinds of shit about Detti but I'm not the kind to betray a brother in blue." He forced the mug back to his lips. "Trust me, there's no one I'd rather talk shit about than that greaseball dick."

And he did, just not there and then in my office.

Houck invited me to drinks with Mulligan after work.

The more he drank.

The more he dumped. "I shouldn't tell you this. I shouldn't tell you that."

But he did

It wasn't the alcohol alone that made him talk. He held his liquor better than that. It was hatred he held for the man that pushed the words past his lips and into my ears, infecting me with the poison that was Detective Cal Detti.

Chapter Fifteen

8010 Liberty Avenue, Brooklyn, was the scene of the Palm Sunday Massacre. The address fell inside East New York, which, as I said, was an awful, rotten place, a real shithole with some of the highest crime rates in the country, rife with drug dealers, pimps, hoes, mobsters, and what have you. Numbers were run, grannies mugged, cars jacked, loans sharked—the innocent murdered. East New York was certainly right up there with the worst of the worst.

East New York is also uniquely situated between Ozone Park, where the Italian mob had a big presence, and LaGuardia Airport, where tempting swag moved in and out by the plane load. With all those factors in play, is it any wonder why something as atrocious as the Palm Sunday Massacre didn't happen sooner? Guess it was just a matter of time. On April 15, 1984, the shit hit the proverbial fan.

The Reverend Pointer played on the heartstrings of each and every member of the community, making sure the public's demand for blood was met. He was relentless, appearing in public day and night, rampant and angry, calling for the mayor's and the police commissioner's resignations. The public insisted the NYPD hand over a monster so reprehensible that the mere mention of his name would make blood run cold, a man you could hate with every iota of your existence.

The police served up Dennis Wayne Tyrone, and they took it.

Mulligan corroborating D. Wayne's story shocked the shit out of me. When he told me the "Bulldog" cop could alibi him, I figured he was full of shit because, nine times out of ten, he was.

But Mulligan did as D. Wayne said he could and seemed pretty willing to spill.

I wasn't fooling anyone and wasn't trying to. I was no detective, no Sherlock Holmes, mystery-solving sleuth. I was a rookie parole officer, and that was all. But I'd made my way through college by being persistent and focused, and I figured I was capable of doing it again. It was the best and only tool in my arsenal, so I'd better make damn good use of it.

Mulligan liked the ponies, and now that we were drinking buddies, invited me to join him at Belmont Park over the weekend. I told him I didn't have money to burn, but he seemed happy when I agreed to come along. We shared a mutual dislike for Detective Detti. With me, he could rag on the man all he wanted without getting backlash from the job. That and the sun in our faces made for a nice afternoon.

"I just like the ponies, you know? I'm not going to get rich at it. I'm not addicted. It's just nice to spend an afternoon at the track," Mulligan said. "God bless the missus—she understands. Gives me a little alone time." He slapped me on the knee. "Got to exorcise those demons, am I right?"

"Have you seen any big races?"

"Did I?" The question seemed to set him aglow. "I was here in seventy-three when Secretariat won the Stakes in two minutes twenty-four—fastest time ever, even now. I've seen a lot of close ones, and there's this three-year-old, Swale, I like for the Triple Crown. Been watching him like a hawk."

He wasn't a big better, two dollars here, a five there. With his help, I bet a few horses and came away a twenty-dollar winner, enough to cover our drinks.

"How are you liking the parole game?" he asked.

"Figure it's an easy way to make it through to a pension. Won't get rich, but I won't end up eating dog food in my eighties."

"You just told me *why* you do it, not if you like it."

"Too soon to tell, Mike, but…most of these cons, they spend a few months struggling to turn their lives around, then go back inside. They don't have the strength to make it work. Seems kind of pointless. Guess I learned that firsthand when they arrested D. Wayne for the eleven-kill. Me and him, we've got history."

Mulligan put down his cocktail. "No shit. I know you knew this guy, but you're telling me you *really* knew him. Does Houck know that?"

I shook my head. "Hasn't come up."

"Don't be cute. Harry Houck's no dummy."

"I never said he was."

"Don't try to play him for a fool."

"Trust me, I won't."

"Look, I won't tell him. But it does explain why you're so bent out of shape over this dirtbag's arrest."

"We both know he didn't do it."

He gnashed his teeth. "Fucking Detti claims he can prove the murders happened around five o'clock, two hours later than the coroner says the shootings took place. For my money, he changed the time just in case I somehow get subpoenaed by the defense and have to testify that I saw him boosting the radio around three. Testimony like that coming from a cop... that would really sink his battleship."

"How is it this guy has so much clout? He's only a second-grade detective, and he seems like the man calling all the shots."

"Detti's got an impressive record."

"Lots of collars?"

"It's more than just the number...it's the caliber. He broke some high-level cases. On top of that, some of the collars offered to buy him off with money and jewelry. Detti cuffed them all the same and added attempted bribery to the charges. The muckety mucks get a real woody when a cop proves himself incorruptible—sent him a letter of commendation from the Bribery Review Board, which is a panel of super chiefs."

"NYPD's got super chiefs? They fly or something—stop bullets with their bare hands?"

Mulligan laughed. "Chief of D's, Chief of Ops—high ranking officials like that."

"So, Detti's a son of a bitch, but he's a great cop—is that the story?"

"Allegedly."

"Now I'm confused."

He'd said he wouldn't trash talk a fellow cop, but we were drinking again, and liquor was the lubricant that made the venom flow. I guess he figured a little more dish couldn't hurt. "Word on the street is that he's mob-dirty. He keeps them out of harm's way, and they return the favor. There was this high jingo case a couple of years back. You probably read about it in the paper. An East Harlem nun was raped and murdered. Detti broke the case, but the word was that the tipoff came from 'Johnny Boy' Buratti."

That one knocked me for a loop. "'Johnny Boy' the Mafia crime boss."

"He's only a captain, but yeah, one and the same. I'm far from an authority on the subject but…" He leaned forward. "After saving all year long, I was able to take the missus and my two girls to Lake George last summer, and we had a friggin' blast. I was all set to tell everyone in the squad about the trip before the morning briefing when Detti saunters in just back from PTO he spent in Cannes-fucking-France. The Sultan of Brunei comes to town—guess who gets the call for the private security gig? TV reporters want to discuss a case…they call Detti. Thousand dollar suits, bling up the yin-yang, convertible Benz. Brooklyn detectives don't pull down Fortune 500 salaries, capisce?"

"So he's dirty."

"Like a goddamn earthworm. Money's rolling in from so many directions he probably has to hire Price Waterhouse to balance his checkbook."

"So why hasn't he been brought up on charges?"

"It's complicated, and I've said way too much already." He signaled the hostess to bring over another round. "One step at a time, Steady. Today you learned how to bet the ponies and not lose the rent money. Bringing down, Detti…man, that's a conversation for another day."

Chapter Sixteen

etti was, indeed, a conversation for another day—getting my arms around D. Wayne's case wasn't. While watching the balance of the racing card, Mulligan walked me through the eleven-person execution as Detti had explained it to his sergeant, his lieutenant, the captain, the Chief of Detectives, Police Commissioner Canton, and last but not least, Mayor Edward Irving. All were thrilled that NYPD's so-called "Dynamo Detective" had pulled their fat, charred asses out of the fire. The arrest of Dennis Wayne Tyrone extinguished the fire of community unrest faster than a flash flood.

For the time being, anyway.

Before Detti arrested D. Wayne, NYPD investigators were convinced that they were looking for two shooters. They'd maintained that no single assailant could've approached ten individuals and one-by-one put bullets in their heads. I'd learned in my freshman psych course that there's an automatic psychological response most higher-level organisms possess. It's called the fight or flight response, and it kicks in at the drop of a hat the moment danger is perceived. Now, this isn't one of those theoretical psychological applications that only half makes sense. Fight or flight is real. It's part of the sympathetic nervous system, and it's been fine-tuned over the course of millions of evolutionary years. The moment we spot danger, our pupils dilate, our arteries swell, and adrenaline surges. In other words, when we see someone coming at us firing a motherfucking gun, we instantaneously haul ass or fight like a goddamn ninja. You don't sit perfectly still knowing the next bullet has your name on it. You run like hell.

NYPD was sure that one assailant held a gun on the group and kept them motionless while the other did the deed, killing one after another until bullets in the first gun ran low, then they traded places. Slugs from two different guns, a .45 and a .38 Special, were recovered, solidifying the two gun-two gunmen theory.

All that went out the window when Detti collared D. Wayne. One shooter, two guns—so it is said, and so it shall be believed.

8010 Liberty was close to the address of another parolee I had to check on, a medium-length ride on the A Train. Stopping by for a peek at the crime scene seemed like the right thing to do.

Mulligan had already explained the layout of the house, an attached three-bedroom across the street from an Italian bakery. The dining room had a large front window that looked out onto Liberty Avenue. Including the unborn fetus, ten of the eleven killed were found in the parlor, the room adjacent to the dining room. A witness had come forward saying he'd seen D. Wayne in the act. He was passing by when he heard the shots, looked through the dining room into the parlor where D. Wayne murdered ten women and kids who were presumably paralyzed with fear, waiting to be called to heaven. They sat there, watching TV, eating snacks while D. Wayne, a little five-foot-nothing, ended their lives, firing kill shots at point-blank range like Wyatt Earp with a chrome-plated six-gun in each hand—all while possessing the cat-like reflexes of a heroin addict.

Tell me this shit is believable.

Where I come from, they call that selling someone a bill of goods. Bullshit.

And they bought it, everyone from Detti's supervisor to the district attorney to the mayor.

Hook, line, and sinker.

I didn't have any details on Detti's witness. However, I'm a big man, and seeing past the dining room into the parlor was close to impossible. All I could make out was a small portion of the ceiling. The dining room was built over a crawlspace, and the window was set way up high. The best angle I could manage gave me a view of the parlor high hats. Knowing a little geometry, the witness would've had to be two heads taller than Wilt

Chamberlain to see even the top half of the room.

Like I said, hook, line, and sinker.

Bullshit.

Any defense attorney worth a shit would shoot that witness down during trial. But hearing what I had about D. Wayne's legal representation…I wasn't so sure.

I felt a hand on my shoulder, locked my fist, and was ready to drive my elbow into someone's gut until I heard an urgent, "Whoa. Whoa. Easy."

I looked back and saw a middle-aged man in a white uniform.

The breeze sailed by, carrying the man's scent. He smelled like cotton candy.

"Who the hell are you?" he asked.

I flashed my badge.

He squinted to read the detail. I could see him mouth the words Parole Officer. He lifted his eyes. "Like I said, who the hell are you?"

Chapter Seventeen

Ten minutes later, I was across the street in his bakery, sipping espresso and munching on almond cookies that were about as hard as cement. He called them biscotti, and he'd generously laid out a dish of the jawbreakers for me to enjoy. For my money, they were stale, but he said they're supposed to be like that. His name was Carmelo Rizzo, and he said he bakes them two times to make them hard and crunchy. Tasted more like four times to me, or four squared. I was careful not to chip a tooth.

But the coffee was good, thank God, and the air filled with wonderful aromas: freshly baked bread, powdered sugar, vanilla, and cinnamon. Trays filled with cannoli were visible in the glass display case. I'd rather have had one of those, but he hadn't offered.

What's that they say about beggars and choosers?

He sat down with me at a small café table and set down an espresso of his own. Using a finger, he toggled a lemon peel from the rim into the cup and took a sip. "You'd think the lookie-loos would've lost interest by now, but *no*, it goes on all day long, idiots gawking into the window just like you did, hoping to see the blood or brains of a bunch of innocent women and kids." He wrinkled his nose. "It's disgusting. What makes people so low? What makes something so awful so goddamn interesting?"

"People are like that, I suppose…crazy like that. Maybe they're trying to see if eleven ghosts are walking around in that house?"

"How long have you been parole officer to this crazy fuck they grabbed?"

"He was just assigned to me. His last PO retired."

"Lucky you. How does a piece of shit like that get out of prison in the first place? An animal like that shouldn't be around normal people."

Knowing I could've spent the last three years in the cell next to D. Wayne loosened my tongue. "He hasn't been tried yet."

"Yeah, come on, I've seen his record. It's in all the papers. He's been in and out of the joint for years.

"Never said the man was a saint, but our legal system's got this crazy notion—innocent until proven guilty. Maybe you heard of it?"

His hands got real active, moving around like he was doing pantomime. "Yeah, look, I try to keep an open mind but this guy's rap sheet. I mean, come on."

Maybe that's what they want you to think. "I know how it looks. That's why I stopped by. To take a look for myself. You know they've got a witness that claims he saw Tyrone pulling the trigger. I'm a solid six-four, and I couldn't see shit. You've got to see through the dining room, through an archway, and into the parlor. And with the house being built over a crawlspace..."

"I know. I read that in the paper too—hard to visualize. You know, I was the first one inside after Rico went in and came out—even before the police arrived. Made me sick to my stomach."

No shit? "You up to talking about it?"

He huffed. "I don't know. I already told the police maybe fifteen times. Some of the detectives made me rehash it over and over. All except for this guy in the papers, Detti, the "Dynamo Detective."—I told him once, and he was good to go. Maybe that's why he cracked the case."

"Yeah, maybe. So what do you think...one more time?"

He looked around. There was only one customer in the shop who was being helped by his daughter. He'd introduced me and told me her name, Angela. If we weren't talking face-to-face, my eyes would've been all over that girl.

"All right," he said, "the place is dead right now. But please, listen up—I don't want to have to repeat myself."

"Hand to God. I'm ready."

"I've been on this corner twenty-nine years and the neighborhood...it has really gone downhill. Still, something like this . . .? Someone gunning down women and kids . . .? I never thought…anyway, it's Palm Sunday, and there isn't a loaf of bread left in the store—completely cleaned out. About seven o'clock, Rico Bueno, the guy across the street, he comes in and right away I could tell he's fucked up. He's sweating…jumpy—looks crazy. He tells me he just came home, and everyone's dead, his girlfriend, his kids, his wife's sisters, and their kids too. Naturally, it took me a minute because I figured the guy's lost his friggin' mind. I mean, I always figured him for a drug dealer anyway."

"That must've been quite a shock."

"Ya-think? You heard that his girlfriend was pregnant, right? Poor woman took a bullet to the skull and by the time the police arrived…so sad, so *friggin'* sad. Anyway, she's got cravings like most pregnant women do. She's always running in for something sweet. She's got a thing for caramel and my caramel cheesecake…" He kissed his fingertips. "It's out of this world." I could see he'd lost his place. It took a while for him to find it. "What a night—scariest goddamn thing I ever saw. All those women and kids with holes in their heads—blood everywhere, little…" He was getting choked up. "…lifeless bodies. Most of them were sitting in chairs. One woman was sitting on the couch eating a bowl of chocolate pudding. Do you believe that, chocolate-goddamn-pudding? Her head was down, and the bowl was still in her lap."

I could see that reliving those moments hurt the man like hell. "You need a break?"

"Yeah, take a break, Dad," Angela said. "What are you, gonna drop dead and leave me to run the bakery?"

"No. I'm all right. Just give me a minute."

He needed every bit of that minute and then some, but I waited patiently, and he finally began to speak again.

"I can still see those faces. Sometimes…sometimes I watch TV half the night because I'm afraid to go to sleep. Nightmares, you know? Just awful." He turned to his daughter. *Bambolina*, two more espressos, *grazie*." He looked down at the full plate of cookies. "You want something else?"

"No. I'm good. Going to meet my girl for dinner after this."

Angela brought the espressos.

"Wrap the biscotti, would ya, honey?" he said. "My friend here is going to take them when he goes. He'll give them to his lady friend."

"Lady friend, huh?" Angela had a twinkle in her eye as she bussed the table. She lingered and gave me a look that was so sultry. . . *Sandy, who?*

"This part you're not going to believe," he said. "I'm looking around the parlor doing my best not to heave when I see this little girl hiding under the couch." He sniffled, his voice crackling. "A precious little brown-eyed girl. She was dressed for church. You know, a little dress, white tights and matching Mary Janes. Oh dear God…" He made the sign of the cross. "Poor thing was in shock. I picked her up, and I could feel her shaking. I could actually hear her teeth chattering."

"Wait a minute. You mean to tell me that Bueno didn't check to see if there were any survivors? He didn't call 911?"

"Do you believe that?" Angela said from behind the counter. "Are you freakin' kidding me?"

"That's the thing," Rizzo said. "He sees the little girl in my arms and asks if maybe he should call for an ambulance. I mean, his pregnant girlfriend is dead, lying on the carpet, and he's not sure if he should call 911? I wanted to take a swing at the son of a bitch. I ran into the kitchen, picked up the goddamn phone, and called myself."

"The hell is wrong with him? Shock? Even so, you'd think his first instinct would be to try to save the baby. How far along was she?"

"Pretty damn far." He demonstrated with his hand. "She was out to here."

"She was carrying low," Angela said as she brought over the bag of cookies. "Bet she was having a boy. They didn't mention the baby's sex in the papers. Now we'll never know." She cracked her chewing gum and walked into the back room just as the bell above the front door chimed.

I saw Rizzo's eyes zero in on the new patrons. "Excuse me," he said and hurried to greet them. A silver-haired gent in a sharkskin suit greeted him with a kiss on each cheek. The other man waited his turn, then did the same. "How's everything, Mr. Buratti?" He brushed a speck of lint off the man's lapel. "Great suit. Italian?"

Holy shit. I'd heard that Buratti operated out of East New York but never thought I'd see the notorious mafia captain in the flesh.

Buratti shrugged. "Does a bear shit in the woods?" He had a robust laugh. The man carried himself with the prominence of a Roman emperor. "How's the family, Carmelo, the missus, and your beautiful daughter?" Angela emerged from the backroom. "Speak of the devil. *Ciao bella.*" He stepped up to the counter, took her hand, and kissed it. "You get more beautiful every time I see you. *Bellissima.*"

She turned red. "Thank you, Mr. Buratti. Some espresso?"

"That would be lovely, doll face." He kissed her hand again. You're gonna make some lucky fuck a very happy man."

She turned to the other goombah. He resembled Buratti but was chubbier and exhibited substantially less polish. He wore a polyester waffle weave leisure suit and a black shirt open to the mid-chest with a mane of dark hair showing. "For you, Gene?"

"Lemon ice in a squeeze cup, dear. Thanks." He tried being aloof but couldn't keep his eyes off her rack. It looked to me like he wanted to squeeze a lot more than a cup of lemon ice. It took a moment, but he finally glanced in my direction, his expression judgmental. "Who's the *moulinyan?*"

He made no effort to lower his voice. In Italian, the word *moulinyan* means eggplant. Eggplants being black, calling me a *moulinyan* was just a hop, skip, and jump from him calling me a nigger. He looked solid but no more solid than a pot filled with six hundred pounds of King Crab. If push came to shove, I figured I could toss the mofo around a whole lot easier.

Rizzo gestured in a manner that suggested that I was okay." "He's all right, Gene."

Gene shrugged in a particular way. I'd seen the gesture before. It meant, *okay, I'll let it slide.* More accurately, it meant *I could give two shits about this guy.*

"I need a nice tray of pastry delivered to the Hunt and Fish Club at noon tomorrow for my weekly meeting—all your best stuff," Buratti said. "Okay, Carmelo? Sfogliatelle, cannoli, rum baba…oh, and throw in a couple pounds of your pignoli cookies. I friggin' love them."

"Like always, yeah?" Rizzo said.

"Like always." He grinned, peeled off a pair of hundreds, and stuffed them into Rizzo's palm.

He refused the cash. "I couldn't possibly. Mr. Buratti, please. Allow me. It's my pleasure."

"You won't take the money? Fine," he said, allowing a hint of the wise guy to surface in the tone of his voice. He handed the money to Angela. "Buy yourself a pair of earrings, dollface. Something nice."

She gushed. "Thank you, Mr. Buratti, but—"

"No buts. Remember—I said something *nice*." He motioned to his associate. "Come on, Gene." They headed out, but Gene's narrow eyes stayed on me all the while he was walking out the door.

Keep looking, motherfucker. I'll bust your ass up.

Chapter Eighteen

I was about half a block from the bakery when I heard Angela call after me, "Excuse me. Excuse me. Wait up."

I turned and saw her hurrying my way. Her big brown eyes sparkled in the sunlight picking up flecks of topaz. And those breasts—bouncing up and down like they were—was enough to give a brother whiplash. I waited for her to catch up.

"Keep walking," she said, continuing past me without making eye contact. "Around the corner where my father can't see us together."

She was on the taller side and took big strides, matching mine. I managed to keep my eyes off her until we turned the corner. It wasn't easy.

She pulled a lone cigarette from her pocket and lit it, then took a long drag and expelled smoke off to the side. She took another. It looked like she needed it, as if her heart was racing. "That Rico Bueno is *such* a friggin' douchebag you have no idea." She took another drag, settling her nerves further. "My father doesn't notice anything except the cash going into the register but that guy, Bueno, he's a real sleaze. Comes in with Connie—she's the sweetest little thing and with the big belly—just adorable. What she's doing with him…?" She shrugged. "And while she's got her eyes on the display case drooling over the rainbow cookies, he's winking and blowing me kisses. Good thing my old man never saw him—he'd wring his friggin' neck."

She was about to put the cigarette to her lips but changed her mind and flicked it into the street. "So, Connie's dead, his kids are dead, and the asshole didn't call 911 or nothing. I mean, can you believe that shit? It's a straight shot down Linden Boulevard to Brookdale Hospital—ambulance could've been there in ten minutes."

"Sounds like a real piece of shit. Was he messed up on drugs at the time?"

"I honestly don't know, but I will tell you he offered to get me a high at least a few times. Told me to come by, and he'd treat me like a *real* woman. Straight up, I can't stand the sight of him. He's disgusting. I see him marching bargain-basement whoas in and out of his place all day long. I see his skanks waiting just down the block. The slimeball waits for Connie to take the kids to the park and then calls them inside."

I couldn't help but shake my head. In the short time I'd been working parole, I'd met any number of scummy dudes, but it sounded as if Rico Bueno was an honors-class douchebag. "He still living in there?"

"Like nothing ever happened—the bodies went out the door, and the whoas marched back in. The guy must be hung like a friggin mule. Oh!" Something seemed to come to her suddenly. "Two days ago, this news reporter walks into the bakery just as I was turning around the sign on the front door. Looked like hell. Poured down three coffees, then went into the powder room to fix herself up. 'Long night?' I ask. She glances over at Rico's and says, 'Honey, you've got no idea.' I hope she stopped at the VD clinic before she went back to the office."

"You're telling me you think she—"

"I think she got the scoop. Two scoops, actually, and a nice gooey cherry on top. Sorry. Makes me angry, is all. He's some kind of sexual deviant."

"I'm glad you told me."

"I heard you talking to pops. Doesn't sound like you think this Tyrone guy did it?"

"Got my doubts."

"That slick detective seemed pretty goddamn sure about it. He know something you don't?"

"Guess he might. He seems to have everyone convinced."

She took out a pack of Wrigley's Doublemint Gum and popped a stick into her mouth. "Pop don't like it when I smoke during hours. He thinks the customers will smell it on my breath."

"He told me he's been in business almost thirty years—I gotta figure he picked up a few things."

"Yeah, you're probably right." Her posture changed. Reading her pose, it seemed like we were less like strangers and more like friends. "You got a business card?" I noticed the twinkle was back in her eyes. She had dimples too—all in all, a pretty sweet package.

I had a stash of freshly printed cards in my jacket pocket. I peeled off the top card and handed it to her.

"I'll give you a call if anything comes to mind. Or…"

"Or?"

She fussed with my tie. "I heard you tellin Pops you were meeting your girl for dinner, but maybe you're a chewing gum guy."

Huh?

She stuffed a stick of Wrigley's into my breast pocket and leaned in close. "Double your pleasure, double your fun…?"

She grazed my cheek with her fingertips before turning to walk away. The view from that direction was none too shabby either, and I enjoyed it until she turned the corner.

Chapter Nineteen

I was daydreaming about those two beautiful white women and rode that fantasy like a Brahma bull all the way across town. I didn't know if Angela was suggesting I see her on the side or if she was up for a three-way, but I didn't see anything wrong with a little erotic make-believe. I don't attend church regularly, but I am a God-fearing man. But the good Lord's got no right to the thoughts in your head. Two snowflakes and a brother in the middle—now, that's the kind of sandwich I've always dreamed of—two slices of angel food cake and me in the middle. Had to make sure my jacket was buttoned before getting off the subway.

Sandy was waiting for me with the door open. Guess she'd seen me coming from her apartment window. She put her arms around me and pressed her lips to mine, hard. "How was your day?"

My day? What day? I knew it was Sandy's lips against mine, but with my eyes closed…guess my illicit-love fantasy wasn't entirely played out. "It was good, baby, real good. There's a lot I want to tell you but first…"

I could see the excitement in her eyes as I scooped her off the floor. "Guess you're not hungry." She giggled.

"Oh, I'm hungry, baby—hungry for my woman."

She gasped, and I carried her to the bedroom with our lips pressed together. I'd spent the last hour getting my fantasy world rocked by two white she-devils and hoped I didn't go too quickly. I was pretty sure she'd overlook a rapid-fire as long as there was another round in the barrel. Two pops were my usual—a hat trick when the stars were aligned.

I don't know if she could pick up on where I was at—when I was with her and when I was with the baker's daughter. Half the time, I didn't know which one I was with. It was an otherworldly experience—like getting knocked to your knees by a love tsunami, only surfacing to draw breath when it was either breathe or perish. The lust only came to an end when we smelled dinner burning in the oven.

"Oh shit, I forgot." She rolled off the bed and raced it into the kitchen, swearing like the guys I'd been with at sea.

She was crying when I got to the kitchen. A roasted chicken had been reduced to carbon—any longer, and it would've been baked into a diamond.

"Baby, with the heat we were generating in the bedroom…" I turned her around and gave her a deep, passionate kiss, but it didn't dig her out of the pit.

"I wanted to make you something special for a change. I'm such a shitty cook, and you never complain. I went to the library and copied the recipe."

Whatever she used to prepare the bird was now completely unidentifiable. A forensics team would've given up and walked away. It looked like some carrots and potatoes had been collateral damage. "Baby, I nourished myself on your love. You think I'm going to make an issue over poultry? Who cares if you can cook in the kitchen as long as you bake me between the sheets like you do?"

I was still holding her tight when her lips found mine again. I carried her toward the goal, ready for my third consecutive score.

Chapter Twenty

I didn't get that life-sustaining breath of air again until morning. It wasn't until I dragged my tired ass into the shower that I knew where sleep ended and consciousness began. The night was like a sexual rollercoaster with highs and lows, peaks and valleys, but as best I could remember, it never came to an end.

I couldn't make up for the lost sleep but calories…they were easy to pack on. We stopped for our morning meal. Also, as usual, she carried her breakfast into the office, and I dined in at the local luncheonette. I wolfed down a massive Denver omelet, home-fried potatoes, and a buttered bagel. Truth be told, I could've doubled up on that meal and not been full. I was utterly depleted, physically, emotionally, and every which way.

I found a racing sheet on my desk when I got into the office. Some of the horses on Sunday's card were circled in red pencil along with two words written in the margin, "You in?"

I called Mulligan, but he was out on his tour. I left a short message, "Hell yes." He didn't have to call back, but he did when he got off duty. I told him about my visit to the crime scene, coffee with Rizzo, and the unexpected meeting with "Johnny Boy" Buratti and his sidekick. I left out the part about Angela's invitation for the two of us to get it on. After the night I'd had with Sandy, I couldn't even fathom being with another woman until my equipment was back from being reconditioned.

"Gene's his brother, rookie. It's a good thing the baker stood up for you. Gene's got a temper, and sometimes he's not too accommodating of blacks showing up in his haunts."

"It was nothing with nothing."

"Glad to hear it. You should practice not being seen by him again...*ever.* It'll be good for your longevity, and I'm just starting to like having company at Belmont. So, you're in for Sunday?"

"Should be okay as long as my lady doesn't have plans otherwise."

"And *what,* that's more important than two guys betting the ponies?"

"You haven't seen my girl naked."

He laughed. "Don't mean I haven't imagined her that way."

Damn, Houck's must've got to yacking to Mulligan about my business. I let it go over my head.

"Still, it bros before hoes, right?"

"No, not right. Whoever said that must've had a face kissed by the A Train and couldn't get any no matter what."

We were about to disconnect when Mulligan asked what I was planning to do to help D. Wayne next. He'd already told me he'd help from a distance but as far as butting heads with his CO again...he had a wife and kids, not to mention a mortgage. He just couldn't risk it.

"I'd like to take a peek at the case file," I said.

"What do you mean you'd *like to?* You really are a rookie, aren't you?"

"I can request it?"

"Tyrone *is* your parolee."

"I know, but he's not on parole anymore."

"It doesn't matter. You've got access to everything in his jacket, and that includes the current case and charges."

I didn't know which reaction was stronger, feeling surprised or stupid. "You're shitting me?"

There's just one possible response to that question.

Mulligan didn't disappoint.

Chapter Twenty-One

Sunday

"Good afternoon, Sunshine," Mulligan said, pushing open the passenger door of his '64 Pontiac GTO with chrome wheels and custom blue paint. It was far from new, but it sure was cherry and turned plenty of heads when he pulled up in front of Sandy's building to pick me up. Made me feel like a millionaire getting in and planting my butt in the parchment-colored bucket seat. He threw the long-throw shifter into gear and pulled out. He didn't leave rubber, but the acceleration was strong enough to throw me back in the seat. The windows were open, and I could hear the throaty sound of the exhaust echo off the tenement buildings as we made our way through the narrow streets. "The pretty blonde could've joined us," he said.

I never told him about Sandy. He either picked up on something during his visits to the office, or as I had assumed, Houck let him on the little secret. I didn't mind Mulligan knowing. It's just...well, first it's one, then two. Before you know it, everyone's whispering behind your back. "You know our relationship is on the q.t., right?"

"And it'll stay that way as long as you don't knock her up? Kind of difficult keeping a lid on things when she's wearing maternity clothes to the office." He punched me on the arm. "You're a lucky-fuck, Steady."

"I'm still waiting on Tyrone's Jacket?"

"Take it easy. It's only been a few days. I'll lay odds there's a four-dollar-an-hour prima donna who's got your request sitting on her desk, gathering dust. PO requests don't go to the top of the list—know what I mean? Let me know if it doesn't come in the next day or so. I know someone I can lean on."

"You've got clout?" I asked.

"Me, clout? You've got to be kidding. I'm a patrolman, a nothing. I've got no business asking for anything from anybody. But chits…I've got a bag full of 'em—citations I didn't write, scaring off punks and douchebags." He turned to me with a mouthful of white teeth as he hit the entrance ramp on the Northern State Parkway. "Mike Mulligan isn't without his charms."

"Not Taking the LIE?"

"Does it look like I am?"

"I think the Long Island Expressway's faster, and it's got much longer on-ramps."

"It's also got eighteen-wheelers and debris-carting shit-haulers. One paint chip on this baby, and I'm in the garage two days touching up, sanding and polishing. And I'm not too concerned about the on-ramps." He gunned the GTO to get up to speed on the stub-length Northern State on-ramp. I saw the speedometer shoot past seventy-five. He grinned. "Love this car—it's got real balls."

The ramps were short and the overpasses low because Robert Moses, the city planner, didn't want trucks and buses filled with riffraff blacks and Puerto Ricans driving on it in their panel vans and such. He wanted to maintain the serenity of the Northern and Southern State Parkways for his well-heeled country club buddies.

Bigot motherfucker.

"Can't wait to hit the park and fill my lung with the musk of horse lather and earth," he said. "I feel like I'm going to be a big winner today. How about you, Steady?"

"I feel like a winner just driving in this fancy blue car. You must give it a lot of TLC."

"Right behind the missus and the girls. She's my blue-eyed baby. Wax it once a month—oil changes every fifteen hundred miles." He ran his hand over the dashboard. "Armor All—makes the upholstery shine like new. Hey, I've been meaning to ask—how did it feel to get the stink eye from baby bro Buratti? Couldn't' have made you feel warm and fuzzy."

"You know my background, right? I've been to sea with all kinds of crazy bastards. Most of them didn't wear silk suits like that palooka. Compared to some of the lowlife seadogs I've known, Gene Buratti is a cream puff. I'd dropkick a nasty prick like that—no problem whatsoever."

"There's one important difference, my friend. That nasty prick, Gene Buratti, wouldn't think twice about putting a bullet between your eyes. And that nice baker you met, Carmelo Rizzo…Someone put your lights out…? He'd say he didn't see a goddamn thing if some wet-behind-the-ears detective came by asking questions about your disappearance. He'd say, 'What parole officer? Steady Groove *who?*' It would be like you never existed. And with big bro running the crew…? He wouldn't even have to ask permission. Worst case scenario, he gets a slap on the wrist from 'Johnny Boy' and goes back to BAU."

"Huh?"

"Business as usual.

"Just for sitting at a table sipping coffee?"

"For *noth-ing*. For not liking the way you look—the shine on your shoes. You don't get it. The only ones safe around these guys is another made man and, to a lesser degree, the police. These guys are ruthless. They have a code, and it doesn't include Steady Groove or any of the members of your tribe. The stuff you read about in the papers, those are only the high rollers who got whacked, the names that sell newspapers. Guys like you…*ha*. It would be like you fell off the face of the earth."

There was a short line of cars getting into the parking field at Belmont. I handed Mulligan a few bills. "For the parking," I said. "Look, I'm not going to lose any sleep over this greaseball, but I appreciate the heads-up. What's the punishment for shacking up with one of the neighborhood ladies?"

He seemed stunned. "You're not serious?

"Better to be forearmed, you dig?"

"Don't even think about it. Dead is dead, my friend. They'd cut off your dick and toss you in a shallow grave. *And* they don't use anesthesia. It's strictly field surgery with these guys. *Comprendo?*" He handed cash to the parking attendant and drove to the very last spot where I suppose he felt confident the GTO would be safe from door dings. He checked to make sure both doors were locked and set the alarm before we began our walk to the track.

"That entire area from East New York to Ozone Park is Cosa Nostra-filthy. Buratti does a lot of his business out of the Bergin Hunt and Fish Club on 101st. The only guy above "Johnny Boy" Buratti is "Big" Paul Gromaggio, the don himself. And from what I hear, he's lost a lot of control to Buratti."

"You seem to know a lot about the mafia. Are all cops as savvy as you are?"

"Cops know more than most, but—" He stopped abruptly. "You tell anyone about what I'm about to say, and I'll kill you with my own two hands."

"I'm a black rookie parole officer. Who am I gonna tell? Who'd listen?"

"All the same—you know what they say about loose lips, right?" He looked around. There wasn't anyone within one hundred feet in any direction. "No names, but my cousin…he's a Westie."

"I've got no idea what that is. Wait, is that like the Royal Canadian Mounted Police? You know, from that Dudley Do-Right cartoon."

"Geez, Steady—maybe you watched too many cartoons as a kid."

"Say what you want but that TV kept me off the street and out of trouble more than I care to admit." *For a while anyway.*

"Happy to hear it. Anyway, the Westies are an Irish mob, Steady. They operate out of Hell's Kitchen. They're not big, but they're deadly-fucking-dangerous. And they've thrown in with Big Paul."

"Irish mixing with the Italian mob—how come?"

"They get Big Paul's protection, and he gets access to the Irish torpedoes. It's a marriage made in the dark fucking abyss."

We started toward the track again. "Gromaggio doesn't have enough hit men of his own? And sometimes a don doesn't want to go through channels. You get me? Covert operations"

"Why doesn't the head of the Gambino crime family have enough of his own hitmen to go around? Did the State Department impose some kind of embargo on the Sicilian Mafioso? One torpedo per family?"

Mulligan had a deep, rumbling laugh. "You're a pisser, Steady. The thing is, you don't know the landscape. When Gromaggio took over from Carlo Gambino as head of the Gambino Crime Family, he got the nod because Carlo thought it was in the family's best interest to go into *legitimate* business. Gromaggio engineered big construction and carting contracts that brought in tens of millions, but he wasn't from the street, if you know what I mean. They call him the Howard Hughes of the mob. He's stays hunkered down in his ivory tower mansion on Staten Island. Rumor has it he walks around in silk pajamas all day long like Hugh Hefner. When he took over, it caused a big rift in the family, and guys like Buratti—they're more old school. They support drug dealing and all the other shady goings-on the old mob is known for. From what my cousin tells me, Buratti thinks that 'Big' Paul is too isolated and too greedy. Thinks he's getting the short end of the stick on the trucks they hijack out of JFK. Gromaggio and Buratti—*shit*, if you ask me, it's just a matter of time who gets dead first."

"Tangled web shit, huh?"

He slapped me on the back. "Yeah. Tangled web shit." His hearty laugh returned. "Shit, Steady, you crack me up."

Chapter Twenty-Two

There are thousands of sayings about Monday mornings, some good, most bad. There are the bullshit uplifting messages and the straightforward man-in-the-trenches sayings. Seemed this was going to be the latter. I hadn't sipped coffee yet, and Houck was already in my face. He held in his monster grip a four-inch-thick folder that he pounded on my desk.

"I know what you're doing, Steady. I just don't know *why* you're doing it."

No point in playing dumb. It was D. Wayne's folder, and it had grown ten-fold in thickness since the last time I'd seen it.

Houck closed my office door, then turned around and slammed his fists on the metal desktop like he wanted to jackhammer it into the floor. Up until now, I'd only known happy Harry Houck, but I'd caught glimpses of his Mr. Hyde persona a few times, slamming doors and eviscerating POs. Seems like I was going to get a taste of his dark side.

"Is this the part you hinted at when you interviewed—when I asked if you'd ever been arrested? 'Should've been…but no, never.'"

"You're close."

"You sure you want to be telling me that? You're still probationary, Groove. I can sack your ass in two seconds flat."

The only way I knew to extinguish Houck's four-alarm blaze was to kick down the dam and let the truth burst through—dowse the sucker. "I've known Dennis Tyrone since I was eight. Used to be his partner in crime."

I could see the scenario was playing out in his mind—playing out like a napalm attack during the battle of Khe Sanh. It looked as if his lungs had deflated. His ruddy complexion turned white, then he hammered the desktop with his big right fist, not once but twice times—left a divot so deep you'd need a chassis straightener to level it out. "Why in the name of Christ didn't you tell me that on day one, when I handed you Tyrone's folder? I had plenty of files on my desk. All you had to say was that you had a relationship with Tyrone, and that would've been that. *Fuck*. I knew it was too good to be true. *Why?*"

"I didn't want to open Pandora's Box."

"Your background check came back clean as a whistle—not so much as a parking ticket. What the hell were you afraid of?" He yanked out a chair and sat down. He was weighing options, and it looked as if the gears in his head had ground to a halt. "Badge and gun, on the desk, now!"

I had them out and in front of him in a flash. He slid them over to his side of the desk.

"Did you have any knowledge that Tyrone was involved in the shootings before he was arrested?"

"None, Harry. Absolutely not."

"You're sure?"

"Yes."

"You're not lying to cover your ass, are you?"

"No way."

He studied my eyes before moving on. "Tyrone went away for three years on a felony robbery charge. You involved in that?"

I wanted to answer immediately, but my throat had turned to stone. I nodded and took a sip of java. "Yes, I was."

"But you weren't arrested or charged?"

"No."

He was relentless, coming at me like a bull, seeing red. "Look me in the eye and swear you didn't cut a deal with the DA and had your record expunged because I'm going to check and if you're lying…there's a perjury clause in your contract. You could do time for lying on your application. You aware of that?"

"I'm telling you straight up. I've never been arrested, and I had no clue

Tyrone was involved in killing those women and kids."

"So, I ask you again, *why?*"

I tried to crack my neck, but it was locked up, stiff as a steam pipe. "I owe the man. He got popped for robbery and didn't say a word to anyone about me being involved. That kind of loyalty runs deep, man. He did jail time, and I spent three years on the Bering Sea—straight up, just like I told you."

"That's your motivation, not your reason." He picked up the hefty file and held it above his head. "What are you doing with—" He dropped the brick, and it came down with a jarring thud—"this? He's no longer a free man. He's not your responsibility. Are you some kind of ghoul? You want all the gory details? See the blood? The crime scene photos of those cut-down women and kids?"

I lifted my hand high. "Hand to God, boss, it ain't nothing like that. I...I don't believe he did it."

The color was returning to Houck's face. He seemed a shade more rational. "Why, Steady, because he's established such a fine record? Because he's such a solid, upstanding member of the community? He's a junkie, man. He's trash. Throw him away."

I don't play a brother like that. "I've got good reason to believe he's being framed. Some of the allegations against him—they're just horse shit."

"Oh yeah? Like What?"

"First off, Mulligan—"

"*Motherfucker.*" He pressed his hand to his forehead. "Mike? Mike Mulligan?"

I nodded.

"*He's* your source?"

"For some it, yes, but not all of it."

"This hole just gets deeper and deeper, doesn't it?" He grabbed my coffee and gulped it down, then looked me dead in the eye. "*Explain.*"

Chapter Twenty-Three

Houck didn't fire me. He didn't even put me on suspension. Not because he was such a great guy and not because he was so understanding. I think it was because he wasn't sure what to do. Yes, he liked me. And yes, he and Mike Mulligan were asshole buds. Still, the man wasn't going to cover up anything, and certainly not for a junior PO. He appeared ready to file a report until I mentioned Detti. Then, just like that, his switch flipped. His expression soured at the mention of the man's name.

"I know Detti," he said like he had spoiled milk in his mouth. He slid my gun and badge back across the desk. "This isn't over, Groove. I need to confer with my rabbi. And if I find out you're doing anything other than PO work while you're on the clock…"

"Absolutely not."

"You'd better not. I want your daily log on my desk before you go home at the end of each day. Are we clear?"

"Totally, Harry."

He blew out of my office, and I got busy with my other files. Sandy stopped by my doorway. Her eyes were the size of jumbo eggs but she made no other attempt to communicate with me. Somehow she already knew that I was tainted goods and was smart enough to stay clear. No doubt I owed her a lengthy explanation and a healthy apology. I'd mentioned D. Wayne to her in passing, the arrest he'd done the three-years for and such, but my past ties to the man…Uh-uh, I was going to eat crow over that. Forget the damn crow, she'd have me choking down a big-ass buzzard for messing up on the new job.

I needed to get out of the office and made haste slipping into the elevator before Sandy could corner me for interrogation. One of my ex-cons had missed his last check-in, and I hadn't been able to get him on the phone.

Salty Monroe was a ladies man, a gigolo of sorts who occasionally crossed the line and confused the cookie jar for the honey pot—the brother got caught with his hands in the cashbox. He stood about five-foot-six—his hair, fried, dyed, and laid to the side like Sammy Davis, Jr. He could've passed for the man, and I'd read in his file that he sometimes used his resemblance to Mister Show Business to snooker some of the more gullible ladies. For the most part, no one got hurt in a Salty Monroe sting except for the egos of the ladies who got shystered out of their hard-earned scratch. His stints in jail were never long, but he'd already been sent away four times, which made him a three-time loser and then some. His next trip up the river was going to be a long one. Magistrates don't play nice with brothers that can't learn their lessons.

The most surefire way to find an ex-con is to start with Big John over at the tavern. Big John sold everything, information included. The problem was that his prices were steep as hell. I grabbed a seat at the bar and dropped a five-dollar bill from a foot up in the air to see if the flypaper bar top would suck it out of the air.

Close.

Big John peeled it up immediately and dropped a glass on the bar. It looked like the same glass I'd used months back. The smudges and grime made it look as if he'd stored it for me, unwashed.

What the hell, I thought. *Alcohol kills everything, don't it?*

He poured the requisite two fingers and went right into his sales pitch. "You back for the RCA?"

"Maybe when I get a place of my own. I'm seeing someone, though. What about those Rolex watches you used to carry? I saw Salty Monroe, and he told me nothing spreads legs faster than one of your counterfeit Taiwanese watches."

His eyes grew, kind of looking like a sale getting rung up on an old-fashioned cash register. *"Ab-so-lute-a-men-tay.* Got you covered, college boy." All the small trinkets were kept behind the bar. He pulled out a cigar box. The name *Romeo Y Julietta* was printed on the face of it, and it still reeked of tobacco. Those stogies were cheap and popular in the hood. When he set the closed box on the counter, I could tell that it weighed too much for a box of rolled tobacco. He flipped the lid, revealing a box of gold-plated watches, men's and women's versions of the Rolex President.

"These run?" I asked.

"Like sunny-side-up eggs."

I picked up two of the ladies' model—both appeared to be keeping proper time. They didn't feel heavy like solid gold, but I didn't expect them to.

"These ain't those cheap-shit windup watches neither—little battery keeps 'em running a year, plus. *Fit-e,*" he said, lying his open palm on the bar top. "Pick any one you want."

"Fit-e my ass. They're thirty everywhere else."

He slammed the lid closed. "So, go somewhere else."

He began to take the box off the bar, but I put my hand on top of it. "That what you charged Salty?"

"No, he buys in bulk, so I knock ten off each. How many you want?"

I only wanted the one for Sandy but figured it couldn't hurt bringing my doting Auntie a gift. After all, she'd been like a second mama to me all this time. I wouldn't bullshit either of them—I'd tell them the watches were knockoffs and not a solid gold Swiss timepiece. Knowing Auntie, she'd think I'd committed some manner of street crime if I handed her a real one. "How about two for sixty?"

"Two for seventy."

"Okay, but you have to tell me where I can find Salty. We've got business to discuss."

"Fine—show me *da'green.* And not a word to Salty I gave you a better deal than I gave him."

I paid the man and got a verbal list of Salty's favorite haunts.

* * *

I caught up with Salty at one of the Tad's Steaks locations in the city. In his monogrammed blazer and silk ascot, he seemed out of place sitting among the tourists and Time Square denizens who'd hustled just enough cash for their once-every-third-day meal. They'd wolf down a cheap steak and be back out on the street resuming their liquid and intravenous diets.

Salty was sitting alone with a numbers sheet and a nub of a pencil. He looked over the top of his black frame glasses when I approached, then back down at the paper. He scratched his numbers on the paper before looking up again.

"The law really does have a long arm. How are you, Parole Officer College Boy? Can I buy you a succulent T-bone?"

"Too early for lunch, Salty."

He took a glance at his watch. "Oh come on—here we are, two handsome men of the world. Live a little."

The place had nothing going for it other than its hash-house look, which I guess appealed to some. The smell of strong ammonia disinfectant drifted out of the nearby men's room, killing whatever portion of appetite I might've had. A tray of filled wine glasses sat on the bar covered with Saran Wrap, showing that the staff had a handle on fly control. "Doesn't look very tempting. In fact—"

"Seven-dollar lunch special—how can we go wrong?"

"I don't know…food poisoning, ptomaine?"

"Come on, Mr. Groove. I'm *buying*. How do you take your steak, rare, medium, or incinerated? Personally, I like my meat bloody rare."

"Against the rules, Salty. I can't accept gifts. You know that."

A waitress came over. She smelled like Big John's cigar box and looked like a Popeye in a wig. "Can I take your order?"

"Two lunch specials," Salty said.

"Just coffee for me," I said. "Two separate checks."

She seemed pissed but took the meager order and did so without thanking us for it. She left, leaving a wash of Camels in her wake.

"You fall on hard times, Salty? I expected to find you in The Russian Tea Room. But here…? I'm sorry you're down on your luck."

"No, *baby*, I just dig the beef. I grew up on rough cuts of meat like they have here. Like to give my jaws a workout when I eat. How'd you find me here anyhow?"

"I asked around. Found out this is where you come when no one is picking up the tab." My coffee arrived along with a sneer. It, too, smelled like tobacco. "You missed your check-in, my friend. What's up with that? You so far up a divorcee's cooch you couldn't pull out in time?"

"Not a chance, Mr. Parole Officer, sir. I'm like the Erie Lackawanna—always pull out of the station on time."

"So, what about the appointment?"

"Oh shit, I must've forgotten. Last Wednesday, right?"

I took a sip of the coffee. It tasted weak as if it had been cut the same way the a greasy spoon bartender cuts whiskey. "You know, you beat the odds so far—four trips to the pokey, and you're still going strong. I don't have to tell you how long you could go away for if you get caught messing with another old darling's savings account, do I?"

"No, man, I'm done with that. You've seen my employee record—twelve weeks straight and never missed a day."

"Just want to make sure you're not involved in any extracurricular activity. You feeling me, Salty?"

"I'm down, College Boy—down like a clown, Charlie Brown."

"Don't miss your next check-in. Cool?"

"Like the ice under a Zamboni."

I took out my appointment book and wrote down a date. "This coming Tuesday—you be in my office by ten a.m., or I'll be on your ass like flies on shit." I threw a couple of bucks on the table and walked away.

I held the door for a sister on my way out. She looked way too classy for a joint like Tad's, but you know…she looked like she was on her lunch break, and maybe Tad's was close by. To the eye, she clocked in around fifty and looked well maintained. She wore expensive clothes and tasteful bling. Her hair was pulled back in a bun and held taut with a fancy ceramic pin. I lingered at the front window just to see Salty's expression when the darling cruised by.

She wasn't anywhere near Salty's table, but he kind of came to life all the same. It was almost as if he had a sixth sense and was able to detect opportunity in his immediate vicinity. He looked up and licked his chops.

Chapter Twenty-Four

I would never call Auntie's place a doghouse, however, the doghouse was where I'd been sent. Sandy hadn't taken kindly to all the gaps in our communication and had unceremoniously shown me the door. She wouldn't even let me curl up next to her in bed. I left without having dinner—wearing the same clothes I'd worn to work.

Auntie wasn't expecting me, and made me a sandwich from leftover meatloaf and toasted a stale roll. It wasn't elegant dining, but it hit the spot. I felt lousy for showing up hat in hand after being kicked to the curb.

All I had in the closet were jeans, tees, and underwear. Saint that she was, Auntie washed my work shirt in the sink and hung it up to dry on the clothesline. I'd have to wear the same suit again, not exactly a cardinal sin.

I could see she was worn out as she plopped into her favorite chair, her head sinking into the cushion, her eyes struggling to stay open. "I don't suppose you feel like telling me what's happened between you and your lady friend?"

"I do not."

"Good, because I'm too damn tired to drag it out of you. Your uncle stopped by twice, asking if you had moved out for good. I wouldn't have told him even if you had. The old weasel was angling for an invitation, and once he gets through the door…getting rid of his lazy ass would be like trying to pull an embedded tick out of your backside."

"Thanks, Auntie. Things are kind of up in the air with Sandy and me. Okay if I let you know my plans in a few days?"

"Just don't have me waiting up worrying about you. Drop a dime if you're sleeping out. Fair enough?"

"More than fair, Auntie. I'll try not to be a pain in the ass."

"You better do *more* than try."

"Where's Barney been staying?"

"What kind of fool do you think I am? You think I asked him, knowing he'd guilt me into submission? 'It's cold out on the street. I haven't had a decent meal since you tossed me out.' You know your uncle has the conscience of a field rat. By the time he got through guilting me, I'd be the one sleeping on the floor and him in *my* bed."

I could see she was almost out. "Why don't you head off to bed?"

"Now, there's an idea I like." She pried her weary body out of the chair and gave me a kiss on the forehead on her way to the bedroom. "Now, don't wait too long to mend fences with Sandra Dee, you hear?"

"I won't, Auntie."

"Good. Having bacon and eggs for breakfast, Steady. Don't make me call you twice."

I was tired enough to go to bed, but there was too much on my mind. The day had started with an argument with Houck over D. Wayne's file. Seemed like the day was going to end the same way. I took the heavy folder over to the dining room table and dug into it where the new arrest records began—Detti's reports to be exact."

Police reports are supposed to be concise and to the point, but Detti's entries were long and detailed. It struck me that he was trying to bury the important facts beneath an avalanche of excessive details and that an underpaid, overworked public defender would be too lazy and without sufficient motivation to sort through it. The case against D. Wayne seemed to hinge on just a handful of points of evidence.

My eyes were burning, my brain begging for sleep. It was after midnight, but I had made a commitment and was determined to get a solid handle on those points of evidence before I turned in.

The newspapers and TV had withheld the names of the witnesses, but here in the official police record, they were plain as day. I began reading the names of the witnesses. It was a matter of seconds before I hit the wall.

The witness who'd viewed D. Wayne through the window of 8010 Liberty Avenue was listed as Bernard A. Booker. I was stunned and, at the same time, confused. It took a moment for anger to push the cobwebs from my head. The man whose statement had helped lock away D. Wayne was my flesh and blood, Uncle Sockeye.

Chapter Twenty-Five

I might've just as well have spent the night walking the street. When the alarm went off, I was already showered and dressed. I'd been unable to sleep little more than a wink. A couple of short cat naps in between forging through the file as far as I could.

Uncle-mother-fucking-Sockeye was the brute that had stomped through my head all night long. He'd somehow gotten tied up with Detti, a somehow I had no trouble figuring out. To prove it, though, would be like trying to hotwire a car wearing boxing gloves. The first thing I had to do was find the SOB.

It wasn't half-bad having a familiar connection out on the Bering Sea, but I always knew that Sockeye's reason for being on the ship was not the one he'd stated. I knew he had a colorful past, colorful as in stained with shit. He'd always been a five-and-dime hustler. Guess there was no reason to believe he'd changed.

I had to put Sockeye on the backburner when 9:00 a.m. came around. No way in hell I wasn't going to give Houck a new reason to suspend or fire my ass. For the next eight hours, I was Parole Officer Stedman Groove, civil servant extraordinaire. There were parolees to meet with and cases to work. I put my nose to the grindstone, hoping the workday would pass quickly.

There was no doubt I was still on Houck's shit list. He gave me a coldhearted stare every time he walked by. I was hoping the man was still torn over what to do, that he still hadn't made a decision. The other alternative was that he'd already written me up and had decided I was to be shit-canned. I could sometimes navigate Houck's mood from the signals

Sandy gave me, but she didn't seem eager to help. She was aloof, pissed off beneath the surface. I was amazed at how well she managed to avoid contact with me.

Maybe she's been here before? I thought. Parole officers were slimy by reputation. You don't sleep with dogs and not wake up with fleas, right? It was the nature of the job, dealing with the dregs of civilization. A guy's bound to pick up a few bad habits. Houck had already told me he preferred I be with her than the other skirt chasers.

"We need to talk," I said when I cornered her in the file room. "When are you taking lunch?"

"I'm not sure I'm ready for that."

"Still hot, huh?"

"What's going on here, Steady? I thought you were different."

I thought you were different is what a woman says when you've been a dick, when you've let her down. It's a long climb back to the top once you've fallen off the mountain. "Just give me a chance to explain. After that..."

"Not today."

"Tomorrow?"

"Don't push your luck." She closed the space between her thumb and forefinger until the gap practically disappeared. "From the way Houck's grumbling, you're this close to getting fired."

"Yeah, I hear you." What's worse is that I was a heartbeat away from becoming a cliché, an unemployed black man who'd just been kicked to the curb for lying to his woman. That was the beginning of the end for my moms and father. The nightclub life, booze, and broads—Earl Groove did my mother like that and I didn't want to fall down the same sinkhole that he had. The thing between Sandy and me was casual, just two adults having a good time. But what Earl Groove did to my moms—I wouldn't wish it on a dog.

"Good. Now get out of here before Houck catches us alone and fires us both."

"Message received, loud and clear." I yanked on the door and hustled back to my office. *Almost noon and still employed—fingers crossed. Focus on your work, Steady. Focus on the damn work."*

The phone started ringing the moment my pants hit the chair. I picked up the phone. "Parole Officer Stedman Groove."

The response was slow coming back. "Mr. Groove, this is Angela Rizzo. We met last week at the bakery."

Mother-fucking Angela Rizzo—now what does she want? The same thing I wanted. *Goddamn black man's cliché, here I come.* "How can I help you, Ms. Rizzo?"

"I heard something about the murders. I think you should know."

"Did you call the police?"

"You think I'm stupid? No friggin' way."

"I'm not sure what you're trying to tell me."

"Can we meet? I don't trust the phones."

This broad thinks the bakery phone line is bugged? "Where, at the bakery?"

"Anywhere *but* here. How about seven o'clock at—" She gave me the address of a bar on South Conduit Boulevard off the Belt Parkway as well as the closest subway stop. Guess she wanted to make sure I didn't get lost.

"This is important, right?"

"No, I'm calling to waste your friggin' time. Of course, it's important."

"All right, I'll see you there."

Hell of a day so far, I thought as I hung up. I was wondering what Angela Rizzo had to tell me that demanded we meet in person and if it involved the Burattis? The hairs on my arms began to tingle.

I'm ashamed to say that the call from Angela fired me back to fantasyland. A suggestive scenario began to play in my head, real as life, just as Sandra walked by in the corridor. She seemed less angry than she had in the file room. *Hope she can't see what's in my mind.* My mind flooded with guilt, then another thought smacked me in the back of the head. *You're already thinking like your no-good father. Don't piss everyone off—pick up the phone and tell Auntie not to wait up.*

Chapter Twenty-Six

My new shoes weren't broken in, and a blister was growing on the side of my toe. If that wasn't bad enough, I sensed the dew point was rising even before I spotted the first clouds in the sky and nothing aggravates a pain in the ass faster than an approaching storm. It felt like someone was squeezing a channel lock on my right leg just under the cheek. The pain was radiating from there and traveling down my leg to the calf. I chewed up a couple of Doan's but I'd waited too long to take the painkillers and they were slow to lend a helping hand.

I'd walked another block before I noticed I'd begun to limp. Headwinds had picked up, enough that some were hurrying home in anticipation of the rain. I liked the breeze and the smell of ozone in the air, that electric tang that smells like the sparks coming off the tracks of subway cars pulling into the station. That downdraft from the stratosphere where ozone resides filled my nostrils, invigorating me.

Although I was new at it, part of me felt like the parole officer job was like being a babysitter. *Were you a good little ex-con? Did you go to work last week? Stay out of trouble?* True, there were the troublemakers, the ones that couldn't stay clean—you had to stay one step ahead of those. But for the most part, the job wasn't challenging. Gathering facts about D. Wayne felt different, like I was making good use of my brain and doing it because I wanted to.

The walk from the railroad to the bar took me past 8010 Liberty. Someone was sitting out on the front steps. Getting closer, I recognized the man's face. Rico Bueno had a mop of tight curly hair and mustache like Yosemite Sam. A white wife-beater accentuated his big paunch. He jumped up when a woman approached, a skinny brunette wearing a denim jacket over a sundress. He gave her a hug and a buss on the cheek, then gestured toward his front door, and she followed him into the house.

Catch of the day, I mused, *a sunfish in a sundress*. Sunfish are notorious chumps. It takes no effort at all to catch one. Stick a worm on a hook and bang, you've got a hit on your line, no know-how needed. And this woman looked like she wouldn't require much work at all, maybe none. They called them rock stars, gals that screwed for drugs—women looking for love for all the wrong reasons in all the wrong places.

And Bueno's home, the recent scene of eleven murders, was nothing if not the wrong place. Like a good fisherman capable of sensing the slightest tug on the fishing line, Bueno could spot the easy marks. He'd cast his hook and hauled in an easy catch, a fish that would fall for his macho charm, hook, line, and sinker. My thoughts ran to the story Angela had told me about the news reporter and her walk of shame. The new sighting corroborated what she'd said about Bueno's ravenous hunger for the ladies. I walked into the meeting with Angela, believing she liked to play it straight.

She was out of her white uniform when I spotted her at the bar getting chatted up by the bartender. She wore a white tailored blouse over dark slacks and pumps. Her clothing was much more formfitting than the all-white bakery uniform she'd worn when we first met. She was a big sexy gal, voluptuous, and her curves were obvious the moment I walked through the door.

She cut off the bartender the moment she saw me come through the door. Picking up her drink, she motioned for me to follow her toward a booth away from the bar—two vinyl-covered bench seats fronting the entrance to the dining room area.

"Right on time. What are you having?" she asked as she slid into the booth.

"Beer works."

She called out to the bartender. "Bobby, a Peroni."

"What's a Peroni?"

"That's the kind of beer they serve in a place like this."

"What kind of place is this?"

"A goombah place, a place heavy Italians come to."

Heavy didn't mean weight. Heavy meant Italians were slow to abandon old ways and traditions. "Peroni any good?"

"If you like that Budweiser crap, you'll love Peroni."

She had a pretty smile. Her makeup looked freshly applied, but what did I know. I was always amazed by the way makeup could change a woman's appearance—like they could use those powders and creams to conjure up any kind of appearance they wanted: demure, modest, businesslike, sexy. Angela had opted for sexy. No complaints. Her dark brown hair was no longer pinned back but now cascaded in soft waves to the mid-back.

Maybe she's going on a date after this, I thought. *Maybe she's planning to light up her boyfriend like a Vegas billboard. Lucky guy.*

I thought about Sandy and the good times we were missing out on by being apart. I couldn't help wondering what Angela was wearing under her shirt and slacks. *"Don't be a dog. Try not to think like that.* "So what do you have to tell me that I had to ride the subway to hear?"

"Right to it—just like that?"

The bartender brought my beer to the table, a light amber ale in one of those pilsner glasses. "First Peroni?" The man had thick hair, like strands of Kevlar, dense enough to stop a point-blank headshot.

"Guess it is."

"Italian beers are much better than domestics. Trust me, you'll see." Angela's cocktail glass was half-empty. "I'll bring you a fresh one, Ang," he said and headed off.

I raised my glass. "Here's to being helpful." The beer had a distinctive taste. It took a few sips before I was able to appreciate the nuances.

"What do you think?" she asked.

"Different."

"Different, how? Different good or different bad?"

"Just different."

"Different like you'd order it again or different as in you don't need it in your life?"

"A little of both. I'm guessing it's a lot more expensive than domestic."

"Like double."

"I'm not exactly a caviar and champagne kind of guy."

"So it's good but not good enough to pay extra for. I don't understand that kind of thinking."

I stuck my foot out to the side. "I paid extra for these shoes, and I'm still getting blisters."

She glanced at my loafers. "Bet they're not made in Italy. You get a pair of calfskin Italian loafers, and you'll feel like you're walking on air."

It wasn't hard to see she was a dyed-in-the-wool paisan. "Maybe you'll come shoe shopping with me next time," I said.

"Maybe I will. Not for nothing, but you look like you could use a woman's touch."

"What kind of touch?" The adolescent part of my brain enjoyed that one.

Bobby dropped off Angela's cocktail and walked into the backroom restaurant. I looked around and saw that the bar was empty. "If I didn't know better, I'd be worried that we were about to get gunned down."

"Yeah, that's right—I set you up to get whacked. I think you've watched *The Godfather* too many times." She slid a bowl of cashews in front of me. "Here, the last supper. Eat up if you don't want to end up sleeping with the fishes."

"I used to sleep above the fishes."

"Huh?"

"Spent three years on the Bering Sea swinging crab pots."

"Oh." She reached across the table and squeezed my bicep. "Didn't do you any harm."

She's definitely flirting. Don't be like your old man, I told myself yet again. *Change the damn subject.* "You had something to tell me?"

"Oh yeah, that's right. I remembered something I forgot to tell you the first time we spoke."

I inched closer in my seat.

"Back when all this happened, I overheard someone telling one of the detectives something?"

CHAPTER TWENTY-SIX

"Which detective?"

"*You* know which one, the one that looks like a mob enforcer—stocky, receding hairline."

"Detti?"

"Yeah, I guess. He looked Italian."

"Who was he talking to?"

"Some guy. I don't know…another guy. Look, you want me to tell you what I remembered, or are we gonna play twenty questions?"

Angela Rizzo was anything but a wallflower. "I'm listening."

"You'd better because I've got a temper, and I hold a grudge."

"I'd better stay on your good side then."

"And don't you forget it."

"I won't."

"Good. So, this guy, he was kind of worked up. He wanted to know what the skuz bucket was doing living in Brooklyn."

"Skuz bucket—that's Bueno, right?"

"Right, the man-whore."

"Why was the other guy so worked up?"

"Something about Skuzzo being on parole in Rhode Island."

"*What*? Bueno's out on parole?"

"Yeah, that's what I said, isn't it? In Rhode Island. I guess that's some kind of problem?"

"It most definitely *is*." Having just completed training, I knew the ins and outs of parole like nobody's business—those details were fresher in my mind than bakery bread on Sunday morning. Bueno had to live in the county where he was paroled. Living on the wrong side of the Queens-Brooklyn border might not have been a large issue, but Queens to Rhode Island? There was absolutely no way. "He was living out of the state he was paroled too?"

"I mean, it's not as if I was part of the conversation. I had to snoop, you know? Good thing I've got exceptionally fine hearing."

And that's ain't all. "You happen to overhear anything else."

"No, but from where I stood, I could see that detective's notepad was blank—nothing was written on it whatsoever. He kept nodding and pretending to take notes in his notebook but he actually wrote *zippo*. *Nada. Nothing*. So, unless he's got one of those photographic memories…"

"Thank you, Angela. I really appreciate it."

She seemed pleased with herself, pleased because she'd been helpful. Her body language changed just as it had at the end of our first meeting. I could almost see her shifting gears.

She leaned in close and spoke in a most manner-of-fact manner. "And now it's time you anted up."

Sure, I'll pay for the drinks. I reached for my pocket, but she grabbed my arm.

"Not that." She smiled playfully. "I'm gonna take you shoe shopping."

The hell? Shoe shopping? "Now? It's too late. All the stores are—"

"You're a little slow on the uptake, Mr. Groove. Don't you want to slip into a nice soft pair of Italian…?" she whispered, then caressed her neck with the tips of her fingernails, allowing them to fall until they came to rest at the apex of her cleavage. "Well, handsome, are you ready to walk on air?"

Chapter Twenty-Seven

I was angry, angry because Angela made cheatin' so easy, but more so because falling into that cheatin' routine never felt so damn good. I mean, I was still walking on air when I left Angela's apartment the next morning. Let me tell you, that woman understood passion, how to satisfy and *be* satisfied. She made her body mine to do whatever I wanted with it, and I did, over and over until all the air was out of the balloon. If that wasn't enough, she wouldn't let me out the door without making me a big breakfast, pancakes, eggs, and coffee—the whole Sicilian…manicotti. Manicotti, that's Italian for enchilada, right?

And get this—she made a chicken cutlet sub for my lunch. I tell you right now—when I get married, I'm going Italian. Between her curves and her cooking, you'd have to be nuts to look anywhere else.

I was still gazing into Angela's big brown eyes when I walked to the subway. It was about then that guilt gave me a second kick in the head—I'm talking an enormous Clydesdale kick, two horseshoe-clad hooves to the head. I started thinking about Sandy, sexy, flirty Sandy, and how badly she'd be hurt if she knew where I'd spent the night—how I'd spent the night. Now, Sandy and I were casual. I mean, we'd only been together less than a month. It's not like we were in a committed relationship. No matter—I still felt like a dick.

The next ten brothers I passed on the street would say that I was nuts. They'd say something like, "Two white bitches? Damn. Play, playuh, play. You don't want 'em? *She-it*, I'll take them off your hands."

Knowing how most guys would handle my problem helped mitigate the guilt a little but it seemed I was still distracted. I was a few yards from the subway entrance when I took a shoulder in the back that sent me flying. It wasn't one of them itty-bitty bumps. I was one of them how-dare-you-get-in-my-way collisions, the kind that makes your fist ball up. "Hey!"

Mr. Hit-and-Run was a few steps past me. He looked angry. "What?" It was Detti.

"You got a problem, Parole Officer *Groove*?"

So it's gonna be like that, huh? "I'd say you ought to look where you're going, but you knew exactly what you were doing."

"No. Honest to God, it was an accident." He approached and grabbed a handful of my lapel. "You live around here, Groove?"

I smacked his hand off me. "No, just slumming. That all right with you?"

He got up on his toes. I guess he thought he had to meet me eye-to-eye to intimidate me. Shit, he was so close I could smell his luxury store cologne. "You're starting to be a pain in the ass, Groove. Whatsamatta, you don't like me taking down your homeboy?"

"I've got no idea what you're talking about, Detective."

"Of course, you don't. Then why are you asking questions? You visited the crime scene and talked to people in the neighborhood."

"I got the motherfucking right to go anywhere I please, talk to anyone I want. Got something in this country called freedom of speech."

"And you pulled Tyrone's case file."

"I sure as hell did. He's my parolee."

"Your parolee's not on the street—he's in the goddamn hoosegow. He's not your responsibility anymore."

"I'm real conscientious, Detti. I'm crossing all my "T"s, dotting all my "I"s. You have a problem with a man doing a proper job?"

"Don't shit me, Groove. You and Tyrone are thick as thieves. You're in league with each other."

"Oh yeah, what league is that?"

"The Black Bandits League. I know all about you and your mass-murdering friend. He'd get the needle if it were up to me."

"Good thing it's not."

I guess he couldn't prop himself up on his toes any longer. I saw the top of his head fall. "I thought you were smarter than that, but you're just another dumb black kid. Do yourself a favor. I'm Gerry Cooney to your Ken Norton. All I need is fifty-four seconds to put you on your ass. You have any idea who you're messing with? I'll bring so much hurt down on you, you won't know what hit you. Go ahead, test me. Motherfucking test me, you fish-smelling piece of shit!"

"Where's all the hate coming from? All along, I thought you wanted to be friends."

"*What?*"

I pushed past him hard. Almost put him into the street. "I've got a train to catch. You feel like flapping your gums a little longer, you call my office and make an appointment. You want a pissing war, you're sure as hell gonna come up short."

Chapter Twenty-Eight

Sandy was standing out in front of the office building when I arrived for work. She was holding a brown paper bag saturated with grease, looking up and down the street.

"That for me? I already had breakfast." *Home-cooked.*

"You want it, you can have it. I told Houck I missed breakfast and snuck out so that I could give you a heads-up before you were blindsided."

"A heads-up about what?"

Her eyes were sad, full of disappointment. "What's going on with you, Steady? Was I wrong about you? Seemed like you were different, but—"

"But what?"

"Houck's is burning mad. He got a call from Detective Detti the minute he walked in the door. I've got no idea what Detti said, but I've rarely seen Houck this mad."

"Oh, I know *exactly* what Detti told him, that I'm a nasty-ass piece of garbage. Detti accosted my ass on the way to the subway this morning. Blind-sided me about snooping around in Dennis Tyrone's case."

She looked away. Seemed like she was holding back tears. "What is it with you and this guy. You in love with him or something? Honestly, I don't understand what this is all about."

"Told you—Detti's trying to railroad Tyrone—using him as a fall guy."

"Steady, you'd better be careful. Don't give Houck cause to fire you. Once that happens, you won't see another civil service job again, and I mean ever."

"I've done nothing wrong. I accessed records I'm entitled to see, and I'm doing it on my own time. If Houck's got a problem with that…well then, he can kiss my ass. The only one I care about is you, Sandy. You gonna let me explain? Didn't feel good you kicking me out." *Shit, I'm going to burn in hell, saying that after spending the night in another woman's bed.*

"I need more time."

I said, "okay," but I was gut-twisting angry. "Take your time."

"Houck's in with the higher-ups for the next couple hours. Maybe you should make yourself scarce today."

"Yeah, we'll see. I've got a ten o'clock appointment upstairs. If Houck wants to butt heads…so be it." I walked past her and through the revolving doors. We rode the elevator together in silence.

Her intel was good—Houck's door was open, and the conference room door shut. I didn't know who he was in with and didn't care. My day had been on a downhill slide from the minute I walked out of Angela's apartment. Still had the chicken cutlet hero, though. The sandwich had been out of the refrigerator for a while, and the fragrance was calling out to me. I ate half and stowed the rest in the refrigerator to have for lunch. With every bite, I was reminded of the night I'd spent with Angela, her tan Mediterranean skin, and her warm red lips. The daydream enhanced the taste of the sandwich—made it something special.

For some reason, I'd forgotten what she'd told me about Rico Bueno, about him owning and living in a house in Brooklyn when he was supposed to be a resident of Rhode Island. Didn't make sense to me.

* * *

9:30 a.m.

Salty Monroe was due in my office in a half-hour. I had some busy work I could've attended to but I picked up the phone and got the number for the Rhode Island Department of Corrections. The operator rattled off several regional offices, but the main administrative office was in Cranston. I jotted down the number and dialed.

A woman picked up on the eighth ring. "Rhode Island Department of Parole and Probation—how can I help you?"

"Good morning. This is Parole Officer Stedman Groove with the Brooklyn Parole Office. I was wondering if you might help me with some information on a rehabilitated former offender?"

She cut right to the chase. "Name?"

"Rico Bueno"

"You have an address for the parolee?"

"Not in Rhode Island."

"I need your shield number and phone number. Someone will get back to you if he's in the system."

I gave Ms. Impersonal the requested details. She verified the spelling of my name and hung up.

I checked the time, 9:55. *Salty should be walking through the door pretty soon.*

10:00 a.m. came and went.

10:05 too.

10:10

10:30 saw me still sitting at my desk with a thumb up my ass.

Faced with planning the rest of my day, I was torn between getting reamed out by Houck or tracking down Salty Monroe. To tell the truth, I've never been a big fan of getting my ass stretched, so pressed as to which I'd enjoy more…I opted for tracking down the debonair old weasel. I retrieved the other half of Angela's dream sandwich. The time was right for getting out of Dodge.

Chapter Twenty-Nine

Salty was full of shit. He didn't enjoy the steaks at Tad's so much as the lunch special price point and only frequented the establishment when he was eating out on his own coin. When wining and dining with one of his graying fillies, he did so only at Manhattan's most renowned eateries. I'd committed Big John's list of Salty's favorite haunts to memory and knew where to begin my search. A quick stop at Delmonico's revealed that he'd eaten there on Saturday night but had no future reservations booked. A dime in the Ma Bell coin slot revealed that he wasn't at Luger's, and a second well-spent dime disclosed that he wasn't at Fraunces Tavern either.

I was surprised that the hostess at P. J. Clarke's didn't know Mr. Monroe by name, but the description I gave her yielded an affirmative response leading to a quick ride on the subway.

I'd eaten at Clarke's once, a couple of years before I went to sea. It took me a week to save up enough for burgers and drafts for my girl and me. But it was worth it—for my money, one of the best burgers I'd ever eaten. The red gingham tablecloths and painted wrought iron décor were permanently etched in my mind, as was the long wooden bar where we sat when I took Joyce Cook for dinner. Good old Joyce—she's the one Auntie said had a backside big enough to serve lemonade. I wish she'd been there to see Joyce's rump hanging off that flimsy wooden barstool. Men were stopping to ogle those chops through the glass storefront. She practically caused a pileup on Third Avenue.

The hostess told me there was only seating at the bar and that all the tables were booked for lunch. The badge came out, and she left me alone. "I'll be cool," I told her. "Ten minutes tops."

Salty and his gal were at a table smack dab in the middle of the floor. She had that Queen Elizabeth look, pinned gray hair, and a Chanel suit jacket. A tasteful black handbag sat on the table next to her coffee cup.

I could see that Salty was in the zone, talking with his mouth and his hands—his cheekbones pinned to his eyes. He'd touch her arm and laugh, then do it again. He had that Svengali *thang* down cold.

He looked so smooth I felt bad about disturbing his action. He saw me coming and tried to ignore me, but I sidled up to the table with a shit-eating grin. "Hello, Salty. Aren't you going to introduce me to your lady friend?"

"Well, look who's here," he said. "Janice, this is my dear friend Stedman Grove. Steady and I go way back."

To last week. "Nice to meet you, Janice." She offered her hand, and I gave it a dainty little shake. It was like a mackerel succumbing to rigor mortis. She wore a thick gold bracelet but no engagement ring or wedding band—all the signature attributes of a Salty Monroe mark. Pawning an expensive bracelet like hers would keep Salty in T-bones for months. "This place has the best burgers in town."

"Nice to meet you, Mr. Groove. That is a very interesting name you have," she said.

"I have my dad to thank for it." *That and little else.* "How do you and Salty know each other?"

"Why Salty and I met on the Roseland dance floor. Mr. Monroe is quite a dancer."

"Well, it's nice meeting you, Janice," I said. "You mind if I borrow your dance partner for a few minutes?"

Her hands said, "I guess."

"Can't this wait, old friend?" Salty asked. "Our food should be here any minute now."

"Wish it could." I gave him an I-mean-business nod. He excused himself and followed me to the men's room. "I don't have to tell you why I'm here."

"I know, I know, but you see, Steady, looking this good takes time. You don't think I wake up fully groomed, do you? I'm in the bathroom a good three hours working on this masterpiece. And Janice…getting her well-heeled fanny into that seat was a long time in the works. Don't screw it up for me."

"What do you want me to say? Wake up earlier or figure out *a look* that's lower maintenance. You've got a bad track record, Salty. I'm afraid—"

"No, no, no, don't say it. I can't go back inside. Why, don't me knowing your uncle count for nothing?"

I could feel the muscles in my face stiffen. "Don't shit me, old man. You don't know my uncle."

"The hell I don't. Why I fenced for Barney for years—watches, rings, and such, anything he brought in off the street."

I tried to rile him. "The *hell* you say."

"Why he—"

"He what?"

He looked guilty and measured his words. "This is off the record, right?"

"I ain't decided yet. Let's hear it."

I saw his chest rise and fall. He was so close I could smell wine on his breath. "He came to me with some jewelry just last week. Naturally, I told him I don't do that kind of thing anymore."

"Last week, huh? Where?"

"My place. He showed up out of the blue. Knocked on the door just as I was ready to retire. Looked pretty shabby."

A scheme hatched in my brain, and I didn't like what I was thinking, means-to-and-end thinking, the kind that would almost definitely get me in trouble. "You know how to find Barney?"

"Well, I don't know, Steady—ain't like he gave me a phone number. And boxes under the highway, they tend to be temporary. Know what I mean?"

I knew exactly what he meant. Barney was in a bad way, squatting here and there. Finding him would be like looking for a needle in a haystack. *Better Salty do the legwork than me.*

"Here's my offer. You find Barney for me, and you do it fast. You've got until Friday. If I don't hear from you by then, I'm revoking your parole.

That plain enough?"

"*You* can't do that, man. It ain't ethical."

"Who are you to talk to me about ethics? You're already counting the green you're gonna haul in from pawning Janice's solid gold bracelet."

"I am not."

"Say anything you like, but the offer goes away in five, four, three—"

"All right, all right." He nodded, but the look in his eyes told me he was still weighing options, like where he'd run to if he didn't turn up with Sockeye by the end of the week.

"Enjoy your lunch and the old doll's company. Maybe if you talk her deaf, dumb, and blind, she'll visit you when you're back in the joint."

Chapter Thirty

I'd found Salty too damn fast and was back in the office before 4:00 p.m. Now, most POs would've stretched their outing past quitting time but not me. Guess I wasn't that bright. I was back at my desk in time to fill in my daily activity log so that Houck would know I wasn't off on a mission I had no business being involved in.

There was a message from Lloyd of the Cranston, Rhode Island Corrections Department with a 401 area code. I called him right back, got the receptionist, and was transferred to his desk. "Lloyd, please," I said.

"This is Phil Lloyd—how can I help you?"

Phil Lloyd? Hate those tricky two-first-name names. "Phil, this PO Stedman Groove of the Brooklyn, New York Parole Office. How are you doing today?"

"How am I doing? Let's see…it's Tuesday, which means I've got three more days of riding roughshod over some of the nastiest fuckers this side of Providence. Now, if you'd called me Saturday at about noon…What's up, Groove, Groovy Groove? Is that what they call you?"

"My friends call me Steady."

"Steady, huh? *Hmmm*, I didn't see that one coming. Guess it makes sense—Steady, from Stedman, that is. All right, Steady, it's not getting any earlier. How can I help you? Oh yeah, wait, you wanted some info on Rico Bueno. Is that correct?"

"That's right. Can you tell me why…?"

"…A Rhode Island parolee has a residence in Brooklyn, New York?"

"Uh-huh."

"Wish we were talking face-to-face, Steady. That way you'd see the egg on my face. But our office sent an official report down to NYPD. Guess you didn't see it?"

"Wasn't in the file."

"There's red tape everywhere, my friend. It's probably still worming its way through channels."

"Channels, huh? Suppose you give me the rough and dirty?"

"Can I ask you why you want to know?"

Tell the truth, I figured. *Either he's going to tell me, or he won't.* "I'm the doer's PO in the Palm Sunday Massacre."

"No shit—you're Tyrone's PO?"

"Like I said."

"You poor bastard—I'd hate to be you. Taking some shit, are you?"

"Have been and still am. I'm starting to get used to it."

"Still, what's your interest in Bueno? You playing gold-badge cop?"

"Just professional curiosity."

"It's simpler than you might think, Steady. Bueno's got an apartment and a job delivering dry cleaning here in RI. He shows up for all his check-in appointments when he's supposed to, just like a goddamn Boy Scout."

"What did he do his time for?"

"Felony drug possession and distribution—two-time inmate at D. W. Wyatt Detention Facility—model prisoner."

"You ever figure he's delivering more than just starched shirts?"

"Look, I'm not a detective. Bueno shows up clean and stays out of trouble… as far as I'm concerned, he's John Wayne. As far as him having a place in Brooklyn…? There's no way for us to know about that. Would you know if one of your parolees had a second residence? Not a chance in hell."

"No, but none of my parolees can afford a second place. Bueno paid for the house in Brooklyn, all cash. You hear that, no mortgage? Now how does a Rhode Island ex-con delivery boy come up with fifty large?"

"Son of a bitch! You sure about that?"

I rattled off a phone number. "Recorder of Deeds, Kings County—tell you anything you want to know. What, NYPD didn't share that little tidbit with you?"

Lloyd was silent on the end of the line, and I was quiet on my side as well. Why didn't anyone know what was going on? Why was a five-and-dime drug dealer operating multistate without so much as getting a slap on the wrist? Close as I could figure, there was only one person I could ask who would give me a straight answer. But before I got to the asking, there was something standing in my way: A drill sergeant-looking, seething Parole Officer Supervisor named Harry Houck. He was standing in my doorway, looking like he was ready to come to blows.

Good thing I can handle myself because after what I'd just heard, I was angry enough to bleed for the truth.

Chapter Thirty-One

D. Wayne looked like the Elephant Man when I visited him in prison. He had a purple knob on his forehead the size of a grapefruit and strips of adhesive tape securing gauze across his cheekbone. He looked like Rocky Balboa after his first knock-down-drag-out battle with Apollo Creed, one eye shut, cheekbone bruised—ugly. His balance was off so badly a guard had to escort him to the table in the prison visitor's room where I was waiting for him.

"Good God, D., what the hell happened to you?"

His lips parted, exposing a pair of broken incisors I didn't remember him having before going into the pen, and he had to turn his head to the left so that he could focus on me. "You should see the other guy." When his top lip rose, I noticed that the chipped teeth met at the apex near his gums, forming an almost perfect isosceles triangle making him look even more pathetic than he looked with his mouth closed.

"Inmates did this to you?"

"Sure, inmates with batons."

"Guards beat you this badly?"

He somehow managed to grin without wincing in pain. There was only one explanation for that.

"They got you hopped up?"

"Yeah, man, they got me hopped up *good*. Peed the bed last three nights straight."

I could feel my nose wrinkle. *Shit*. Didn't look like all the hurt bothered him, though. He must've been strung out as a motherfucker. "Does your lawyer know what happened to you?"

"They say he been called."

"And?"

I could see his focus go off, and he started to zone out.

"*And?*"

"Don't know, Steady."

"When did they call him?"

He shrugged.

I was there on a fifteen-minute lunchtime visit, and with the way D. Wayne was being treated, I figured he'd be lucky if they let me stay a full five. Considering the charges against him, I was fortunate they let me visit him at all. I also knew I couldn't take the prison's benevolence for granted and that I might not be able to see D. Wayne again.

Nor did I know how long I could count on Houck's goodwill. We went at it a solid twenty minutes with him barking like a pit bull for disrespecting an NYPD detective. He finally let me off with a strong warning. I didn't think he was going to let me off so easy, but considering the detective making the complaint was Detti…grain of salt shit, you know?

D. Wayne suddenly came back to life. It was as if he'd been asleep, and someone dowsed him with a bucket of ice water. He blurted, "Tuesday."

"They called your lawyer on Tuesday?"

"Yeah, Tuesday…What's today?"

"Thursday."

He seemed to mull it over, then went quiet. It looked like maybe the dope was preventing him from stringing his thoughts together. It also seemed as if his court-appointed lawyer didn't give a rat's ass if his client lived or died. Muckler, the mofo's name, came to mind. *Have to give that ambulance chaser a call.* I figured I'd better ask D. Wayne what I'd come to ask him before he went blank or got hauled back to his cell.

A dab of drool appeared on his lower lip and ran down his chin. "D. Wayne, you know this Rico Bueno dude?"

He was struggling, his lids opening and closing on and off. "You say, *Wayne-O?*"

"No, *Bway-no, Ree-ko Bway-no.*"

"Right, *No bueno*—it's no good them guards beatin' my ass to a pulp. I got rights. Why my lawyer ain't done nothin' yet?"

I flashed my palms. "Dunno, man. Wish I could tell you." I figured in his state of mind that visual aids were needed. I showed him a picture of Bueno I'd taken from the case file. "This motherfucker—you know him?"

He squinted, his lids so narrow I was surprised any light could get through at all. "Yeah, Rico—I know that Puerto Rican piece of shit."

"How? How do you know him?"

He rocked side-to-side, looking content, then made a hand gesture—thumb and index finger touching at the tips, the remaining three fingers pointing down—the symbol dopers use for scoring drugs on the street. "He sells you drugs?"

He nodded, one eye closed. I wasn't sure how lucid he was, but at least he was conscious. "How long have you been scoring off him?"

"Long as I been a free man."

Several months, I figured. It had been six months since his three-year sentence ended. "When was the last time you saw him?"

It took a while for him to answer, but then he made a gun with his index finger and thumb.

"The day of the shooting?"

He fired off another one-eyed nod.

"Anyone else in the house when this went down?"

"Naw, man, Rico's old lady is devout. She likes to eat them communion wafers. And being Palm Sunday, you know? Must've taken the kids for that church thang."

D. Wayne's info corroborated the testimony in the case file I'd gotten around to reading only the night before. His junkie girlfriend, Vonda Gale, had provided testimony that she'd gone with D. Wayne to Bueno's home on Palm Sunday, earlier in the day. The DA was going to call Vonda as a witness in D. Wayne's trial. Looked like Vonda blew hot and cold. She could love D. Wayne or leave him to rot depending on how well he saw to her needs. "You and Vonda went to see Rico on Palm Sunday?"

He gave me a nod.

"Then what?

"Motherfucking slinger wouldn't front me my bump—talking some shit about having to pay his *big* dog. I had to scram and hunt down some skrilla."

"So you left?"

"Had to. Vonda and me, we needed our fixer-uppers…*bad*. Took a long time to hunt down some street money."

"When'd you get back?"

"Early. Eleven maybe."

Allowing for inaccuracy, his return was still a good four hours before Mulligan spotted D. Wayne stripping a car, the same time the coroner pegged the time of death.

"What, then?"

"Came back to a bad scene."

"Bad scene? Why? You had the money you needed, right?"

"Yeah, but Vonda, she couldn't wait for me. She swapped stank puss for *her* fix. Came back and caught Rico hittin' her ass. Seeing that…? *She-it*, I grabbed my stash and bounced."

Chapter Thirty-Two

I still hadn't heard anything to implicate D. Wayne in the mass murders. Yes, he'd been in Bueno's house on Palm Sunday, but not at the time of the murders and not when any of the victims were home. So far, all they had on him was the eyewitness testimony of my loser uncle and being placed at the scene of the crime by Vonda Gale, a bipolar heroin addict.

And yet the police weren't looking for anyone else.

Why was Detti so damn sure D. Wayne was guilty? Two sets of bullets had come from two distinctly different guns. How did a shaky runt addict gun down all those women and their kids with a .38 Special in one hand and a big-ass .45 in the other? Seemed to me, D. Wayne was getting the shit end of the stick.

It was close to quitting time when the phone rang. Salty Monroe got on the line crowing about his prowess in tracking down my Uncle. He told me to come to his apartment at 6:30, and that Sockeye would be there.

His timing could not have been better, and yet it couldn't have been worse. Angela was expecting me for dinner, and I presumed that dinner with Angela Rizzo meant a full belly and a drained sack, a night of hot delicacies, and even hotter sex. I left a message on her machine explaining that I was going to be late because of the job.

Houck and I had kept our distance throughout the afternoon. I didn't see our truce as anything more than it was, a respite from arguing for him to see how long I could walk the straight and narrow. I was trying to navigate that highwire, but the wind, it sure was blowing, and that tightrope was getting rougher and rougher to negotiate. I was putting one foot in front of the other, eyes straight ahead, with the balancing bar level in my palms when Sandy blew into my office, grabbed that tight wire, and plucked it like a sting on a cello. She dropped a short stack of files on my desk and looked up at me with her soft doe eyes.

"I'm ready to talk," she said. "Do you have plans tonight?"

Chapter Thirty-Three

Damn, I hated lying to that girl.

So, I didn't.

I came clean. I told her I had a late meeting with one of my parolees and a date. I told her I didn't know where things stood between us and that I'd made plans to have dinner with a woman I'd recently met.

She didn't take it well, but at least I hadn't lied. Sure, I left out the part about Uncle Sockeye being a key witness in the case against D. Wayne, but there's a limit to the number of bitter pills a man can swallow, and I was close to gagging already.

The subway was hot as hell. Instead of blowing cool, conditioned air, it was blowing smelly warm air. I walked from the middle car to the last one hoping one of them was less of a furnace. No such luck. By the time I got to my stop, I was soaked through and through. Walking to Salty's, I wondered if Angela would let me take a shower before dinner. I was daydreaming about boning that Sicilian beauty in the shower when I came off the stairs at the second-floor landing and knocked on Salty's door. He lived in a four-story walkup. It wasn't luxury but he sure wasn't living in squalor. I passed a mature could on the way in. They looked well-heeled, the kind that didn't want for much. I guessed that Salty was more successful at the con game than I'd imagined.

Salty opened the door and was dressed to the nines. "We square?" he asked.

I could see Sockeye sitting in a club chair near the window. "Yeah, we're square, but that don't get you any extra credits. You miss one more check-in, and your right back where you started from, knee-deep in shit. "You understand me?"

I could see he was unhappy. I didn't care. One hand had washed the other. I wasn't going to give him a damn sponge bath. "Do you *understand* me?"

He nodded and walked out of the apartment toward the staircase. "Lock the door when you're done. Push the button on your way out," he said and disappeared.

I checked before closing the door. It had a pushbutton on the edge that would allow me to lock the door when I left.

Sockeye was out of the chair when I turned around. "Steady, my man, it sure is good to see you, nephew." He put his arms around me and squeezed tightly, adding some serious body odor to my sweat-drenched suit. "Y'all still staying with Carrie Mae? Shit, my little sis is a strange woman kicking me to the curb the way she did. You'd think she'd miss her brother not seeing me so many years. What did I do to deserve being treated like that? You'd think I did something hellacious."

"Where have you been staying?"

"Here and there—any place I can lay my head, mostly. Say, Steady, how you fixed for dough? I ain't had a solid meal in days."

I'd spent most of three years on a fishing boat with Sockeye, day in and day out, breaking bread and jawing about the mates, the sea, and anything else we could think of to pass the time. He'd been good company on a boat of strangers. I had to reach down deep for the strength to show him my serious side. "Have a seat, Sockeye. We need to talk."

"So you're gonna play old uncle Barney like that? Seems none of my family wants to show me no love."

"Have a seat."

Salty must've left a half-bottle of Schlitz on the coffee table. Sockeye noticed it and put the bottle to his lips. "What's this about?"

"You're an *eye* witness against Dennis Tyrone? How'd that come about?"

"What you mean, how'd it come about? I *seed* him going bang, bang, bang like some kind of one-man killing machine putting bullets between everyone's eyes."

"Bullshit, Sockeye. You're six inches smaller than me, and I couldn't see shit through that front window."

"Maybe *you* didn't want to see shit, but I *see'd* him. I *see'd* him real good. I know that boy since he was a little street rat—always up to no good. I knew it was him straight off. Runty little motherfucker."

"The police report said you couldn't pick him out of the lineup until they had him turn to the side. You know Dennis so fucking well but couldn't identify his ass until you saw the side of his face, his profile? Come on now—cut the shit."

"Oh yeah, that was the detective's idea. But that was all it took—I saw the side of that big old schnoz and knew it was him. That's how I saw him through the window. It was a motherfucking match."

"How the hell did you get together with Detti?"

"How? Reward money is how. I figured I'd help those poor, poor dead women and kids—pick up some scratch at the same time."

"Then how come you're flat busted broke. You plow through all the reward money already?"

"No, man. That cop, Detti, he played my ass. Told me I had outstanding arrest warrants. Said he'd make them disappear but took the reward money off the table."

"You're a fool. You should've let him arrest you. At least you'd have a roof over your head and food in your belly. Now you've got jack shit." I pulled a pair of twenties out of my wallet and waved them in his face. He grabbed for them, but I reeled them back before he could get his dirty little paws on them. "You want the cash, and I want the truth—pay for play, Unc. Did you really see Dennis kill those people, or was that just Detti, putting words in your mouth?"

"What you mean, words in my mouth?"

"Did you actually see those women and kids getting shot, or are you lying to stay out of jail? Which is it?"

His hand shot out for the twenties faster than a striking, fangs-bared viper.

"Did you see Dennis Tyrone kill those people or not?"

I could see how disappointed he was with the paltry hall. "What's it matter to you anyhow? That boy always was a piece of—"

Someone was pounding on the door. *Who's that?* I wondered. *Salty, back already?*

I left Sockeye and moved to the door. "That you, Salty?" I was reaching for the doorknob when someone burst in, slamming the door into my forehead. The cold steel security door crashed into my skull, knocking me down. I heard the sound of footsteps scrambling past me as consciousness began to fade. It was about that time the lights went out.

Chapter Thirty-Four

The next thing I heard was the roar of a mob. I slowly opened my eyes and realized I was in a hospital bed. I had an I.V. in my arm and oxygen in my nose. A machine was beeping, and my head hurt like hell, as if an elephant was sitting on it. Light was streaming through the window. I recognized a landmark building across the street, placing me in Brookdale Hospital with a view of the buildings on Linden Boulevard. *Must be some kind of demonstration going on*, I thought. *Wonder if it's Pointer doing his goat and pony show.*

What the hell am I doing in the hospital?

Auntie entered the room a minute later, carrying a paper cup of coffee. "Praise the Lord," she said as the coffee cup hit the floor. She rushed over to the bed, took my hand, and held it to her cheek. "Steady, oh thank God. You know how long I've been waiting for you to open your eyes?"

I shook my head, causing it to ache all the more.

"More than two days. Someone whacked you upside the head. The doctor thinks you were pistol-whipped."

It was a hell of a long nap, but I still felt exhausted, as if I hadn't slept in days. I felt my head and realized it was bandaged. "Auntie—" My throat was too dry to speak. I touched my throat. She poured water into a cup and helped me to drink through a straw.

"That better, honey?"

"Yeah. What's going on outside?"

"Protests, Steady. The Reverend Malcolm Pointer is calling for the mayor's and police commissioner's resignation. Dennis Tyrone is right here in this very hospital, clinging to life. Got beat to within an inch."

"Let me guess—Pointer's playing the race card?"

She smiled sympathetically.

"Hey, Auntie, you think they've got any Excedrin around this place? I'm in Brookdale, right?"

"Uh-huh. They brought you here Friday at about three o'clock in the morning. You were out cold. It's a good thing you had my phone number in your wallet. What were you doing in that man's apartment anyway? He came home after a date and found you lying on the floor with your head bleeding."

Tumblers were beginning to fall into place. "What about Barney?"

"*Barney*? My *brother*, Barney? Why the hell are you asking about him?"

"He wasn't there?"

"There? Why would he be?" She touched my forehead. "You're warm. I'm going to find the doctor."

I watched her hurry out the door. *No Sockeye*, I thought. Dead *or taken*? My head began to swim, and the lights went out again.

I wasn't sure how much time had passed, but the next time I opened my eyes, it was dark outside. It sounded like the protestors had gone home and Pointer to a five-star restaurant. He pandered to the poor, but I heard that he lived like the rich. *Wonder who's footing his tab?*

Someone was sitting in a chair off to the side. I could see the outline of a man's head, short hair, buzzed sidewalls. "I made your aunt go down to the cafeteria for a snack, Steady. I think she's been living on coffee since you're here."

I didn't expect to see Houck. "I figure you'd be the last who'd want to see me."

He got out of the chair, walked over to the bed, and pretended to graze my chin with his fist. "Aw, come on, Steady, you know I love you. Besides, a PO goes down… one of mine…we're family, Steady. Whatever made you think differently?"

"Been on your shit list the last few days."

He waved his hand. "Water under the bridge. I questioned Salty Monroe.

He said you've been keeping him on a tight leash. He said he forgot you were coming to see him and went out. How long were you in his place waiting for him before someone put your lights out?"

"Not long. I heard someone knocking on the door and went to answer it. The door swung open and smashed me in the head."

"That's not what caused the concussion. You took a hunk of iron to the back of the head."

"So, I got it front and back."

"I'd like to say it was a doubleheader, but that would be downright insensitive."

"Next thing I knew, I woke up here. Close as I can figure, I got in the way of a robbery. Or maybe someone stopped by to settle a debt with Monroe. Both explanations suck. Salty didn't have any idea about who it could've been?"

"Not a one. Hey, I'm sorry you got your clock cleaned. I put you out on medical leave with pay. Take all the time you need to get back on your feet. Spend some time at the beach."

"Sounded like a protest was going on outside when I first came to."

"It's over for today, but that fat ass reverend's been making everyone crazy. Says he's got evidence that Police Commissioner Canton was shacked up with a call girl, booze-blitzed for three straight days. Not sure you knew this, but Canton was nowhere to be found when the Palm Sunday Massacre went down and for days afterward. That's why he wasn't at any of the early press conferences. Between you and me, I think he's gonna get the boot. Rev Pointer is saying Canton and the mayor are using this punk Tyrone as a scapegoat to take pressure off the mayor in an election year. Looks like you know more about this case than I gave you credit for. I'm sorry about that. I jumped to conclusions sometimes. Anyway, how are you feeling?"

"Like Mantle used my head for batting practice."

"Glad to see the concussion didn't hurt your sense of humor."

"You have any idea how long I'm going to be in here?"

"Not a clue, young man, but like I said, you've got a concussion. That means lots of bed rest, and I don't mean—"

"You know that Sandy and me…" I could feel a frown dragging down the corners of my mouth. "Guess you don't know what you've got 'till it's gone."

"Gone? Surely you jest. The fair-haired maiden is out in the waiting area. She's come here the moment she heard about you. You're either far more charming than you let on or…know what, I'm not going there. The department is cracking down on racism." He checked his watch. "I'm happy to see that you're among the living, but I'm sure you're tired of looking at my dingy old puss." He slipped on his suit jacket. "Let me get you someone prettier for you to look at."

Chapter Thirty-Five

I was only in Brookdale three more days, but it felt like forever. There wasn't much to do in the hospital except read the newspaper and wait for visitors to show up. My room had a TV, but I was never much for the tube except for watching that Roger Grimsby dude on the evening news. "Here now the news." He said that every night at the beginning of the show. There was something I liked about that guy. He was either deadly serious or cracking wise, and you never knew what would come out of his mouth. Must've been a combination of the two I enjoyed so much. I like people who don't take themselves seriously.

The nurses were cool. They brought me doubles of chocolate pudding and were diligent about monitoring those beeping machines and changing the dressings on my head wounds.

Auntie came by every day, as did Sandy when she got off from work in the evening. Seems the beat-down I caught bought me a load of sympathy. That and what the papers were saying must've demonstrated that I was somewhat close to the truth. She asked me to move back in with her right after being discharged, but I'd already promised Auntie I'd let her nurse me back to health. She said she'd never forgive herself if something happened to me.

I had plenty of time to read the newspapers, and it seemed that there was lots of pressure on the DA to pursue the charges against D. Wayne. The DA's name was Leah Altman, and from what I read it, she was very aggressive and hadn't lost many cases. Mulligan came to visit, and he confirmed that Altman had an outstanding conviction rate but added, "She nails 'em, guilty or not." He said she was some kind of legal steamroller, a wheeler-dealer who'd do anything to get a conviction, win another term, move up the ladder—wash, rinse, repeat.

Guilty or not, I wondered if they'd inscribe those words on D. Wayne's headstone. Here lies Dennis Wayne Tyrone, convicted of murder—guilty or not.

Poor scrawny D. Wayne was handcuffed to a bed three floors above me, surrounded by police living one heartbeat to the next. He was toxic. He was the street animal who slaughtered eleven women and kids, two six-guns blazing. Mulligan told me that despite the way heroes and desperados were depicted in action movies, ambidextrous shooters were few and far between—practically nonexistent. And D. Wayne with his mad junkie shakes—his hands must've been as steady as a bobblehead on a go-cart dashboard over a cobblestone street.

Mulligan came by the hospital for a visit. "So, who do you think cold conked you?"

"Been thinking about that since I woke up. Close as I can figure—"

"Detti?"

"Yeah. Who else has motive?"

"He doesn't like you sniffing around his case. And with Reverend Pointer stirring up all kinds of shit, the last thing Detti needs is a cowboy parole officer shining a light on all the inconsistencies in his collar. You know, back in the day, they used to pull this malarkey all the time. If the brass wanted a case closed badly enough, they just closed the fucking thing. Someone got thrown under the bus, and everything went back to normal—all except for the poor schmuck who spent the rest of his days in the state pen."

"You think that's what this is?"

"Why not? You've got the mayor, the police commissioner, and the DA all on hot seats. Pointer's got the black and Puerto Rican communities whipped into a frenzy. The Puerto Ricans are screaming bloody murder—and rightly so. The Hizzoner and the DA are both up for reelection. I wouldn't put it past either of those dickheads to pin the massacre on a scapegoat to save their fat asses from the fire. I mean, you've got to be pretty scummy to get mixed up in politics in the first place, no? I never met a one of 'em that wouldn't eat their firstborn. I've told you that I hate Pointer because he's a filthy dirty opportunist, but you've got to admire the way he gets things done. He's got all the city's top players by the short hairs, and that ain't easy to do."

"I hear tell that Pointer goes home to some palatial estate in New Jersey every night. How does a man of the cloth spend his days on a soapbox and make that kind of scratch?"

"That's easy. He's on the dole, Steady. Let's say the mob wants a construction site shut down to pressure the developer into handing out jobs to their goombahs. Pointer gives all of his low-wage followers a ham sandwich and a cup of coffee to come down and raise hell. The mob gets what they want, and Pointer gets five K in an envelope. Shit like that."

"That is one slick dude. He must be a hell of a lot smarter than he looks."

There was another part of the equation I had to figure out—what happened to Sockeye? If Detti was the one who cracked me over the head, what did he do with Sockeye? He wouldn't kill him—he needed him to testify against D. Wayne. The only thing that made sense was that he had him squirreled away, locked up in a safe house where he couldn't be found.

At the same time, I was now completely sure that the case against D. Wayne was a put-up job. Sockeye hadn't eye-witnessed the murders. That was bullshit. D. Wayne's girlfriend placed him at the crime scene on the day of the murders but so what? She was a lying, two-faced junkie who'd say anything she was told to say for a syringe full of dope. Detti making sure she was well supplied…? Wasn't much of a stretch.

The most damning piece of evidence was a spent slug Detti had recovered from a flophouse D. Wayne had rented short term, a place that burned to the ground. Detti's slug matched some of the rounds recovered from the victims during the autopsy. Detti being the Boy Scout he was, it seemed likely that slug was planted. And who was going to argue in D. Wayne's defense, Muckler, a bargain-basement public defender who'd already proved his lack of worth by standing idle while his client was almost beaten to death, not on one occasion but twice? And even if he was intent on doing his job, Muckler up against a dirty, mob-connected cop, a flimflamming DA, a pervert police commissioner, and the highest-ranking politician in the city.

Good-fucking-luck!

Chapter Thirty-Six

Auntie couldn't have been more caring. The doc said I needed bed rest, and she was all over that shit. He said headaches and dizziness were common after a concussion and if a second concussion occurred before the first one was completely healed…The damn fool said the "D" word, the dead word right in front of her sending her into a full-blown panic. From that point on, there was no reasoning with her.

She wouldn't let me lift a damn finger.

Not to do anything.

She shopped and cooked, brought me snacks and the newspapers—fluffed my pillow if she thought I looked uncomfortable. I couldn't get off the couch without having slippers magically appear beneath my feet.

I tell you what—all that attention can wear pretty thin after a couple of days. Wear thin? It can drive you out of your ever-loving mind. She was underfoot every time I turned, twitched, or sneezed, offering a tissue, a drink, nuts, cookies, and what have you—water, juice, tea, even some anemic beverage called postum because the doc told me to stay away from coffee. It was a hot beverage made from grains. I tried that concoction once, and that was enough. Best I could describe it was a taste like a sad nothing, a drink with no flavor, no jolt, and no reason for being.

Auntie even baked a mouthwatering pecan pie. Now, who can say no to that?

Between the inactivity and the goodies, I was starting to look a little doughy. One thing a young black man doesn't need is a gut. Folks start talking behind your back, asking if you've gotten lazy or drinking too much beer. I probably shouldn't care what other people think, but I like to look sharp, and it's hard to feel crisp with a paunch hanging over your belt. I tried to cut my portions, but that just made her worry about my loss of appetite. Lounging around wasn't my thing.

Sandy came over after work. I could tell straight off that Auntie was a fan because Sandy wasn't one of those gals who just sat around and let someone do everything for her. She was up and down every two minutes helping Auntie in the kitchen, clearing the table, anything she could do to lend a hand. She never came by empty-handed either. Dessert, a bottle of wine—anything she thought we'd appreciate.

Now, don't hate me, but while all the loving and devotion was happening, I couldn't help thinking of a way to see Angela. Almost a week had passed since I missed our date, and I hadn't gotten around to calling, mainly because I figured she'd call bullshit. "Sure, you got ambushed. Did the dog eat your homework too?" I'm not sure why I thought she'd doubt me, but I did. I wanted to see her in person and tell her face to face.

Auntie made pan-fried pork chops in gravy, and Sandy helped her with the sides. I could feel my pants getting tighter with every bite. I had a recheck with the doc at the end of the week, but I didn't think I'd last that long. When Thursday morning rolled around, I woke up planning to leave the apartment for a while even though Auntie had me under house arrest. Her nostrils flared the moment she saw me step out of the bathroom wearing slacks and a button-down shirt instead of sweats.

"That doesn't look like your lounging-around-the-house outfit. You planning on leaving the apartment?"

"Just for a while. I feel fine, and I figured I'd stretch my legs. I haven't hardly moved a muscle since waking up in the hospital, and I could use some fresh air."

"The doctor told you to be careful. He said—"

"I know *exactly* what he said, Auntie—I'm not going to get another concussion walking around the block."

She was preparing to bake something—eggs and flour were on the counter along with one of those motorized Mixmasters. She wiped her hands on a dishrag and squared off with me, pumping up her tiny little frame to look as imposing as possible. She did a damn good job of it too. "Stedman Groove, look me in the eye and swear to me that's all you plan to do."

"Auntie, I'm fine. I'm used to swinging giant crab pots around like bags of laundry, sliding this way and that with the ship lurching and crashing over pounding surf. A little stroll ain't gonna hurt me none."

"So, which is it, Steady? You gonna do more undercover work and get your skull split again or are you off to see your outside woman?"

"Auntie—"

"Nephew, please. Your Auntie's no fool. Mr. Houck called to check up on you and told me some woman been calling your place of work looking for you. Said she's been asking for your private information, your home phone number, and where you live. He told her he couldn't give out that information, and it's a good thing he stuck to his guns. Can you imagine this outside woman showing up while sweet little Sandy's here? Nephew, those two girls would fight to the death, and the survivor would turn on you and shred your cheatin' ass to the bone. Is that the kind of thing you want to see happen?"

"Why didn't you tell me about the calls?"

"Tell you what, about the home wrecker calling like a damn stalker? As if I might ever."

"That's not your decision, Carrie Mae."

"Oh, so now I'm Carrie Mae? Is that how you address your aunt, your mama's sister who looks after you like you're some kind of royalty?"

"Sandy threw me out, and I'm not sure where I stand with her. And Angela, she's a fine woman. You'd like her."

"I'd like her to mind her damn business. You see the way Sandy cares for you? You gonna be like your father, forsaking his wife and child for his own good time. I'm disappointed in you, Steady. I never figured you to turn out like that man's sorry ass. I'd be happier if you were going out to fight for your friend's innocence than being a womanizer. Is that the way you want it? You want to break a good woman's heart the way Earl Groove broke my sister Kitty's?"

She was on the verge of breaking down, tears welling under her eyes. I was completing college while my moms was losing her struggle. I did all I could for her, but Auntie, she was there for her little sis night and day, and that last year of my mom's life was tough. Auntie was so desperate and depressed that I was worried she'd follow moms into the grave.

Of course, she'd react strongly.

I hugged her and kissed her on the head before leaving the kitchen and walking out the door. I told her there was something I had to do. The words didn't come out of my mouth, but somehow I think she knew that she'd given me the strength to do what I had to.

Chapter Thirty-Seven

Fresh bread must've been baking in the oven because the aroma overpowered me the second I walked into the bakery. Angela was at the cash register making change for a customer when she saw me walk in. She counted out singles and handed them to her customer before hurrying around the counter.

"Have a good day, Mrs. Cologne," she said as the old woman left the store.

"You friggin' stood me up…" she said, sassing me, "but you had a good goddamn excuse." She threw her arms around me and gave me a kiss before pulling away to examine the wounds on my head. "You got quite a wallop there. Must hurt like a bastard?"

"Only when I breathe."

"Don't be such a baby. Those war wounds give you character," she said and cracked her chewing gum. "You know we're going to have to take care of the guy who did this, right? No one messes with my man and gets away with it. I'll make a few calls, and this guy will end up on ice."

"You almost sound like you're serious."

"What makes you think I'm not?" She winked at me. "Say, aren't you supposed to stay off your feet? Your boss told me you were in the hospital with a concussion."

"I was. Heard you spoke to him…more than once."

"I didn't want to be *that* girl, the one who stalks a guy, but you had me worried sick. It was either my sanity or your privacy, and guess what? You came up short." She stroked my arm. "Of course, now that I've known you in the biblical sense, I'm not worried about coming up short." She winked at me—it was one of those Lucille Ball slapstick winks. "Want some coffee?"

"I'm supposed to lay off caffeine and alcohol for a while. The doc says it could mess me up."

"How about a cannoli and a glass of milk? Fix you right up."

"Hard to say no. Your dad around?"

"He went home for lunch. It's just me right now." She went behind the counter and stuffed a cannoli shell with thick cream from the refrigerator, dusted it with powdered sugar, and poured a glass of milk so cold that condensation formed on the glass before it was full. She served me, then sat down with me at the small café table.

Damn, she was pretty.

"I'm glad you came in. There's something I've been meaning to tell you."

"Sure. What's up?" I took a bite of pastry and washed it down with cold milk. "That's *really* good. Don't think I've ever had one with such intense flavor."

"My dad makes the filling from scratch. He starts with fresh ricotta cheese. Makes a fresh batch every morning, and when it's gone, it's gone."

"Amazing. Anyway, you had something you wanted to say?"

"Yeah, I do. John and Gene Buratti were here when you were, so you know this area is heavily mobbed-up, right?"

"I never really thought about it, but now that you've brought it up…"

"Oh yeah—come on. When The Burattis want pastry, they come to my dad and nobody else. We fill an order for Buratti's club once a week like clockwork. They don't have to come in and place the order in person, but they do. It's part of their tradition. Sometimes Gene comes in to pick it up in person. If they want beef, they go to Louie, the butcher. Vino, Santangelo's Liquor Store. See what I mean? We're like one big happy family. And when something is going on in the family, everyone knows about it."

I'd devoured the pastry and licked the cannoli cream off my fingers.

"Want another?" she asked.

"No thanks. I'm getting a little thick around the middle. Besides, knowing your dad only makes so much, I wouldn't want to deprive your regular customers."

She eyed me up and down. "You look all right for a guy who almost got his head knocked off. You must be a quick healer or something. Anyway, things haven't been right ever since these protests began. Normally "Johnny Boy" wouldn't give a rat's ass about the Reverend Pointer and the blacks and Puerto Ricans, but for some reason…I don't know what it is, but there's all kinds of tension. It's like they sounded general quarters or something."

"General quarters? That sounds strange coming from you."

"It means battle stations or prepare for attack."

"I know what it means. It's just not something I ever thought I'd hear you say."

"And I thought it conveyed the message perfectly. Pops was stationed in the Pacific during World War II, and he loves war movies. I've seen *Run Silent, Run Deep* about fifty times."

"Any reason you know of for the Burattis to be on *red* alert?"

"Can't say, but what I do know is that John has his guys out looking for this guy, Angelo Felipe. He's one of the crew, a torpedo, but no one's seen him in weeks."

"But you don't know why they're looking for him?"

"This guy, Felipe, he's been in the store a few times. Believe me when I tell you I don't want anything to do with him. He's this big *jadrool*. Kind of looks like Lurch from *The Addams Family*, and he gives me the creeps. I met his girlfriend once. She carried herself well, and I remember asking myself, *what's this class act is doing with a chooch like Felipe?* People say he lives in an apartment with all manner of mutts and mongrels—all strays, anything from pigeons, to rats and raccoons…opossums, dogs, cats—you name it. A freakin' weirdo, right?"

"And Buratti doesn't have his address?"

"No, no one does. I guess when you're a hitman, it's better to operate on a need-to-know basis."

"That doesn't explain what Buratti wants with him."

"No, right? I know. They're saying he disappeared in advance of *getting* disappeared. You understand what I'm saying, right?"

"And you think it has something to do with all the protesting?"

"I can't explain it, but *yeah*, call it intuition. This all started when the Reverend Fat Ass started bitching about that guy Tyrone being a patsy and that the cops are throwing him under the bus to cover up something."

Her demeanor changed suddenly. She reached out and touched my hand. "Anyway, you heard enough?"

"I don't know. You have anything else to tell me?"

"Yeah." She motioned with her finger for me to get closer. "Who's to say I can't close the store for fifteen minutes. Why don't you take me in the back and hang me on the dough hook?" Her eyes were soft and inviting. Her hand wandered. "That's if you're up to it."

Chapter Thirty-Eight

Angela seemed quiet as she ushered me out the door. I turned to wave goodbye and saw her taking up her place behind the counter, ready for the next customer to enter the store. She was once again the dutiful shop-girl holding down the fort while her father was away.

Not tapping that fine Sicilian ass was one of the hardest things I have ever had to do. I wanted to. I ached to. I ached real badly. But I didn't. At the same time, I loved and hated my auntie for suggesting that I needed to take a stand. Thinking about what she said, about my father ruining my mom's life…Breaking it off with Angela was the right thing to do. The truth be told, I felt overwhelmed with disappointment as I walked away. My johnson was downright pissed off at me—would've probably slit my throat if it could.

I noticed a police cruiser pacing me as I walked along the avenue. The window finally opened, and a cop called out, "Hey, Dark Horse, what are you doing in this neck of the woods?"

Not too many men, cops or otherwise, could get away with calling me a name like that, but Mulligan was one of the few. He waved me over to his car. "I'd wager big money on the trifecta that you either tapped or been trying to tap that Italian cookie's ass. What are my odds?"

"How are you doing, Mike?" I said neither confirming nor denying.

"You're not answering, huh? Well, you look guilty as hell." He looked up and down the avenue with a suspicious eye. "Hang a right at the corner and meet me in the middle of the side street."

He pulled away, and I followed at a leisurely pace. As soon as I turned the corner, I saw his car pulling to the curb between two private driveways.

The street was lined with mature trees that blanketed attached houses with shade. Mulligan got out and leaned against the fender of his cruiser, waiting for me with a thermos in his hand.

"Please tell me you're not actually *doing* Angela Rizzo too? What's the matter, Sandy's ain't woman enough for you?"

"It's nothing like that. Angela knows things."

"Oh yeah, like what, how to make you hee-haw like a donkey? Putting yourself between two women like that ain't smart, fella. You either lose or you lose. There's no other outcome. I know you're a young stud and think you can handle the two of them but trust me, you can't. One way or another, it'll come back to bite you, and when that happens, no one sympathizes with a two-timer. That the kind of guy you want to be?"

"You know from experience?"

"Let's call it street smarts and leave it at that."

"Can we change the subject?"

"Sure, tell me what Angela knows other than your erogenous zones."

I checked the street—it was empty except for a solitary elderly woman pushing a grocery cart. "I think the mob might have something to do with the Palm Sunday Massacre."

"Get real. I know you want to see your homeboy cleared, but…come on, Steady. How do you figure?" He unscrewed the thermos and took a gulp of coffee.

"I'm not sure, but Angela tells me that Buratti has his crew out looking for some hitman named Angelo Felipe. That name familiar?"

He gritted his teeth. "Yeah, the name Angelo Felipe is synonymous with trouble. He's a Gambino torpedo—works for Buratti now, but he used to work for Jimmy 'The Gent' Burr and Henry Knoll, the two geniuses—and I use the term lightly—who orchestrated the Lufthansa fuck up. Of all the mobsters associated with the heist, Felipe is the only one who's still alive—except for Knoll and Jimmy Burr, that is. You want to know why?"

I felt like an idiot knowing so little about a crime that had been in the New York newspapers for months, but an insider like Mulligan was sure to know much more than the average Joe, and let's face it, I'm an average Joe. "I can hardly control my curiosity. Tell me."

"Felipe's alive because he killed everyone else involved in the heist. Felipe and 'Two-gun' Tommy Simon, under the direction of Jimmy Burr, that paranoid motherfucker, whacked everyone that could've possibly tied Jimmy to the heist." He screwed the cap back on and tucked the thermos under his arm so that he could tick off names on his fingers. "Parnell Jones, Marty Kruger, Lou, and Joanna Forma, Bob McCann, and Joe Manzo—all dead, all killed by Felipe or Simon on orders from Jimmy Burr. Felipe's also the nephew of Ralph and 'Shorty' Perditio, two Colombo capos. That makes him Cosa Nostra royalty and another reason he was never touched."

"Wait a minute—didn't you say he's a Gambino torpedo?"

"I did. For some reason, he prefers to work for the Gambinos—probably because he was so close with 'Two-gun' Simon. They graduated Lewisburg together with advanced degrees in brutal murder."

"Why's Buratti looking for Felipe if he can't be touched?"

"Because 'Johnny Boy' has a big brass pair and don't give two shits about the rules. He'll either end up dead or at the top of the heap. Still, how this ties to your homeboy, Tyrone and eleven murdered women and kids…that's way above my pay grade. All I'm saying is be careful. I'm deadly serious—your life ain't worth a plug nickel to these animals."

Chapter Thirty-Nine

There was no way for me to know if Angela was right about Buratti and Felipe having something to do with the massacre. It was just her intuition, and it could've been miles off. Buratti might've wanted Felipe for any number of reasons, none of which I understood. Buratti might've wanted to settle an old gripe that had nothing to do with the murders. Maybe he thought Felipe had been murdered. For all I know, he might've wanted his family recipe for osso buco. Still, I couldn't help feeling there was something there.

I didn't want Auntie getting bent out of shape, so I went back to her place right after speaking with Mulligan. As it was, I'd stayed out longer than I knew she'd be comfortable with. I stopped at the market for fresh bread and wine. I picked up a bouquet because I'm no fool.

I was surprised when I opened the door expecting to be hit with a powerful aroma from the kitchen. Nothing was going on in the kitchen. Nothing was being sliced, diced, baked, or fried. The kitchen light was off, and Auntie was nowhere to be seen. Her bedroom door was locked. I knocked and called out to her.

"Come on in, Steady," she said.

She was sitting in a club chair, feet curled underneath her legs, reading a paperback. An empty wine glass sat on the floor next to her. I knew she liked to read, but for some reason hadn't seen her with a book since coming back to town.

"What are you reading?"

She showed me the cover. "Danielle Steele's latest."

"What's it about?"

"What they're all about, a woman who's lost everything, a knight in shining armor, and a villain who threatens to take everything away from her. This one happens to be pretty good. The heroine's an Italian princess, but they don't call her princess. They call her *principessa*. I just love the way that rolls of the tongue, don't you?"

I nodded. "Has a nice ring to it."

"Speaking of which…how's your *principessa?*"

I knew a cross-examination was coming the moment she mentioned the Italian princess. The name of the book she was reading was *Remembrance*. I'd have to check it out of the library to see if Auntie had been truthful about the way she described it or if she'd made the whole thing up as a segue into an interrogation.

"I'm not going to lie. I saw her for a few minutes at her place of work. I figured I owed her that much."

She got out of the chair, snared her wine glass by the stem, and walked toward me. She sniffed my shirt. "You owe her a fuck as well? Was it a glad-to-see-you fuck, an I-missed-you-fuck, or an I'm-horny-as hell fuck? I know it wasn't a goodbye fuck. I can tell by the way you smell. I hope you didn't do her on any surface they use to decorate the cakes—the Department of Health will have to come in and shut the place down."

"*Auntie*, I'm a grown man."

"Then you damn sure should know better."

She was nagging me so badly I wanted to let her go on believing what she wanted to but didn't. "I broke it off, Auntie. I told her I wasn't going to see her anymore."

"Then why do you smell like women's perfume and powdered sugar?"

"We hugged. We kissed goodbye. Can't do that with a postage stamp."

She seemed pleased and was about to open her mouth when we heard a knock on the door.

Damn, I'm missing out on her apology, I thought, *and those are damn few and far between.*

I should've looked through the peephole but didn't. The man at the door looked like a chubby alter boy version of Wayne Newton and smelled like talcum powder.

"How can I help you?"

"Steady Groove? Mr. Gromaggio wants to see you. I've got a car parked out front."

A lump formed in my throat. "Gromaggio? Big Paulie Gromaggio?" *The don?*

"*Bingo.*"

"Who's there?" Auntie asked, calling from the bedroom.

"It's for me. Stay put."

Telling Auntie to stay put was a bad choice of words—I heard her footsteps on the parquet flooring, gathering momentum. *"Who's* at my door?" she asked.

Gromaggio's driver grinned at her. "Hello, dear. Young Steady here is gonna take a ride with me." He turned to me. "You ready to go?"

"Wait a minute. What makes you think I'm just gonna—"

He brushed aside his jacket, revealing a holstered revolver, then checked his watch. "Shit! We're gonna hit the rush hour heading back to Staten Island. I friggin' hate that."

Auntie staggered back at the sight of the gun. "Steady, should I call—"

"No, I'm fine—just don't wait up for me."

Auntie's courage rallied back. She stepped forward and pointed her finger in the man's nose. "I've got a photographic memory, young man, and—"

"And I've got a gun and your address." His grin was menacing. "*I* win."

Auntie backed behind me.

My service carry was locked in my bedroom closet where it belonged when I wasn't on duty—a good thing too because he stepped forward and began patting me down.

"*Let's* go," he said.

"*Steady,*" Auntie said warily. "Are you sure this is a good idea?"

"I'll be fine, Auntie. Just lock the door after me."

"Are you completely sure?" she asked.

"Ain't that sweet?" Newton said. "I wish I had someone who was worried about me the way she worries about you. Hurry up."

I nodded. "I'll just get my jacket."

"No," he said. "Come as you are. I already frisked you once, and I don't want to have to do it again. I got too close to Steady, Jr. patting you down, and I'm not eager for that to happen again." He gestured toward the hallway with his head.

I closed my eyes momentarily and sighed a big, anxious sigh before following him out into the corridor.

Chapter Forty

It was a solid hour getting over the Verrazano Bridge, bumper-to-bumper all the way with rain falling on the upper level. From there to Gromaggio's estate on Todt Hill didn't take long. Newton didn't tell me his actual name and was silent throughout the trip. His choice of music wasn't bad, though, and the Lincoln's sound system was first-rate. His taste in music was diverse—a mixtape played everything from Prince to Marvin Gaye, with some Dino and Sinatra thrown in.

I expected Gromaggio's home to be large, but I wasn't prepared for what I saw when we pulled up to the sprawling home on Benedict Avenue with wrought iron gates and marble columns. There was an ornate fountain out front. I wondered if Gromaggio would let me fish for pocket change before I went home. That is *if* I was going home.

A small Latin woman opened the door and showed me where to sit. She was unremarkable and dressed more like a servant than the lady of the house. She told me her name was Gloria. I wondered if the visit would help me figure out why D. Wayne was being framed or if I was going to be told to keep my big nose clean under threat of death, then quickly booted out the door.

The house was ridiculous. I couldn't even guess how many rooms there were, how many bedrooms and bathrooms. How many toilets does a man need anyway?

"Maybe you want to freshen up before Big Paulie sees you," Newton said.

He wasn't' asking if I had to pee. He was suggesting I wash off some of my ghetto grime before meeting the big cheese. I told him *no* just to bust balls, but he insisted. I was directed to the washroom on the main level, one I guessed would be immediately sanitized after use. I was tempted to take a big putrid dump on Big Paulie's throne and skip the deodorizer, but my GI tract wouldn't cooperate.

Newton was just outside the powder room, waiting for me to come out. "You all done in there?"

No, I think I'll take a pee in the sitting room. Hey, what's a sitting room? "Yeah, I'm done."

"Good. Follow me. Big Paulie's ready for you."

Better hurry along then. Wouldn't want to keep the don waiting.

Gromaggio had his fingers wrapped around a thick cigar. He was sitting in a wing chair and looked quite at home in red silk pajamas. He didn't get up when I entered.

"You can leave us, Tony," Gromaggio said, revealing the name of his tight-lipped driver.

Tony Newton, I mused. *Nah, that doesn't work at all.*

"Close the doors, will ya?" Gromaggio said. He stared at the doorway until the double doors were completely shut. "Sit down, Mr. Groove," he said. I began to sit on the sofa, but he stopped me. "Not there...*there.*" He pointed to a leather recliner in a way that inferred I should know where the commoners sit. I guess my skin pigment wouldn't be visible if I shedded a few cells on the brown leather. "Groove, that's an interesting name. Doesn't sound like a plantation name."

Oh no, Massa, me great grandpappy got that name from scoring grooves in the cotton fields with his hoe. "My father had it changed. Used to be Graves, but he didn't care for the sound of it."

"That's quite a jump from Graves to Groove."

"He used to collect records."

"You don't say? I've got a record collection, all the great Italian tenors. Pavarotti, Caruso, I've got them all. What kind of records did your father collect?"

"Duke Ellington, Count Basie...Coltrane." *All the great ones.*

"You still have your dad's collection?"

Still got all my bottle caps. Dad couldn't hock them for hooch. "No—he hasn't been around in years."

He shook his head. "Typical."

"What's typical?"

"Black patriarchs, they cut and run—either chasing drugs or chasing pussy. Tell me I'm wrong." He picked up a demitasse cup and sipped with his pinky extended. "Sure, Italian men keep a piece on the side, but we have dinner with the family every Sunday. *La Famiglia.* Fuck all the women you can handle, that's your right as a man. But at the end of the day, you come home to your wife and children. You hold your family together. That's the key." He put the cup back on the table. "You coloreds would do well to remember that."

That's it—two thousand years of collective Roman insight, and that's the best they could come up with? "Inspired thinking."

"I think so. You want something to drink, Groove?"

"I don't want to be a bother."

"It's no bother." He called for his servant, who entered so quickly she must've had her hand on the exterior doorknob. "You like beer? I've got draught."

"Beer's fine." *I wonder if the don is this hospitable to everyone he intends to have whacked.*

"Beer for the gentleman," he said with his eyes glued to the sway of her rear end as she left the room.

Something told me he appreciated Gloria for more than her cooking. Regardless, I had a frosty cold amber in hand in little more time than it took for the second hand on my Timex to complete a rotation. "Delicious. Thanks."

Gromaggio lit his cigar and eased back in his chair. "Nice, right?" He puffed out a perfect ring of smoke. "Mind if we talk shop?"

"I assumed that's why I'm here."

"You're direct. Good, I like that. No bullshit. What's the deal with you and this Palm Sunday thing? You're not an investigator. Why's your nose up everyone's ass?"

"Dennis Tyrone is my parolee."

"Come on, Groove, I thought we were past the smoke screens. Your responsibility ended the second this Tyrone character was arraigned for murder. You should've dropped his file like it was a hot potato, which it was."

"I don't believe he did it."

"Why not?"

"Lots of reasons—unreliable witnesses mostly."

"What else?"

"The man was spotted in another part of town at the exact time he was accused of committing the murders."

Gromaggio poked the air with his cigar. "And this witness is reliable?"

"Rock solid."

"I see. This testimony of your witness should be enough to create reasonable doubt. All it takes is one dissenting juror, no?"

"It was buried, covered up."

"Why?"

"No clue, Mr. Gromaggio. I was hoping maybe you..."

"*What*, you think I know?" He looked up at the coffered ceiling, reflecting.

"Mr. Gromaggio, can I ask how this matter came to your attention?"

"You may not." It seemed he was still evaluating the information. He pointed at me with the cigar, his gaze slicing through the smoke. "Why do you care? You're new to the job. No history. Why do you give a shit what happens to this piece of street garbage?"

"I grew up with that piece of street garbage."

He placed the cigar in a glass ashtray. "Loyalty?" His nod expressed respect. "Bravo, Mr. Groove. That's music to my ears." There must've been a sip of espresso left in the small cup. He put it to his lips and angled it so that the last little bit of coffee trickled onto his tongue. "Let me know if you need any help opening doors. I'm good at that."

"At opening doors?"

"Need I repeat myself? Tony will take you home now."

Huh? "Wait. Are you offering to—?"

The doors opened as if Gromaggio had sent Tony a message with his brain waves. Tony's gesture told me not to dawdle. My moment with the don was over, and I was no longer welcome in his home.

Chapter Forty-One

My bedroom was dead quiet but something woke me up in the middle of the night. I must've felt Auntie's presence. I opened my eyes and noticed her standing by the door checking on me. Coffee had been poured by the time I emerged from the bedroom, showered, and ready for the day.

"How'd you—?"

"Sleep? Seriously, Steady? I was up every fifteen minutes until you finally walked through the door. I figured the police were going to come knocking, telling me they found your body floating in The Narrows. Goddamn it, you trying to give your old Auntie a heart attack?"

I saw pain etch into her face the moment the words came out of her mouth. Mama had died of cancer, and she was only fifty years old. "I'm sorry, Auntie—"

"What was that all about, Steady? Who was that hood who showed up last night, and what in the hell did he want with you?"

I wasn't sure what information Gromaggio was after, but it sure as hell seemed he'd heard what I was after. "Let me know if you need any help opening doors," the man said. *Geez, just what I need, an alliance with the Capo dei capi, the head of the most powerful crime family in New York.* The question was why. What did a powerbroker like Gromaggio need from a fledgling parole officer that he couldn't obtain himself? "I believe it has to do with Dennis Wayne and the murder of those women and kids, only—"

"Only?"

"Only I don't know. I drank a beer, answered a few simple questions, and was driven home. I don't get it."

"Who is this guy you were taken to see?"

I didn't want to tell her who I'd met with, but she saw the goon who came to the door, and she saw the gun. "Paul Gromaggio, Auntie. He's a mafia boss."

She wrung her hands, and I could see that tears were fighting their way to the surface. Mobsters had killed the love of her life. The connection was too powerful for her to bear. I watched her crumble, her knees buckling as her hand shot out to brace herself against the doorjamb. "Oh no," she said, and the tears rushed forward. "My Meyer…and now you. Steady, you've got to break free of these people before it's too late. I'm scared, Steady. These people, they'll eat you alive. My husband's gone because of people like these. My kid sister is gone too. I can't lose you, Steady. I just can't."

I hurried to her side to steady her. "No one's gonna eat Steady Groove, alive or otherwise. This old sea hand is a lot tougher than you think." *And I didn't steal from the mob like your crooked husband Meyer did.*

Gromaggio had left me with a lot of unanswered questions, more than I had begun with. *Angela must've been right about this Angelo Felipe character,* I thought. Buratti wanted him for some reason, a reason I assumed also interested Gromaggio. *Got to figure it out, quick.* Powerful people were making moves, moves that might alter D. Wayne's fate once and for all.

And who was standing between these titans and D. Wayne?

Just me, little old me.

Chapter Forty-Two

D. Wayne's hospitalization delayed his pretrial and the way things were going…D. Wayne was being hit with one complication after another. His liver was failing, his kidneys too. Infection set in. The reports that filtered back to me from Mulligan made it seem like D. Wayne was living on borrowed time, and perhaps he always had been, almost from the moment he was born in the hood. Thinking about D. Wayne and the miserable life he'd had brought to mind an old blues song my father used to listen to on his record player about being born under a bad sign.

D. Wayne never had any luck. I believe he never had a chance. Sometimes I hated the hood for that, for the opportunities it denied us and everyone that would follow. Sure hope he lived long enough to be acquitted.

But with his bad luck…

The protests led by the Reverend Pointer continued like clockwork. Despite his staunch attack on the mayor and every important city official down the line, outrage over the Palm Sunday Massacre lost steam. It was no longer the hot news item it was when the crime was raw, and the mass murder was in the news forefront. A serial killer named Michael Silka was now vying for the top spot along with Dennis Wayne Tyrone. A manhunt for Silka's capture continued and sucked the attention of the public like a fresh-out-of-the-box Hoover. It was believed that Silka had murdered as many as nine people in Manley Hot Springs, Alaska. The press was closely following the manhunt and bringing the attempted capture into everyone's home. The tension was so thick it was palpable.

Pointer was determined not to be upstaged by the Pacific Northwest spree killer. He continued daily demonstrations in front of Brookdale Hospital. His focus was the mistreatment of a black man being railroaded into prison, a man who laid unconscious in ICU while *Whitey* conspired against him.

The reverend must've been making a bundle on D. Wayne's plight. Knowing what Mulligan had told me about Pointer being in league with the Jersey mob, it made sense that he wasn't so much interested in D. Wayne as he was in his personal agenda, fighting for minorities and advancing his own, very lucrative career. Still, the man was moving mountains, and if he was capable of such miracles, he might be capable of getting me useful information, real facts that would support the case for D. Wayne's innocence.

But why would an ambitious opportunist like Pointer waste his time with me? There was Mike Mulligan's D. Wayne-sighting, but I'd promised Mulligan I wouldn't tell anyone about it or do anything to jeopardize his NYPD career. I knew that Sockeye's testimony was pure BS, but the old fraud was nowhere to be found. I assumed that Detti had planted the slug that matched one of the murder weapons, but how could I prove it? Detti was a hotshot detective with several impressive collars to his name.

It seemed that I had nothing going for me, and the possibility of discrediting Detti was as likely as winning the lottery until I walked out of my bedroom the next morning and found an envelope under the front door.

I heard water running in the shower and hustled back into my bedroom before Auntie spotted the envelope.

It contained five snapshots of Detective Detti standing in front of a luggage locker. He was wearing a different outfit in each, a gray suit, slacks and a red sweater, a brown suit, and so on. Detti had been photographed on five separate occasions in what looked to be the same location. Looking carefully, each photo depicted him with an envelope in his hand. I thought about what Mulligan had told me about Detti's extravagant vacations, his fancy cars, and expensive suits. The implication was obvious.

As was the source.

The photos had to have come from Gromaggio. Who else would've given them to me?

He was helping me discredit Detti and, by extension, Detti's case against

D. Wayne. How, I wondered would Gromaggio benefit from D. Wayne's acquittal?

Nothing obvious came to mind. I slid the envelope into my jacket pocket and found my freshly showered Auntie setting the table when I walked into the kitchen. She was still dressed in her robe but was smiling and singing "Let's Do It." If you closed your eyes, you'd swear you were listening to Ella Fitzgerald.

"Sounding fine, Auntie. Good to see you with a smile on your face this morning."

"I'm not dead, so I figured I'd better stop acting like I was. You haven't had any more meetings with the mob, have you?"

I thought about the envelope in my jacket pocket. No one would ever define an envelope of pictures as a clandestine Cosa Nostra meeting. "Nope, I sure haven't."

"I've got a big day planned. I'm meeting some of the gals from my old crooning days for lunch. We're gonna drink, and laugh, and talk about those good old days." She placed the last dish on the table and took my hand. We danced around the kitchen for a beat or two.

"How 'bout we flip the script, and I cook you breakfast today?" I said. "How do you feel about Spam and eggs?"

She was pensive for a moment, then let out a robust, "Yes. *Hell* yes. Doc says my blood pressure is fine, and I haven't had Spam and eggs in a dog's age. I'll get dressed. You best not give me food poisoning, Steady. I already told you I'm looking forward to seeing my girlfriends, and I don't want to spend the day yacking into a commode."

"Trust me, Auntie, You're in good hands. Go pretty yourself up, and I'll fix us some grub."

I adored Auntie, but I was happy she was going to be out of the house because she made me feel as if by working on the case, I was sneaking around. I owed D. Wayne, and he had no one else in his corner.

And with fresh incentive in my pocket, I was more eager than ever to renew my efforts.

Chapter Forty-Three

Mulligan was out with a bum shoulder. He'd visited me in the hospital and I figured I could do the same. He'd torn it while chasing after a crackhead. He'd smacked the doper in the back of the knees with his baton, but it was like trying to take down a polar bear with a peashooter. The assailant pounced on him, sending them both down a flight of marble stairs. Mulligan was dazed but still managed to grab the dope fiend by the belt as he was about to flee. With adrenaline pumping through the doper's veins like high-test gasoline through the carburetor of a top fuel dragster, the crackhead pulled him down a second flight of stairs. That's when he felt his shoulder tear. He received a cortisone shot and some paid time off. The doc told him he'd probably need surgery if the shot didn't do the trick. Fortunately, it was his left shoulder and didn't inhibit him from washing and waxing his GTO.

He handed me an applicator pad and showed me how to apply wax in a small circular motion. I handled the fenders while he worked on the long hood because he didn't trust me to work on the glamor area of his pride and joy. When we were done, he let the back of his hand glide over the glistening paint to feel how smooth it was, then spritzed water on the hood and watched it bead up.

"Looking good, Mike," I said.

"Yeah, thanks, Steady. I love this friggin' car. Always wanted one. When I was a kid, this older guy, Richard, had one, and I used to eat my heart out watching him and his girlfriend cruise around the neighborhood. His folks owned a clothing store—lots of money there. They gave the spoiled brat whatever he wanted." He wrapped the hose around his arm and stowed it on a hook mounted to the side of the house. "Come on inside. I'll introduce you to the missus."

Patty Mulligan was a beefy gal. She wore a housecoat and had her hair wound into a bun. She was tidying up the kitchen when we walked in. "Who's this?" she asked in a welcoming tone, "one of our long-lost relatives? Mike, is he one of the Tir MacCarthain Mulligans or the Fermanagh Mulligans? He kind of looks like your great uncle Dingus, the great potato bandit of County Donegal."

"You're a riot, Alice," Mulligan said. He gave her a buss on the cheek and a swat on the ass.

"'You're a riot, Alice?' You not only sound like Gleason, you're starting to look like him." She extended her hand. "Like Mike said, I'm the missus, but you can call me Patty. There's no need to be formal." The wound on my forehead was healing but was still obvious. She studied it and winced. "You a cop too? You get the same time off as Mike to lie around and collect dust?"

"Funny. Say hello to Steady Groove, Patty. He's a parole officer and my new buddy. We've been betting the ponies together." Mulligan opened the fridge and retrieved a pair of cold Millers. He handed me one.

"Nice to meet you, Patty."

"How'd you get the welt on your head? I thought PO gave pee tests."

"He got pistol-whipped while checking in on of his parolees," Mulligan said. "He's on PTO too, just like me."

"Another lazy loafer just like my husband. Guess the two of you are birds of a feather."

"Birds of a feather?" I said, "I ain't ever seen no white crows."

She laughed. "I like this one," she said. "You can keep him."

"Say, aren't you supposed to be at your sister's about now?" Mulligan asked.

She picked up a pale yellow cardigan and her purse. "Just leaving."

"Patty watches her sister's kid until three so she can start her shift at the diner."

"What are you two goldbricks going to do while I'm out, polish the hubcaps again, or drink your weight in suds?" She gave Mulligan a peck on the lips. "Love you," she said. "And nice to meet you, Steady." I watched as she headed out.

"She's all right, Mike. Great sense of humor."

"Oh, she's a barrel of laughs. She keeps me on my toes too—trust me." He pulled out a kitchen chair and sat down. "You said you had something to show me?"

I tossed an envelope on the table and sat down while he removed the snapshots and viewed them one at a time.

"Jesus." He went through them once then examined them more slowly before settling back in his chair. "I don't like to jump to conclusions, but..."

"Looks like an expensive sports car and a closet full of handmade suits, don't it?"

I knew he didn't like Detti but seemed reluctant to agree. "You know what would happen if these got into the hands of one of the vampires at IAB? Detti would get flushed down the toilet, stuck-up attitude and all."

"Couldn't happen to a nicer guy."

He stuffed the photos back into the envelope and handed it back. "What are you going to do with them?"

"Haven't gotten that far."

"Any idea where they came from?"

"I don't want to speculate, but..." I took a swig of beer and told him about my chauffeured ride to the estate on Todt Hill."

He began to rub his temples. "*Geez*, you met with Big Paulie? You might be right about the mob being tied into this mass shooting. But how? And why is this important enough to get the attention of Big Paulie Gromaggio, the highest-ranking don in the country? This guy farts and people drop. Why would he align himself with a nobody?"

"*Hey*. That hurts."

"Sorry, no offense, but if the shoe fits..." He stood and paced the kitchen. "Come on," he said. "I feel like taking my spiffy GTO for a ride."

"Aren't you afraid of getting bird shit on it?"

"My friend, I've been getting shit on all my life. Never kept me off the streets before."

Chapter Forty-Four

Mulligan complained about the drizzle falling on the GTO as we drove into Manhattan. He said that Mother Nature was sabotaging all his hard work. I was hypnotized by the dance of the small beads of water on the hood colliding with one another to form bigger and bigger beads that were ultimately pushed off the hood by the wind. The Brooklyn-Queens Expressway led us to the Queens-Midtown Tunnel into Manhattan, then crosstown to Hell's Kitchen. He stopped in front of an apartment building on 50th Street between 10th and 11th Avenues. It wasn't exactly the high rent district. Sandwiched in between two apartment buildings was a horse stable and with the car windows open… A street prostitute cruised the block, her fishnets torn, wobbling on a broken heel.

"Wait here," Mulligan said as he piled out of the bucket seat. "I'll be right back."

It was still drizzling, but the rain didn't stop some kids from playing skully in the space between two parked cars next to a fire hydrant, far enough away from the stable that an errant checker wouldn't accidentally sail into a pile of horse flop. The blue chalk they'd used to outline the skully court almost seemed fluorescent from the rain, and the bottle caps seemed to sail easily across the wet street. I was watching the bottle caps hydroplane over the water when the driver's door opened. Mulligan pulled the seatback forward, and someone piled into the rear seat. He snapped it back into place and dropped into the driver's bucket seat.

"Steady, say hello to Frankie Irish," Mulligan said.

I looked back and offered my hand. Frankie Irish acknowledged the gesture with a raised palm and an averted-eye expression that made me feel like a leper. His eyes and mine never made contact.

"Show him the pictures," Mulligan said.

"Are you sure?" I asked.

He nodded.

Mulligan had explained about his cousin once before and repeated the story on our ride in. Tall, dark, and deadly was a member of the Westies, an Irish mob that had aligned with Paul Gromaggio.

"Keep your mouth shut," Mulligan had said on the drive in. "Let me do the talking."

Whatever.

I shuttled the envelope over my shoulder and waited for Friendly Frankie to grace us with his wisdom. I heard the friction of paper against paper as Frankie rotated the photos, front to back.

"What do you make of them?" Mulligan asked.

"This looks like the international arrivals building at JFK," Frankie said. "Me and my buddy Reed spent five years working cargo over at the airport."

Mulligan snorted. "Working, yeah, *right.*"

"Don't be a wiseass," Frankie said. "I recognize the concourse."

"Does it look to you like it looks to us?"

Frankie eyed Mulligan warily. "Cuz, it's all right the brother hears everything?"

"No worries, Frankie. I vouch."

"You vouch, huh? Okay. Sure, Detti's dirty but so what?" He dropped the photos on the center console. "Everyone knows Detti's a bottom feeder. He's been in bed with Buratti's Bergin crew for years. Big Paulie says no drugs—focus on legit biz, and Buratti turns a deaf ear. Detti clears the way for him. One of Buratti's men gets pinched for dealing, Detti cashes in an IOU, a get-out-of-jail-free card. Have to say, I've seen some tough bastards in my day, but Johnny Boy takes the cake. Gromaggio has a standing order that made men are not to deal drugs—under penalty of *death.* But Buratti ignores him like Gromaggio is powerless or something. Meanwhile, little brother Gene and crazy Angelo Gugliami were arrested for dealing, and

Buratti's drug biz is still expanding big time. Push is gonna come to shove one day soon, and either Buratti or Big Paulie is gonna swallow a forty-five."

"How'd baby bro and this guy Gugliami get arrested with Detti looking out for them?" I asked.

Mulligan's glare drew blood, telling me to keep my mouth shut, then answered for his cousin. "The big bad wolf can't blow down every house he sees. Some collars are just too big to sweep under the carpet."

I realized I could see Frankie Irish in the rearview mirror. He looked as if he ate, drank, and slept his assassin's job, as if the killer's mentality had penetrated all the cells in his body.

"Hence the regular trips to JFK." Mulligan smacked my elbow. "I told you that sack of shit Detti was living too good." He looked into the back seat. "Buratti helps Detti with intel for his cases too, doesn't he, makes a mediocre detective look like a friggin' genius?"

"Oh, you know it. You remember that Harlem nun that got raped and murdered, back maybe…three years?" Frankie asked.

"Of course I do—took so long to wrap up, the mayor threatened to clean house, from the chief of Ds all the way up to the commissioner. Detti got the collar on that one. Made him a rising star."

"Of course," Frankie began, "only Detti did exactly *nothing*. Johnny Boy was so furious over a nun getting raped that he put twenty-five Gs out on the street. His crew turned the guy up in almost no time and dropped him in Detti's lap, gift wrapped—*bam*, instant hero."

"Some way to make your bones," Mulligan said. "Sometimes I think Detti's the smart one, all mobbed up, snatching undeserved credit and living like a robber baron."

"No argument from me," Frankie said as he cleared his throat. "Cuz…I was kind of in the middle of something when you showed—you need anything else?"

"No. Thanks, Frankie. I owe you." They got out of the car and bro-hugged. Mulligan got back in. "Don't take the cold shoulder personally," he said. "Frankie's a genuine tough guy—know what I mean? You don't want to know some of the shit he's been mixed up in."

"What are you talking about? He's a peach of a guy."

He smiled. "Trust me, you don't want to know Frankie 'Irish' any better than you already do. It wouldn't be good for your health. Sometimes I worry it ain't good for *my* health." He picked up the photos. "So, what are you going to do with these?"

"Actually…I was hoping we could spitball ideas."

"Hold that thought. The smell from the stables is starting to get to me." Mulligan started the car and shifted into gear. "There's a great Irish Pub about three minutes from here where the air doesn't gag you with the smell of horseshit. You can tell me all about it over a cold one and burger."

Chapter Forty-Five

The pub Mulligan took me to was a great choice. The burgers were cooked on the griddle, and the chopped meat had just the right amount of fat. The fries were extra crispy, and the beer ice cold. The pub was filled with lots of boisterous young people who'd just gotten off from work, serious about blowing off steam and having a good time.

Mulligan had roaming eyes. "Lots of eye candy in here. Ever wish you could…what am I talking about? You don't have to wish for anything. You've got Sandy *and* Angela Rizzo face down, ass up. If I was smart, I'd wish that I were you." He took a big gulp of beer. "I shouldn't complain. Patty's great, and the girls keep me in stitches. I sowed my wild oats—back in the day." He gestured to a redhead with long legs wearing a short skirt. "You think God would forgive me if I gave that ginger lass a quick poke in the pants—not a long and sordid affair, just a blip on the radar?"

The woman he pointed out was drop-dead gorgeous. "God? Yes. You… I'm not so sure. Guilt can be a motherfucker."

Mulligan raised his glass. "Here's to walking the straight line. Now look me in the eye and swear you're not getting it from Angela Rizzo."

"You don't give up, do you? All right, yeah—I had a one and done, a moment of weakness when Sandy kicked me out of her place."

"Moment of weakness, huh? With the tits on Angela, who could blame you?"

"I don't want to be that kind of guy, not until I figure out what Sandy and I mean to each other. I told Angela I didn't feel right about stepping out on my lady. She wasn't happy, but…I think I did the right thing."

"You, you're a better man than I am. Turning your back on that sexy Sicilian doll…that's willpower with a capital W." There were a few fries left on his plate. He used one of them to plow ketchup to the end of the plate, then scooped it up and popped it into his mouth. "So what's the plan? Are you dead set on running afoul of Detti and the mob? You got a Superman suit on under that J.C. Penney button down?"

"Being bulletproof wouldn't be so bad. Best I can figure, this Angelo Felipe is the lynchpin. Seems both Gromaggio *and* Buratti have an interest in the outcome of D. Wayne's trial. Buratti's crew is out looking for Felipe. Gotta be something there, right?"

"Sure, but if Buratti can't find Felipe, what makes you think you can? Buratti's got a couple dozen street-savvy guys in his crew, and they're pretty good at turning up rats. They don't have to play by the same rules we cops do. They get shit done, you know? Like they put a gun to an informant's head, and they either spill information or their brains."

"I hear *that*. Honestly, I don't have a clue. I'm only one guy, and I don't have a lot of experience chasing down missing people. Now if you needed to track down some Pacific halibut…"

"I kind of figured. I wish I knew how to help. The basic rule is pound the pavement and talk to all his known associates, but being a wiseguy, his wiseguy friends aren't going to give you the time of day and may end up cleaning your clock while they're at it." He slapped me on the shoulder. "Still, this was a hell of a lot more fun than watching the Mets drop a third straight game to Houston." He drained his glass and threw a twenty on the counter. "I've got this."

"Thanks for dinner."

"Don't mention it."

"Gromaggio told me he could help me open doors."

"Better be careful with that. Some of those doors, buddy, may be one way in and no way out. Gromaggio might wear silk PJs, but that doesn't mean he won't order a guy like Frankie Irish to blow your brains out. You know, loose ends. I already told you about Jimmy Burr and all the blood he spilled so that he wouldn't be connected with the Lufthansa heist. If Big Paulie decides he wants you gone, you're gone. Come on, I'd better head home before Patty sends out a search party."

"Feels kind of hopeless," I said on our way back to his car.

"You're a smart guy, Steady. You'll figure something out." The envelope of photos was still lying on the center console. "Mind if I hold onto these pics for a while?" he asked.

"Knock yourself out. It's not like I know what to do with them."

He started the car and turned on the radio. "Let' see how bad the Mets got shellacked."

The dial was set to 1010 WINS, the news station. He was about to reach for the tuning knob when a broadcast began. "This just in—the body of reputed mobster Angelo Felipe was fished from the East River some thirty minutes ago by the NYPD Harbor Unit. Felipe, a longtime Gambino soldier was removed from the river by the police scuba team after being spotted by a commercial tugboat…"

Mulligan's jaw dropped. "Son of a bitch." He turned to me. "Did you hear that?"

I squeezed my eyes shut and shook my head. One of those doors Gromaggio had offered to open was now permanently sealed. Someone wanted to make sure that nothing got in the way of D. Wayne taking the fall for all eleven murders, and I was helpless to do anything about it. Whether or not Felipe was involved in the Palm Sunday Massacre had yet to be demonstrated, but proving it was going to be that much harder because the man had taken the secret to his grave.

Chapter Forty-Six

"Too many people got too many fish to fry," Mulligan said as we came to a stop near the East River in Greenpoint Brooklyn at the periphery of the crime scene area. It was a lousy turn of phrase but one that didn't seem to bother him. He unplugged a power cord from the cigarette lighter jack, then got out of the car and removed a magnetically attached fireball strobe from the rooftop, careful not to scratch the paint.

It was twilight, and the East River was lit up like the Fourth of July by mobile lighting units and the powerful beacons of overhead police choppers.

"Stay put," Mulligan said. "Let me see if I can find someone to chat up."

I waited by the car while he strolled off. It looked like he was searching for a familiar face, someone who wouldn't immediately shut him down by prying. In a moment, he was gone, swallowed up by the throngs of police and special teams that had descended on the area like vultures on a dead carcass. The scene seemed less chaotic than I had anticipated, mostly officers mulling about or paired off in groups, chatting, sipping coffee, and talking on field radios.

Mulligan returned a few minutes later. "Not a lot to tell you, Steady. He wasn't in the water long. Two officers who'd had dealings with Felipe positively ID'd him. It appears the body is still here and under review by the coroner. Felipe took two to the chest and one to the head at close range—you know, mob-style."

"Mob style?"

"Two shots to the heart does the trick, but the mob always puts one bullet between the eyes, just to be sure."

A big black Ford SUV screeched to a stop about ten yards away from us. A second SUV followed behind the first. The doors on both SUVs flew open.

"Vehicles like that transport NYPD brass, department chiefs, deputy commissioners, and *the* commissioner," Mulligan said.

He wasn't wrong. He pointed out the man emerging from the first car. It was Police Commissioner Canton, and someone Mulligan called the first deputy commissioner. The chief of detectives emerged from the second SUV, his expression solemn as his direct reports hurried after him to fill him in on the situation. All three high-ranking officials moved off toward the riverfront to view the body.

"Isn't this a lot of attention for one dead mobster?" I asked. "I could understand if he was a don or something, but Felipe was just a soldier, right? Sure, he was a made man, but there are tons of those, aren't there?"

"Too many, Steady, way too many."

A mobster gets made if he's a good earner and has shown some initiative. He gets a small crew, say three or four guys, to order around. Most of them don't go any further than that. They report to a capo who reports to a boss or an underboss if one is in place. Either way, being *made* is nothing to make a fuss over.

"So, why did three of NYPD's highest-ranking officials fall out of the sky just to be here? What makes Angelo Felipe so goddamn special?"

Chapter Forty-Seven

Two days later

A nor'easter had slowed my progress as an amateur investigator. I'd been out walking the streets talking to every two-bit user who might've scored drugs from Rico Bueno, but there wasn't much to learn. They bought, he sold—Bueno and his customers weren't exactly fast friends. The few urchins I managed to speak with knew where to find Bueno and what he sold. Beyond being their supplier, they didn't give a rat's ass about the man.

For my troubles, I'd ruined my spiffy black loafers. I'd gotten them good and soaked from trudging around in the rain. When they dried, the soles separated from the uppers, which had warped badly. If a bell had been sewn to the toe, they would've resembled jester's shoes.

Still, I had a roof over my head and a job that was paying me to stay home. Houck had called and asked how I was feeling. I told him I could come back whenever he needed me, but he told me to stay out until the end of the month. "A concussion is nothing to mess with," he said. "Don't rush it."

My life could've been worse, far worse, D. Wayne kind of worse. He was still in Brookdale Hospital and was thankfully conscious. He had been stepped down from ICU to the critical care unit. I'd learned that the beatings had caused severe neurological tremors and such that the docs felt might be permanent. D. Wayne was hardly salt-of-the-earth material. He was more of a salt-in-an-open-wound kind of guy, but he didn't deserve the hand he'd been dealt, not by a long shot.

Auntie seemed to be walking on air. It seemed she was still thrilled to have me under her roof while Sandy and I took our time figuring out what we were supposed to be. She and her gal pals had decided to take their act out of mothballs, rehearse a bit, and see if they could get a few local bookings. "Win, lose, or draw," as she put it, was more than good enough because it was the renewed camaraderie with her friends she enjoyed so much. The girls were meeting two and three times a week to rehearse their old standards and discuss wardrobe. She'd been lonely for years after my moms passed away. It was good to see her embracing life again, looking forward to waking up each morning.

We'd had dinner together, and she'd gone out to rehearse afterward. I was working on my elf shoes, trying to determine if they could be fixed, when the phone rang. It was my unlikely partner in crime, Mike Mulligan. "How you doing, Steady?" he asked.

"High and dry, Mike. Actually...scratch that, just dry. You?"

"It's raining like a cow pissing on a flat rock out here. You believe that, all the years of seniority I got, and I'm still out on a night not fit for man or beast?"

"Can't believe you're back at work already."

He sounded tired. "Yeah, well, life's a bitch. Mine anyway. Listen, I thought you'd be interested—a call came in late afternoon. One of the tenants in an apartment building in East New York called complaining about a commotion, animal noises. A unit responded and found an entire fucking circus in an apartment: mice, raccoons, dogs, cats...you name it. The place stunk to high heaven. The report back to central said that the place looked abandoned and that the animals had turned on each other to survive. Took three ASPCA units to clean the place out. The way I figure it—"

"Felipe's hiding place."

"Hey, you're getting good at this, Steady. You're a regular Sherlock Holmes. It was too late in the day for them to check with anyone as to who lived there, but...anyway, it's probably been three or four days since Felipe got yanked out of the river and with no one around to feed the critters…? Maybe you want to slide in there before one of my astute colleagues arrives at the same or similar conclusion. Maybe you'll find something that might help your homeboy's case. Write this down, will you?" He provided the address. "Just remember, don't be seen, and don't make it obvious you were there. You got that, Steady? And if someone slaps a set of cuffs on you, you didn't hear about this from me."

"Appreciate it, Mike. Stay dry."

"Yeah, fat chance."

I still had a pair of sneakers that were in serviceable condition. I figured they'd hold up against the deluge and laced them up. They were on borrowed time and wouldn't be much of a loss if I had to toss them in the trash. I borrowed a flashlight from Auntie's kitchen drawer and headed out, eager to play gumshoe.

Chapter Forty-Eight

The apartment, if it had been Felipe's, was on the top floor of a six-story hi-rise, a prewar building with a painted stucco interior, a steel stair rail, and badly worn marble steps. I'd hoped my sneakers would be quiet, but they were soaked and squished with the steps. Aside from the occasional radio or TV noise migrating into the hallway, the building was quiet. Up we went, my gurgling shoes and me, four flights, five… six. *Man, Felipe must've been in good shape.* The door was covered with yellow police tape, and some kind of official notice had been plastered dead center. Despite all the *no entry* warnings, the door had not been padlocked. I turned the doorknob and realized it wasn't connected to any kind of locking mechanism. I figured it had been destroyed when the police broke in.

I flipped on the light after entering the apartment but reconsidered my strategy and switched it off. Mulligan had been clear that I should not be seen or leave clues indicating I had entered and snooped around. Auntie's flashlight got the call. I tried to avoid windows so that no one would see me in the window and notice that I was prowling.

Mulligan had been accurate—without someone to see after the animals, the place smelled like a sewer, the floor a minefield of turds, dumps, and animal-piss puddles. Plastic bins of animal chow were weighted down with gallon bottles of bleach and ammonia. Some of the more resourceful critters had gnawed small holes in the thick plastic tubs and were able to survive. Scattered bloodstains probably meant that the smaller animals became food for some of the larger carnivores.

I spent a good half-hour poking about and nudging things aside with my foot to see if any treasures had fallen behind furniture and subsequently forgotten about.

No such luck.

I forced the bedroom door. It looked like Felipe kept his underwear and socks in paper grocery bags that lined the floor by the window. Dust bunnies were all over the floor, and spiderwebs thick enough to support an aerialist traversed the ceiling. I'd found the door closed and figured Felipe must've kept the bedroom off-limits to his menagerie because there were no signs of animal excrement once inside. It smelled differently—not better, just different—kind of stale as if the sheets hadn't been laundered in months.

The top dresser drawer contained shirts and a shoebox. It was filled with cash, rubber band-bound rolls of bills. The second drawer was filled with sweaters and a second shoebox. More cash. Third drawer, same. And then, eureka, a carbon copy dry-cleaning ticket with the name Joanna Nocaldo written on it. Angela had told me that Felipe had a girlfriend and that she'd been in the bakery with Felipe once. Angela said that she carried herself well. I figured a classy woman like that didn't throw her cashmere sweaters in the Laundromat washer. I stashed the ticket in my pocket for safekeeping. A wave of guilt washed over me for having looted an apartment with D. Wayne, the robbery that had sent him away for three years. I couldn't unwind that clock, but maybe the dry-cleaning ticket might somehow lead to a clue that might somehow set him free. Nothing else I could do.

There were additional shoeboxes on the closet shelves. A betting man would wager that Felipe was not into shoes. I wondered how much money was in that closet—enough to keep his pets in kibble for decades.

Suits and slacks were neatly draped on hangers, but the shoe organizer that hung on the door had cleverly been repurposed. Each of the pockets in the first and third rows contained a handgun. There was an assortment of revolvers and automatics—six in total. The second and fourth rows were filled with ammo. I knew enough about ordnance to figure out that the ammo in each pocket was specific to the sidearm that hung directly above it, .38s, 9mms, and .45s.

This dude was a marvel of organization. I wondered if the jungle outside the bedroom was there because Felipe had a warm spot in his heart for animals or rather, he figured no one had the stomach to brave his monkey militia wilderness and get from the front door to the bedroom where the artillery and moola were stashed.

Damn, you'd think the man would've been better off with a big, heavy safe.

Studying Felipe's handguns I noticed that one of the revolvers in the shoe organizer was a .38 special, the same kind of gun used in the mass shooting—maybe *the* gun used in the shootings.

D. Wayne's get-out-of-jail-free card might be right at my fingertips.

Think, Steady. Think!

I wanted to grab the .38 Special, but I couldn't. I had no right to take it and removing it might've invalidated the evidence. I was a PO, not a detective, but chain of evidence protocol had been covered in my training.

I heard movement outside the front door, then a voice. Someone had been almost as savvy as quick-thinking Mike Mulligan, put two and two together, and had come to check out what was likely to be Felipe's rat hole. The door would swing open in a second. Whoever was at the door was minutes from discovering everything I already had, facts I needed to preserve.

* * *

I was already on the fire escape outside the bedroom window, lying motionless as heavy rain fell when the lights were switched on in the apartment. The drenching rain almost made me feel as if I was back on Mjolnir's deck, out in the middle of the Bering Sea with thirty-foot waves crashing down on the deck. With my sweatshirt hood covering my face, I'd positioned myself against the brick facade where it would be almost impossible for anyone to notice me. There was just enough of an opening in the hood for me to see through the angled blinds into the bedroom if the light was switched on.

I was sure they'd get switched on.

Any minute now...

I was soaked through and through. Out on the sea, I wore layers of rubber to keep me dry, even under the roughest conditions. But here, I was at nature's mercy, and the heavens seemed angry that I would be so defiant as to venture out while the elements were lashing out at the earth and all those who dwelled on it.

"Trust me, God," I said. "The last place I want to be is six stories up on a metal fire escape during a wrath-of-God storm with lightning flashing all around me. Kitty Groove didn't raise me to be a fool." I would've been safer in a bathtub, fixing a faulty toaster.

As if to respond, lightning flashed nearby. It was probably miles away but close enough to scare the shit out of me. It took a moment or two before the flash subsided, then all was dark for a moment before the light in the bedroom came on. It almost seemed as if the man was looking straight at me, but I knew he wasn't. He was just gazing out at the storm. I could see Detti, but he couldn't see me at all. I waited and watched him as he tossed the room, finding the money, guns, and the ammo. He wasn't prepared to find box upon box of bills but stuffed a hell of a lot of cash into his pockets before leaving the bedroom. I waited until all the lights in the apartment were out, and Detti had taken his leave. I needed a moment to make sure he hadn't stumbled upon the .38 Special I'd removed from the shoe organizer and hidden where I figured the douchebag was unlikely to look.

Chapter Forty-Nine

I was still soaking wet but so stoked on adrenaline that I couldn't even think about sleeping. I'd been trying to forge a plan, a way to use the contents of Felipe's apartment to help D. Wayne.

I finally found an all-night luncheonette and drank coffee until the electric circuits began to hum. I had all this vital information to drop on *the man* and no idea how to do it. Detti hated me and was a crook who didn't give a rat's ass about seeing justice served. In his mind, D. Wayne had already been tried and sentenced, sent up the river of no return. No doubt he was counting on collecting a promotion and filling his coffers with gold. *No way I can trust that crooked sack of shit to do the right thing.*

Mulligan, I figured. *Yeah, once more back to the well.* I figured he'd know how to put my discoveries in play.

If not him, who?

My cheapo Timex ran a little fast, but that didn't stop me from stepping into a phone booth and waking his ass in the middle of the night.

He sounded groggy on the phone, annoyed at having had his sleep shattered. "Who the hell is this?"

"Mike, it's Steady. We've got to talk."

"Wait a minute. *What?*"

"It's Steady, and I need to see you, now."

"Now...? he asked in a muted voice. "What the hell time is it?"

"Two-something."

"I heard him yawn. "Holy shit. Are you for real?"

"Look, I'm sorry to wake you, but it's really important. I went to Felipe's apartment, just like you said and…I found out *a* lot."

"You're serious? This can't keep?"

"No."

"Consider carefully, this can't keep?"

"Literally, man, we don't have a minute to spare. I'm just a few blocks away. I'll walk over."

"Fuck." He was grumbling indecipherably. "Okay, but don't ring the bell. Everyone is sound asleep." The line went dead.

I walked into an all-night luncheonette. The short-order cook was already prepping for breakfast, and the air was strong with the aromas of fresh coffee and bacon sizzling on the grill. I bought Mulligan a coffee to go and an obscenely oversized bear claw to appease the savage beast I'd just awoken.

He was already outside, locking the front door when I got there. His hair was wet."

"This better be good, Steady. This better be *fucking* good."

"You took a shower?"

"Had to do something to wake my sorry ass up."

"I brought you coffee."

"I hope it's fucking strong."

He yanked on the garage handle, revealing a faded green Dodge Dart. It didn't look like it received the same tender loving care as his shiny blue pride and joy. Side-by-side with the cherry GTO…? It looked like a frog alongside a flamingo.

"What's this?" I asked.

"My daily driver. You think I'm gonna leave the GTO in the station parking lot so that some numbnuts can open his door into my quarter panel. No-fucking-way. Get in. My house is like an echo chamber. There's a strip mall on the avenue. It's dead this time of night." He got into the car, took the coffee from me, and stuffed the hot cup into the center console cup holder. "What's in the bag?"

"Bear claw."

His eyebrows peaked. "*Nice.* I'm hungry as a bear." He looked in the bag and got a glob of icing on his knuckle. "I hope you took at least thirty napkins. Looks like a messy mother."

He started the car, threw the stick shift into gear, and powered up the sloped driveway. "Not bad, right?" he said as the car hit the street. "Three-twenty horse, three hundred-forty cubic inches—not bad for a car with eighty thousand miles on the odometer. And with the manual stick…a real sleeper. The other day some fancy pants guy pulled up next to me at the stoplight in a two-door Mercedes-Benz convertible—I blew his effing doors off." He chomped into the bear claw. "Hmmm, pretty good—almostr worth the mess."

We were parked in a lot in front of an Aboff's paint store two minutes later.

"All right, so hit me with the details. Was Felipe's place a mess?" he asked. "Got to figure it was a pigsty."

"Oh *hell* yes. I've been knee-deep in thawed-out, rotting fish that didn't smell half as bad as that apartment. Animal crap everywhere—pee and varmint blood. Hard to picture a normal person living there. Think I'll stop by the clinic for a syringe of penicillin just to play it safe."

"Who said Felipe was normal? A guy who kills on order—a guy like that has to have a few loose screws, no? Anyway, what did you come up with?"

"I found a name, a woman's name, and address on a dry cleaning receipt. Angela told me that she'd met Felipe's girlfriend one time. I have to believe that's who this is."

He laughed. "Angela told you, huh? You know, Steady, you're like Brooklyn's answer to James Bond—one trip to the mattress and the ladies spill their guts. You must be one hell of a lover."

"I already told you, Angela knows stuff."

"Okay, no argument. What else did you find up there?"

"Shoeboxes filled with cash."

"*Whoa*. I guess Felipe didn't trust the banks. How much are we talking?"

"Hard to say. I didn't have the time to fan out every roll or open every shoebox but…got to be tens of thousands."

Mulligan whistled. "Wow. I'm surprised the ASPCA guys didn't clean the place out. They've got a reputation for that kind of felonious mopery. You'd be surprised how many cat ladies pass away with a cookie jar full of milk money. Friggin dog catchers live for that shit."

"Maybe the handgun collection frightened them off."

"You said *collection*?"

"I found six guns, including a .38 Special."

His mouth fell open. "No *shit*—like the one used in the Palm Sunday Massacre?"

"Maybe, but I made sure Detti didn't find it when he showed up. He got there about an hour after me. I was cornered in the bedroom and had to bail out the window onto the fire escape. I was out there getting drenched while he rifled through the apartment."

"Shit, Detti was there already. Now I know why you were at my door in the middle of the night. Did he fill his pockets?"

"Yeah, as much as he could carry off."

"But there was a lot more, right?"

"A *lot* more."

"That crooked fuck will go back for the rest. What about the guns?"

"Six guns, six boxes of ammo."

"Which Detti found?"

"Yes."

"But not the .38 Special?"

"No, I hid it along with the ammo so he wouldn't see the bullets and go looking for the corresponding gun."

He grimaced. "*Please* tell me you didn't get your prints on it or smudged up what was already on it."

"I picked it up by the end of the barrel using a clean sock I found in the apartment. I slit the side of Felipe's mattress and stuffed it in there along with a box of shells. Covered it with the sheet and blanket."

"I need a minute to think. I don't know how to play this. We know Detti's going to hustle back there for the rest of the cash. At the same time, he'll take the ordnance out of play. In the right hands, the prints from those guns could be linked to dozens of mafia hits. 'Johnny Boy' will pay handsomely for those. Having those guns in play is a huge liability for him. Detti will score big time for taking them out of circulation. You did good, Steady—real good. I'm just not sure how we work this. How do we get the .38 Special into the hands of a straight-up DT who'll do the right thing?"

I could see how hard he was concentrating. He began to gnaw through the pastry like kindling through a wood chipper.

"Any ideas?" I asked.

"Oh, I've got ideas, but they all suck. By the time we figure out what to do and set the wheels in motion, Detti will be back with an SUV and duffle bags. He'll clean the place out."

"Sounds like we're fucked."

"Oh, *so* fucked."

"Poor D. Wayne, lying in a hospital bed hanging on by a thread. We've got all this sway at our fingertips, and I feel like it's all gonna go up in smoke."

Mulligan's eyes blinked rapidly, then opened wide. "What did you say?"

"I said I fell like—"

"Never mind, I heard you." He was growing animated. "I heard you loud and clear." He cranked the engine and threw the stick shift into gear.

"You got something?" I asked.

"Oh, Steady," he began, "do I ever."

Chapter Fifty

awn had yet to rise, but the building Felipe had lived in had already been cleared. Some of the displaced tenants were milling about in front of the building in groups complaining about being forced to leave the building in the middle of the night. Others waited in their parked cars, dozing.

The staircase and common areas were thick with smoke. Mulligan and I were hidden from sight a half-flight up Felipe's apartment near the rooftop doorway. Craning our necks, we could see the door to Felipe's apartment on the floor below where two brawny, ax-wielding firemen had taken up position.

Mulligan winced and massaged his neck. "If I have to stand this way much longer, I'll need the rest of the week off. My fucking neck is killing me."

"Cop a squat. I'll let you know when Detti shows," I said.

He stretched his neck this way and that, to the extreme left and the extreme right to get the kink out. "Don't get old, Steady—it's overrated."

"No, it's not—everyone says getting old sucks."

"And they're right."

"You're not old? What are you, forty-five?" I asked.

"I'm every bit of forty-two, but my years on the job count double, so taking that into account, I'm coming up on sixty, and I feel like a decrepit seventy-five."

"Too bad they won't double up on your pension."

"Yeah." He laughed. "Ain't that a—"

"*Shhh.* I think I hear something." Had to be Detti—everyone else was being kept out. I signaled to the two firemen and mouthed. "He's coming." One of them acknowledged with a nod.

"The grumbling grew louder. A voice sounded like Detti's. Spying through the center of the staircase, I recognized the shape of his head from the back and saw that he was holding a handkerchief over his nose to filter the smoke. Two large black duffle bags were in tow, one over each shoulder.

"What did I tell you," Mulligan whispered. "The dirty bastard came back to clean the place out."

He came off the landing at Felipe's floor and scrutinized the two imposing firemen before stepping forward. "What the hell?" he said. "You evacuated the goddamn building? Why in the hell did you do that?"

"Marshmallow roast," firefighter Ryan said.

It looked like Detti was studying their nametags. "Ryan and Kelly, huh? I walk into a leprechaun convention?"

Kelly must've been every bit of six-two and a solid two-twenty. He raised the blade of his ax until the thickest part of the stock near the ax head rested in his hand. "I look like a fucking leprechaun to you?"

"Easy, brother," Detti said as he reached into his pocket and took out his gold shield. "This is an active crime scene. I've got business inside."

"Ain't safe," Ryan said. "No one gets in."

"You don't understand," Detti said in a hardnosed tone. "I'm a fucking detective, and I'm going in."

Kelly and Ryan closed the gap between them. "Go ahead, Detective," Kelly said. "Give it a try."

"All right, dickheads, where's your supervisor?"

Kelly rapped on the door three times. The door opened a moment later and a third firefighter stepped out. He closed the door behind him and slipped off his SCBA mask. "Someone looking for me?" His nametag read Battalion Chief Terrence Mulligan. He looked like his younger brother—had the same eyes.

Detti shook his head. "Mulligan, Kelly, and Ryan—what happened, you bogtrotters run out of potatoes again?"

"We're kind of busy here. What do you want?" Chief Mulligan asked.

Detti took out his gold badge again. "Active crime scene," he said in a humorless tone. "Can you get your two pit bulls to stand down so I can go inside? Official police business."

"You're right about the place being an active crime scene," Mulligan said. "We're investigating a possible arson. Give me your card, and we'll let you know when it's safe for you and your blue-clad pansies to go in and look around."

"Arson, my ass. Who are you trying to kid?"

Mulligan stared blankly at Detti, his mouth tightly shut.

"Time of the essence, man," Detti said. "I need in *right now*."

"No can do, Detective. Now, do I have to call your commanding officer or are you going to take a hike like a good little goombah?"

"Fuck you, Mulligan! Call anyone you damn well please. Now step aside. There's evidence I need to collect."

"Already bagged and tagged, Detective."

I wished I could've seen Detti's face. It must've turned white when those words hit his ears. He didn't respond for a few moments. When he did, his tone was subdued. "You're interfering with my chain of evidence. I was here last night. First in, man."

"Protocol clearly states FDNY has jurisdiction over all police agencies until the scene has been deemed safe," Mulligan said. "And this place is far from safe. The cash, the guns, and the ammo—we collected it all. This is a suspected arson investigation, and no one is better equipped to pull and analyze fingerprints under said conditions than FDNY forensics. Now, if you'll leave us to it..."

"Mulligan, huh? I know a Mulligan, a big ugly ape."

"I know—we all look alike to you dagos. Now, are we done here, or do you want to take a few more potshots at my proud Irish heritage?"

"I'm going, but you haven't heard the last of this," Detti said.

"*Bring* it, Detective. You know where to find me."

"*A fanabla!*" Detti swore and dismissed Mulligan with a flash of his hand as he slunk off.

"Can't imagine the look on Detti's face when he found out the fire department collected all the ill-gotten bounty he'd come for," Mulligan said. "The poor rotten prick—what a pity."

"Good job, men," Chief Mulligan said to his men. "Help the others finish up inside." He waited for his men to enter Felipe's apartment then stood by the door for a while, looking around to make sure the coast was clear. He then took the stairs and met us on one floor up. Chief Mulligan and his younger brother high-fived. "I fucking love being Irish."

"Back at you," Mulligan said.

"Yeah, thanks, big bro," I said. "You really saved the day. Tell me, though, how'd you fill the whole building with smoke?"

"That's a trick of the trade, my friend," Chief Mulligan said.

"Ah, come on, you gonna leave a brother hanging like that?"

His eyebrows peaked. "I am indeed."

"Thanks for stepping up for us in a pinch, big brother," Mulligan said. "You got it all, right?"

"Every last roll of bills, every box of ammo, all the ordnance in the apartment—including one very well-hidden .38 Special," he said. "We'll run everything through forensics. When the *arson* investigation comes back inconclusive, we'll hand all our findings over to NYPD. And without Detti polluting the air with his corrupt stink, all the evidence, prints, and forensics will be part of the official record. I'd say Detti will be shit out of luck."

It seemed as if the clouds had begun to roll away, and a ray or two of sunlight was shining down on D. Wayne. Now, if only he could stay alive long enough for the rest of the pieces to fall into place.

Chapter Fifty-One

Stomping Detti's ass felt good, so good that I went home and slept through the afternoon. No use in staying up—Mulligan's brother said that it would take about forty-eight hours for NYFD forensics to process all the material they'd collected.

He'd given specific instructions for the .38 Special to be processed for fingerprints before the rest of the collected evidence. With any luck, the report would be back first thing the following morning. I was hoping the gun had a Felipe print on it, a big juicy incriminating print. I only knew a little about matching prints, but what I did know was that the more matching points they find, the better—a dozen was good, twenty was considered a dead-on match. I was hoping for like fifty, some ironclad shit. I wanted the jury to hear the evidence and say, "Hell no, the homeboy didn't do it. It was that Mafioso dude."

I awoke to the harmony of women's hushed whispers. I was groggy, more asleep than awake, lying in bed trying to decipher what I was hearing. I finally had the voices pegged. They belonged to my Auntie and Sandra. But what they were saying…? No clue. Even stranger, I didn't smell anything cooking. You know, two women in the kitchen and all…? I figured something delicious should be in the works.

"What's all the lollygagging?" I said as I entered the kitchen. "I've got a powerful appetite, and the two of you are sitting around gossiping like hens."

The gals must've been getting on real well because they whispered between them, then both flipped me the finger.

"Now, is that any way to take care of a recovering parole officer?"

"I've got rehearsal," Auntie said.

"Again?"

"You want us to be good, don't cha, Steady?"

"With all those rehearsals, you should be opening for The Jackson 5." I turned to Sandy. "What about you? You part of Auntie's New Supremes vocal group as well?"

"No way, I sing like a chicken." She rested her arms over my shoulders and gave me a small peck on the lips. "My talents lie elsewhere. How about you let me take you out for something to eat? I feel guilty about the way I've been treating you." She gave me another kiss, this time lingering a bit longer. She barely pulled away, her lips just a hair's breadth away.

My cheekbones rose. "Hell, come to think of it, I ain't even that hungry."

"Message received, loud and clear," Auntie said as she grabbed her purse and headed for the door. "I'll be back…much later," she said with a huge shit-eating grin. "You both hear me? I said I'll be back about *much* later, a good long while from now. If you two randy savages are still going at it when I get back, that's on you."

I have a vague memory of Auntie saying she wouldn't be home for a while, but it never really stuck. We were off our feet and in my bedroom before Auntie ever made it out the door.

* * *

I heard a knock on my bedroom door and pried my eyelids open to see that it was morning. Sandy was lying on my chest, sleeping soundly. She didn't budge when I saw my auntie at the door. "Auntie?"

"Your friend Mike Mulligan is on the phone. Get your man-whore ass out of bed and take the call."

"Why are you so mad?"

"I'm not mad," she said with a lilt in her voice. "I'm *jealous*. Been ages since I had a romance like that. Come on now—your friend isn't going to hang on forever."

"What time is it?"

"Seven bells, mate. He said he gave you a lot more time than you gave him. Is your girlfriend gonna be able to go to work, or do I need to bring her smelling salts?"

"She's fine, Auntie. Be right there." I heard the door close, followed by the sound of her slippers on the floor. I heard her say, "He's coming, Officer Mike. Had a tough night, that one."

I lifted her head and torso, swung one leg off the bed, then the other. Sandy was still out cold after I had extricated myself from her grasp and slipped into my sweatpants.

The phone was lying on the kitchen counter next to a cup of steaming hot coffee. "Mr. Mulligan, what brings you—"

"Bad news, hotshot—the .38 Special was covered with full prints, but none of them were Felipe's. A couple of partials might've belonged to him, but they came back inconclusive."

"Shit!" I sipped coffee and burned my tongue. "Shit!"

"You said that already."

"I burned my tongue."

"Whatsamatta, too much cunnilingus?"

"Asshole."

"Doesn't mean Felipe *didn't* do it, but the gun doesn't prove that he did."

"So this was all a waste of time—all the time and effort sneaking into Felipe's apartment and emptying the apartment house in the middle of the night—it was all for nothing."

"Felipe's prints might turn up on one of the other guns. So don't start crying in your beer just yet. The guns and ammo will get turned over to NYPD after the rest of the evidence is processed. They'll check ballistics against slugs they've recovered from past murders. And if even one of these guns turns out to solve a cold case, well, then that's a sweepstakes winner in and of itself, isn't it?"

"Why doesn't the fire department do the ballistics tests?"

"Because we've got nothing to compare the ammo to."

"But that'll give Detti the opportunity to mess with the ballistics reports, and you know he will."

"Maybe, but that's a hell of a lot harder to do. We cut him out of the chain of custody. Nothing's impossible, but he shouldn't be able to get his grubby little hands anywhere near them."

"Oh yeah, right."

"Keep your fingers crossed."

"Why? Felipe's already dead. Nailing him on a bunch of old murders might answer some old questions, but it won't help D. Wayne."

"You don't know that. There's a slim chance but…"

"Yeah?"

"If the ballistics test matches the slugs found at the massacre to the gun we found in Felipe's place, we win anyway. Even though Detti found a matching slug at your friend's old flophouse, the fact that the murder weapon was found in Felipe's home opens a door. Any defense attorney worth a shit, even a lummox public defender, should be able to establish that D. Wayne didn't necessarily pull the trigger. And that, my friend, is what we in the law game call *reasonable* doubt."

Chapter Fifty-Two

Sandy was not at all motivated to go to work. She woke up mellow, and when I say mellow, I mean that she didn't want to move a muscle. I wanted to take her out for breakfast, but neither heaven nor earth was capable of moving that girl. She sat at the tiny kitchen table, nibbling toast and sipping coffee, barely able to balance her head on her hand.

"What are we doing today?" she asked.

"Well, since it's a quarter of nine, I guess you're not going into the office. Do you plan on calling out, or do you expect Houck to figure it out on his own?"

Her eyes were closing, on and off. "I'll call. I just need a few minutes."

"I don't remember you missing a day since I started."

"Well then, I deserve a day, don't I?" She signaled for me to get closer and whispered in my ear. "You *destroyed* me."

"Girl, the way I remember it, you were the one crushing it."

"Either way, there's no way can I whizz around the office taking care of twenty parole officers today. I'm going to tell Houck I woke up with lady problems."

"Harry doesn't strike me as the kind of guy you can say that to."

"Trust me, he's got three daughters. He'll deal way better than you think. Besides, I've got a lot of sick days saved up. So, it's cool. What are we going to do today, being as we're both off?"

It had been a night of healing on both a physical and an emotional level. Along with the lovemaking, there had been plenty of time to talk. And now that she understood why I was so committed to helping D. Wayne, she'd become a strong advocate. I didn't hesitate to tell her what I had planned. She knew about the dry cleaning ticket I'd found in Felipe's apartment. "I planed to run down this Joanna Nocaldo. Her address is on the cleaning ticket. Should be a piece of cake."

"Sure, It'll be exciting, like being private eyes or something. I'll tag along."

"You don't look like you're in the mood for excitement. I think you'd be happier with a couch-and-soap-operas kind of day."

"I'll be fine. Just wait until the caffeine kicks in. I'll run circles around you."

"That's some big talk for a woman who claims to have been destroyed in the bedroom."

She grabbed my face and kissed me long and hard, then I carried her to the shower and shoved her in.

* * *

Sandy was a different person after a cool shower and a tank full of high test java. I'd never seen a woman go from zero-to-sixty as quickly as she did. But I was dreading what would happen to her when she ran out of gas. Mulligan told me his GTO could break from sixty miles per hour to zero in less than five seconds. I was betting Sandy could cut that time in half.

In the meantime, she began whizzing around like a popped balloon and was ready for a second cup of coffee and a donut as soon as we exited the subway. She didn't want to sit and savor the snack but instead nibbled the donut while she walked, a bite from the left, a sip of coffee from the right. She seemed happy with the arrangement.

I described the kind of rattrap Felipe lived in and she was concerned that we might find Nocaldo's apartment the same. Angela Rizzo said that Felipe's girlfriend carried herself well and that she was surprised she'd go with a guy like Felipe. I was hoping she was right—at the very least, I hoped she didn't have any pets.

"Looks like a new building," Sandy said. It didn't have those old-world touches you normally see on prewar buildings in Brooklyn or Queens. The bricks were beige instead of the typical red. It looked like a big tan box with windows. No style or charm—strictly utilitarian.

Her name was on the directory alongside a buzzer button. I buzzed once, then twice, eventually holding the button in for long intervals.

No answer—no access.

Not a problem—there must've been eighty tenants listed. We went at it, buzzing every renter in the building until someone buzzed us in. We were looking for apartment 5F. We took the elevator to the fifth floor, where we encountered two moving men carrying a white sofa. A third mover carrying a cellophane-wrapped lamp followed them. We followed the procession of movers back to 5F.

"This looks bad," Sandy said.

It seemed the couch that passed us on the way out was the last of the furniture. The apartment contained stacked boxes and little else. We walked in hoping Nocaldo was still around, but the only visible remnant of the evacuating tenant was a tray of nail polish bottles in the bathroom, yet to be boxed. I grabbed one of the movers for the big question. I flashed the badge quickly, hoping he wouldn't spend time reading the fine print. "Where are you taking all this stuff?"

His English wasn't good. Actually, his English was Russian. All I got from him was a shrug, and a finger pointed at one of the other men.

I moved on.

"Where's this stuff going?" I asked. The second mover groped in his pocket and handed me a yellow carbon copy form. The heading read Ozone Park Thrift Shop along with the establishment's address and phone number. Joanna Nocaldo's address has been filled in on the body of the form. Along with instructions: See superintendent, Sol. Apt. 1J. Empty entire apartment—all content and furniture.

I showed the form to Sandy, and she shook her head discouragingly. The thrift shop would be our next stop, but the odds were that Joanna Nocaldo had taken it on the lam.

Chapter Fifty-Three

The weather was ideal for walking to the thrift shop, which was about a mile away. Sandy was still holding her coffee cup, but I couldn't imagine there was anything in it, that she'd stretched eight ounces of coffee for that long.

Ozone Park had changed a great deal since I was a kid when there weren't, as I remembered, a ton of black families. It was more Italian and Polish. The streets weren't nearly as crowded. It had become densely populated with apartment houses and shops, narrow streets, and congestion. Lots of black families had moved in, Asians and Hispanics too. I remembered the air being fresher back then without as much traffic in the streets. It seemed as if the avenues smelled of bus exhaust day in and out.

Our route took us down 101st. Scanning the street numbers, I realized we were approaching the Bergin Hunt and Fish Club, John Buratti's place. We were getting closer and closer to it but never quite made it all the way there. The thrift shop was about a block away, and we would've made it in the front door if Mulligan hadn't pulled up in front of us.

"What's this, the Oreo Detective Agency? You two hot in pursuit of a glass of cold milk?"

I wanted to flip him the bird but thought better of stretching the bounds of our friendship in public. "The hell you say, Officer? We're one full brother short of an Oreo. We're more like a black and white cookie. Hey, Sandy, how you feel about a threesome with another virile black man like myself?"

She doubled over laughing so hard she could barely get the words out. "Anything for the job."

"Good to know," Mulligan said with a raised eyebrow. "Does Houck know the two of you are holding hands and picking out furniture?"

"I called out sick," Sandy said. "First day I've missed all year."

"Don't worry, kiddo—my lips are sealed."

"This meet-up planned or coincidental?" I asked.

"I was looking for you," he said. "The forensics workups are complete." He got out of the car, and we huddled around him. "The .38 Special you found in Felipe's apartment turned out to be one of the murder weapons everyone was looking for. It was used to kill five of the eleven victims."

"That means Felipe did the killings, right?" Sandy asked.

I shook my head. "No, I think I mentioned to you—Felipe's prints weren't found on the gun."

"So, what does it mean?" she asked.

"Could mean a lot of things," Mulligan began, "most likely Felipe pulled the trigger, but it could also mean someone else used his gun."

"What about the other five handguns? Any of them tied to the murders?"

"No such luck, Steady. We're still shy one of the murder weapons. Could be anywhere. I'm surprised Felipe never tossed the .38 Special into the river, but maybe that was because he knew his prints weren't on it."

"Even so, you know what they say about possession. He had to have another reason for holding onto it."

"Like what?" Sandy asked.

"That much I don't know—not yet anyway."

"The cash found in the apartment was drug money. There were lots of small bills. The lab found traces of coke and heroin on several bills."

"Which could mean that Felipe and Bueno did business together," I said. "The last time I spoke to D. Wayne, he said that Bueno wouldn't float him his fix. He said Bueno needed the cash upfront because he had to pay his distributor." Something stuck in the back of my head was taunting me. I was just about to give up on it when I remembered. "What D. Wayne said was that he had to pay his *big dog*. Big dog is street lingo for a mob dealer, isn't it?"

"Unsure," Mulligan said. "Never heard that before."

"What's going to happen with all this newly discovered information?" I asked.

"The evidence is black and white—it can't be misinterpreted. Reports will go to the detective in charge, Detti, and his higher-ups—the DA's office as well."

"And what about our theory? How do we make it work for D. Wayne?"

"Ordinarily—I mean, if you had an honest DT heading up the investigation, you could pass it along. But with Detti, that bent dick, it would be like pissing in the wind. He'd thank you for the information, and it would never see the light of day. We have to hope that the District Attorney forces the chief of D's hand."

"What are the chances?" Sandy asked.

"DA Altman *should* push on it really hard, but she's a politician. It all depends if she thinks it will benefit her career. She's the opportunistic type. Know what I mean?"

The throaty sound of a revving car engine turned out heads. A red Jaguar convertible slowed next to Mulligan's cruiser. John and Gene Buratti gave us a disapproving once-over while smoke from their Cuban cigars billowed above their heads like thought bubbles.

I wasn't sure if Buratti recognized me from the bakery or if he considered a brother-Irish cop conference uncool. We were less than a block from his Bergin Hunt and Fish Club. Maybe the look meant, "How dare you consecrate our sacred Mafia holy ground?" From the looks of disdain we were getting, that might very well have been the case.

"Hey, Mulligan," Buratti shouted as his cheekbones rose, "I didn't know you were one of them *black* Irish." He let out a hearty laugh before pulling away only to pull to the curb in front of his club and disappearing inside.

Chapter Fifty-Four

The thrift shop manager remembered Joanna Nocaldo vividly. I guess the lady made an impression. He described her and commented about how classy she was—said something about her being a pleasure to deal with. He told me she was in a hurry to move out of her apartment and didn't want any money from the sale of the contents. She provided her superintendent's name and phone number so that the move out could be scheduled and seemed happy to delegate the responsibility. Our conversation had gone well until I realized he didn't know dick about where she had gone. No forwarding address, phone number…nothing.

We left the thrift shop, disappointed, but the news we got from Mulligan had been enough to keep our hopes aloft.

Sandy seemed determined to make the most out of her day off, and being we had no further leads to track down…She insisted that we take the rest of the day off from sussing out D. Wayne's predicament.

I'd been to Coney Island a handful of times, but she'd been there often. She had fond memories of visiting the resort as a kid and missed it because she hadn't been back in years. She wanted to walk the boardwalk and play skee ball at the arcade, pile up winning tickets and come home with a big stuffed doll.

We were still riding high from our night of reconciliation sex, and our chemistry was *muy* simpatico, so I figured *why not?*

It was a long train ride, over an hour. As often is the case, the A/C in our subway car was nonexistent—I could barely feel the tepid air coming out of the vents. We stood between the cars allowing the ozone-impregnated air to flow around us, cooling us off as sparks crackled on the third rail beneath us.

"That Buratti guy, he's a scary son of a bitch," she said. "Did you see the way he looked at us, like we were peasants or something?"

"He's only frightening because you know who he is and what he's capable of. If anyone else pulled up in a red convertible, you wouldn't think of it the same way."

"Maybe. I mean, I guess you're right. But that face—you can tell he thinks who the hell he is. That holier than thou attitude of his—it got to me, you know? With just a glance, you know he's not someone to be messed with."

And why would we? Buratti had the power to wipe you off the map. "We're dirt beneath his boot—not worth his time and attention. We crossed paths before. He probably recognized me and was wondering what I was doing talking to a neighborhood cop."

"Where did *you* meet John Buratti?"

"When I was checking out the house where the killings took place. I met the baker, and he invited me into his shop to talk about the night the bodies were found. Remember, I brought you those dried-out cookies?"

"You mean the delicious biscotti?"

"I guess."

"I'm glad it was a coincidental meeting and not that you were helping Buratti out with his shylock business."

"Yeah, well, I'm a good earner." We had a good laugh over the absurdity of the implication. "Can you imagine a brother becoming part of the family? They'd have to switch Sunday dinner from meatballs and spaghetti to ham hocks and okra."

The train stopped and started, chugged and lurched. It seemed as if it would never pull into the Coney Island train station. Regardless, the conversation continued to flow, and all that time riding between cars proved worth the wait when I bit into an ear of hot buttered corn. I wolfed down a couple of Nathan's dogs and could've eaten a third. Sandy went for the fried shrimp on a bun along with fries. There was something about Nathan's fries I've never found duplicated anywhere else. Those thick-cut potatoes were magic for the mouth. No one knew the secret. If someone did, they'd surely have duplicated it by now.

Turns out I was a skee ball wizard. Tickets were spilling out of that machine like stock prices on a Wall Street ticker tape. Sandy rolled mostly tens and twenties, but I was good for at least thirty on almost every roll. There were one hundred-point cups on the upper corners of the machine, but those were near impossible to get. I tried a few times, and the ball would fall into the ten-point gutter—sucker bait.

"Guess I've got the touch."

"You sure had it last night." She kissed me, and I got back-to-back fifties on my next two rolls. We came away with a pair of oversized Raggedy Ann dolls and slurped soft serve to reward ourselves.

A strong breeze was blowing off the ocean. We walked the boardwalk back and forth until we were worn out, then sat down on a bench to relax. We were soon joined by an elderly man in a straw hat chomping on a cigar. He told us his name was Louie. "Okay if I sit with you nice people?" he asked. He was a real old gentleman and offered us both a handshake. "I promise I won't light the cigar."

News spilled out of his transistor radio. We were able to ignore most of the stories, but the top-of-the-hour headline grabbed us both.

"Joanna Nocaldo, the girlfriend of reputed mafia soldier, Angelo Felipe, was found dead in the water off the Canarsie Pier. You may remember that Felipe's body was fished out of the East River just days ago. The two mob-style hits have led to speculation that an old-fashioned mob war may be brewing. There are no suspects in either murder."

"You believe this shit?" Louie said. "A bunch of cowboys these mobsters are—lawless vigilantes. They give the Italians a bad name." He tuned in to the ballgame. "Who wants to hear about that mafia crap anyway? Not me and not you young people, am I right?"

We tried not to let on how excited we were about the news, but Sandy was so emotional she practically squealed.

"I know, three's a crowd," Louie said. The next bench emptied. "Oh, look." He stood immediately. "I'll move over and give you kids a little privacy."

"Don't go," Sandy said.

"Don't give it a second thought," he said. "I was young once." He plugged in an earplug and winked at us before turning his full attention to the game.

"You think we'll always feel this way?" Sandy asked. She didn't have to elaborate further. I felt it too, that charge of exhilaration that electrified the circuits in our brains. There's a chemical in the brain that's responsible for the way we feel, but I couldn't remember the name and decided to ride the wave of happiness rather than waste the moment recalling the name of a chemical I didn't care about.

The best I could do was to give her a noncommittal shrug. Life's ebbs and flows hit us with good and bad. For every man on the moon, there are a thousand shit storms we're forced to suffer through. Babies are born, and people die—it's that old circle of life, and it never stops spinning. I wasn't the kind of guy to BS my lady, so I took her in my arms. "One day at a time, baby girl. One day at a time."

Chapter Fifty-Five

Sandy and I were dead on our feet by the time the day came to an end. I was trying to maintain my brave face, but I started limping toward the end of the walk to her apartment, and she noticed. She told me to stay the night, but I could see that she needed to sleep, so I popped my last two Vicodin and hung out with an icepack on my hip until she was ready for bed, then had her lock me out.

As if one pain in the ass wasn't enough, Tony was waiting for me when I left Sandy's building. He was leaning against the fender of the black Lincoln, smoking a cigarette. The car was running with the radio on. Dean Martin was singing "That's Amore."

"You get around, don't you, Groove?" He flicked the stogie into the gutter, still glowing red. "Come on, I'll take you home."

I paused at the top of the steps trying to decide if I wanted to get into the Lincoln. I hadn't given the icepack enough time to work, and the Vicodin...I figured it was time to ask the doc for a stronger dosage. My rump was throbbing. It felt as if someone was whacking away at my ass with a sledgehammer. "*My* home, not Todt Hill, right?"

"Yeah, yeah, yeah, your place. Let's go," he said with a grin. "It's an offer you can't refuse." He opened the rear passenger door for me, then, without waiting, walked around the front of the car and got behind the wheel.

"How long have you been following me?"

He pulled away from the curb. "Better you shouldn't know." It was after one in the morning. Tony looked tired and was acting punchy. "I'm glad you came down when you did. I'm friggin' exhausted. Big Paulie ran my ass ragged today. I started the day running him over to Cherry Hill, New Jersey, then into Manhattan—three stops in Brooklyn before dropping him home in Staten Island. I had a couple of slices and a Coke for dinner before trying to find you and your squeeze, which took considerable time. Where were you? You and that pretty little thing shacked up all day?" He yawned. "A long day, my friend, a *very* long day."

The ride from Sandy's place to mine was quick, and Tony had the air conditioning turned down low enough to frost meat. We pulled up in front of Auntie's building about ten minutes later.

"So, what are we doing?" I asked. "Gromaggio didn't send you so we could catch up on your day's activities."

He reached for something on the adjoining seat and handed me a large tan envelope.

"Another envelope? Does Big Paulie own a stationery store?"

"*Ha*. We figured you might want to start a picture album. Go ahead, take a look."

"Sure. Why not?" It contained eight-by-ten black and white photos, six in total—pictures of a streetwalker soliciting johns in their cars. The girl was average-looking and on the squat side. Still, she used her platform boots and hot pants to their fullest advantage. "I don't recognize her. Should I?"

"These photographs will hit the Times city desk by tomorrow evening if a certain Manhattan DA doesn't do the right thing first thing tomorrow morning. *Capish?*"

"You're planning to blackmail the DA?"

"Those are your words, not mine."

"Who's the woman in these pictures, her daughter?"

"Big Paulie was right about you, Groove. You catch on fast. Her name is Hayden Gummer, Gummer being synonymous with how she pays the rent. The DA's full name is Altman-Gummer, but she goes by Altman, professionally speaking, that is. Poor little Hayden has a few loose screws… more than a few. Poor thing has spent so much time on the analyst's couch she thinks her name is Sigmund. Earns her money on a mattress."

"So, you're going to ruin this girl to get what you want?"

"Hey, Mr. High And Mighty, it's what you want too. Trust me, Steady, this girl is damaged goods. She's plenty ruined already. Besides, if the DA does the right thing…these eight by tens go into the incinerator shoot, and the shameful life of her nutso daughter remains a secret."

"How'd you get these anyway?"

"How we got them is not important. What *is* important is that said district attorney once called in a marker from an unnamed detective she once extricated from a jam. The DA was desperate to locate her runaway daughter and said a detective was eager to provide assistance. The detective, in turn, used family connections, Gambino family connections, to find Ms. Fruit Loops. And all this undercover work took place without the blessing of Big Paulie, the *capo dei capi*. Are you getting the picture?"

"Sure I get it—Altman leaned on Detti, who reached out to Buratti under Gromaggio's nose. And now Altman is in Buratti's pocket. Is that about the size of it?"

Was that the reason everyone was lined up against D. Wayne? In my mind, it had to be. The evidence against him was so flimsy, and still, they kept hammering away at him. The mayor's ass was getting chewed raw over the lack of progress on the Palm Sunday Massacre case. It wasn't looking good for him, getting elected to a new term. The police commissioner was a massive loser, and Altman was under Buratti's thumb. Eleven innocent women and kids had been murdered, and the people were screaming for blood. Buratti decided to give them D. Wayne's, and I had a pretty good idea why.

"Good. You get a gold star," Tony said, "Have a good night." He reached past me and pulled the door handle. It took a moment for me to make the connection, but Gromaggio and his driver were doing exactly the same thing. They were opening a door.

Chapter Fifty-Six

I had to take five aspirin to get moving the next morning. I was fine while lying down in bed, but that sciatic nerve hurt worse than a pile driver to the ass when I tried to stand up. All that walking on concrete city sidewalks…It was a dumb move on my part and I was paying the price. My sciatic nerve was on fire and there hadn't been time to refill my prescription.

I hobbled into the kitchen to find Auntie ready to go out and her bootleg Rolex on the table. "Darn thing stopped keeping time already," she said. "And I got so many compliments on it, too. What am I supposed to say… that my nephew, Steady, gave me a hunk-of-junk knockoff watch? I tried winding it up, but nothing happened."

I picked it up as I sank into a chair, my face contorted in pain.

"What did you do to yourself?" Auntie asked. "You stay on that sweet little girl all night long? You know white girls aren't built for that kind of punishment."

"Say what? *I'm* the one limping, Auntie. Anyway, why do you think my johnson is involved anytime my body hurts? We went to Coney Island yesterday. Didn't you see that giant Raggedy Ann doll I left for you?"

"And I *love* it. Maybe if I carry it around in my arms all day, the girls won't notice I'm not wearing my pretend gold watch."

I studied the dial on the faux Rolex, and it was, in fact, dead. Being the boneheaded man I was, I shook it like a maraca to see if it would start up again. No such luck. "Probably needs a battery. I'll take it with me when I go out and see if I can't get one put in."

"A battery, huh? I think you ought to try to get your money back."

Big John took money in. He never gave it out. "I'll see what I can do, Auntie."

I tried getting out of the chair to answer the phone, but Auntie beat me to it. "Hello. Oh, Officer Mulligan, this is starting to be a regular thing. I hope you can still find time to keep folks on the streets safe…Uh-huh, he's here. I'll put him on…you as well, Officer."

She stretched the coiled phone wire from the wall to the table. "You know who it is. Let me know if you're going to be home for dinner or *walking* with your girlfriend all night long." She bent over and kissed me on the forehead. "Young, dumb, and full of…. Stay out of trouble, Steady."

I waited until I heard the apartment door close before answering the phone. "Mulligan."

"What's going on, my friend? You sound like you woke up on the wrong side."

"My sciatica is acting up again—killing me."

"Maybe you ought to spend more time in an upright position and not so much horizontal."

Another wiseass. "What on your mind, Mike?"

"Steady, *ho-lee shit*, you should've been a fly on the wall at this morning's roll call. Steiner, right? He's the squad commander. I could just tell from the look on his face that he was stressed out of his friggin' mind. Anyway, the first point of order was the Palm Sunday Massacre. The second point was the Palm Sunday Massacre, *third, fourth,* and *fifth.* I don't know how exactly it came down, but the entire department is going bonkers—asses must've been reamed by the carload. They're setting up a special task force to take over the investigation, and our dear friend Detti's been kicked to the curb. They're putting a straight-up no-bullshit cop in charge, this guy Victor Tomlinson—made his bones on the street."

The photos Big Paulie's driver showed me must've really hit home with Altman. I knew those pictures would pack one hell of a wallop. I just didn't know how quickly they would take effect. Mulligan didn't know about my late-night meeting with Tony, the limo driver, and I wasn't sure it was a good idea for me to tell him—not right now anyway. "Man, that's really good to hear. Detti must've gone ballistic."

"People are whispering that Detti's gonna get shit-canned, but something like that, it'll take time. NYPD's got its share of red tape, bureaucracy up the wazoo. The case he built around Tyrone, it's coming down around his ears. Higher-ups don't like cops who make up the outcome of the cases they investigate. Couldn't happen to a nicer guy, right?"

"I think you hate him even more than I do."

"I'll roll you for top honors. If not, I'm a definite goddamn second. Either way, things are getting straightened out. Mayor Irving, the commish, and DA Altman are about to start a press conference. They're going to interrupt regular programming to cover it on all the news stations. Wild, huh? Who would've thunk that an ornery mick patrolman like me and a rookie PO could've done so much damage? I've only got a couple of years left before banging out, but maybe I *will* take the detective's test. I might be pretty good at it."

"Buratti is gonna shit himself. You think he knows already?"

"Oh, *he* knows, Steady—you best believe it. Say, you anywhere near a tube? Switch it on—the press conference should be on almost every station."

Auntie had a small black and white in the kitchen. In all the time I'd lived there, I never saw it switched on—didn't even know if it worked. "Maybe," I said.

"What do you mean, maybe? Either you do, or you don't."

I didn't bother to answer. I switched it on and waited for it to warm up. Nothing appeared to be happening, but I could smell the odor of old electric circuits warming up. I waited for a picture to appear, but there was nothing on the screen. I looked in the ventilation slots on the side of the set and saw that the tubes were beginning to glow orange. A voice crackled from the speaker, and a shadowy picture began to take shape. "Sounds like the press conference is starting."

"Sounds like? Steady, you don't know the difference between TV and radio?"

Looks like…whatever.

The steps of City Hall finally came into focus. The mayor was standing at a podium and was flanked by the DA on his right and the police commissioner on his left. I turned up the volume and held the phone receiver next to the TV so that Mulligan could hear Mayor Irving begin the press conference.

"In light of new evidence, a decision has been made, in conjunction with the office of the Manhattan District Attorney and NYPD, to assemble a task force to further investigate the atrocity the press has labeled the Palm Sunday Massacre. While no decision has been made to drop the charges against Dennis Wayne Tyrone, certain mitigating circumstances have led us to believe that there are greater complexities to the case than had we were originally aware of. While the public will no doubt be displeased to learn that justice for eleven murdered women and children will be longer in coming, we would be negligent if we didn't explore all possible aspects of the crime. In a moment, I'll turn the mike over to District Attorney Altman and Police Commissioner Canton, who will provide in-depth explanations of the new information that has come to our attention as well as NYPD's game plan for carrying out a swift and informative investigation of said new evidence."

"You hear that, Mulligan?"

"We did it, Steady. We fucking did it."

Sure, we helped, but it was Big Paulie Gromaggio who pulled his finger out of the dyke. His photos were the leverage that caused Altman to act. As for Buratti…

Altman had stepped up to the podium. She opened a portfolio and was about to read when the deputy mayor hurried over to the mayor and whispered in his ear. I could see the mayor's eyes growing large.

"Just a minute, please," Altman said to the audience and stepped over to where the mayor and deputy mayor were speaking.

"What's going on there, Steady? Did the old girl forget her standard line of bullshit? Wait. Hold on, Steady. Something's—" I heard a noise on the end of the line. It sounded like static from a police radio. Mulligan was quiet for a time and sounded agitated when he got back on the phone. "Signal thirty, Steady. I've got to jump." The line went dead in my hand. I wasn't familiar with police radio codes, but the edge in Mulligan's voice told me something big was going down. I just didn't know how big it was until I turned back to the TV and saw the mayor, DA, and police commissioner turn and hurry up the steps to City Hall.

The deputy mayor stepped up to the microphone. He took a moment to size up the crowd or, more likely, to work up the nerve. "That's all for now," he said apologetically. "I'm sorry. This press conference is over."

Chapter Fifty-Seven

I hung up and stared at the yellow wall phone, wondering if Mulligan would be able to call back, but quickly realized that, like the watched pot, that sucker was never going to boil. Mulligan's hasty hang-up, along with what I'd witnessed on Auntie's little old TV, told me I'd better drag my broken ass into the shower and run some hot water on it PDQ. I didn't know when an update would come along, but I'd best be ready when it did.

I carried Auntie's little transistor into the bathroom, turned it up to full volume, and angled the wand antenna until 1010 WINS came in loud and clear. Short of a ringing phone, the only way I'd know what was going on would be to hear about it on the radio.

Like most of us, my first thought was to think the worst, that D. Wayne was dead, his wounds fatal. The city brass would have a full chafing dish of egg on their collective faces if an innocent man croaked because he'd been locked up and abused in prison. The civil liberties groups would have a field day with that folly, with the poor street urchin the police had made into a patsy. Hell, the self-righteous Reverend Malcolm Pointer would chew Mayor Irving's ass until it was good and raw. Irving might as well hang up his political career and head to Florida for a retirement ritual of early bird specials. There was no way in hell he'd ever get reelected. I've heard that many old Jews like Irving head out to pasture in and around Palm Beach, Florida, but Altman...? My best guess was that the old Hun would pack up her husband and her head case daughter and make straight for the fatherland, maybe get a job on the Volkswagen assembly line in Wolfsburg.

As for Police Commissioner Canton…I didn't have a clue. I never knew a black man who'd made it all the way through to retirement. Black men didn't retire—they just stopped working, shriveled up, and disappeared.

What I did know was that all three would be washed up…kaput.

The five aspirin and a boiler-full of hot water did me a lot of good. I did some of the stretches the doc had taught me. I still felt like an old warhorse, but at least I could get around. I knew better than to sit down and let everything stiffen up, so I paced the apartment, down the hallway from the kitchen to my bedroom and back—over and over, trying to keep limber.

The big news eventually came. It wasn't anything I expected. I scolded myself because I felt that I should've seen it coming and didn't. I wasn't kidding myself—I was no more than a pawn on the chessboard. But now and then, a pawn plays a hand in toppling a king.

Chapter Fifty-Eight

John Buratti got his at the Bergin Hunt and Fish Club. A sole masked gunman burst in and put two in Buratti's chest before Buratti's men could respond with gunfire. The assassin took one in the leg and one in the back but managed to hobble out the door and into a waiting getaway car.

At roughly the same time, brother Gene was getting peppered with lead on his way out of Rizzo's bakery. He had a piece of pastry in one hand and a cup of coffee in the other. The murky brown coffee and the cannoli cream had blended in with the pool of blood on the sidewalk. First responders found him in Angela Rizzo's arms, his head propped against her white bakery uniform, now soaked red. By the time I arrived, the crime scene had already been processed and the body removed. But a photo of Gene Buratti lying in Angela's arms was captured by a photographer and was displayed on the front page of The New York Post alongside a photo of John Buratti's covered body being carried out of the Bergin Hunt and Fish Club on a stretcher.

I was there, looking on from the periphery of the police barrier, when John Buratti was carried away. Buratti was a local hero with a reputation for being extremely generous to the people in the neighborhood. He threw an annual feast every Fourth of July, treating the neighborhood to barbecued food, music, and fireworks.

The crowd was growing hostile. They were screaming at the police, demanding justice for their fallen champion. Mulligan was one of the many police officers working crowd control. He saw me from the corner of his eye and made his way over.

"It's a real shit show," he said. "Can you believe it—someone actually had the stones to take out Johnny Boy Buratti—in broad daylight no less? Whoever did this had some real balls, Steady, a brass set. I suppose you heard that brother Gene got iced too?"

The rumor of Gene's death had been going through the crowd, but I didn't know if it was true. "Kind of. A single shooter took out John, right?"

"So I hear. One shooter wearing a mask—tapped Buratti twice in the chest and took a couple going out the door. Getaway car was waiting outside. Got away clean."

"And baby bro?"

"Machine-gunned outside Rizzo's bakery. They made his white shirt look like a roll from a player piano."

"I get them hitting John here at his headquarters but how'd they know Gene would be at Rizzo's?"

He shook his head disappointedly. "Geez, Steady, I tried to tell you, but you didn't get it. Maybe you didn't want to understand. Angela was Gene's *goomah*—one of them anyway. Gene couldn't keep it in his pants. He had girlfriends stashed all over town. Why do you think I told you to stay away from her? If he ever found out about the two of you… He picks up the pastry order for big brother's weekly meeting with the captains. He doesn't have to, of course, but like I kind of said, his sweet tooth extends further than the pastry."

I'd had a sense that Angela wasn't a one-man kind of woman. Hearing it from Mulligan made so much sense I couldn't believe I hadn't figured it out on my own. It made me feel a little stupid. I'd been with white women from time to time who were curious to experiment with a black man—see if the legend was true. At the same time, I felt lucky because the news of my tryst with Angela had died on the vine. For my own sake, of course, but…it was a one-and-done, and I was glad Sandy had been spared the pains of my guilty pleasure.

A shoving match had broken out behind me. "I've gotta go, Steady. Shit, a lot of people are going to get hurt today." I'd never seen the big man move so quickly. He ducked under the police barricade and put himself between two arguing men, shutting down the quarrel. No sooner had he addressed the altercation than another broke out a few feet away. The crowd was growing hotter, more violent. More and more cops were breaching the barrier to squash exchanges. Mulligan glared at me, his expression telling me to get the hell out of there. It was about then that someone cracked a bottle over his head, and that big man went *down*.

Chapter Fifty-Nine

Like a sold-out stadium at a rained-out Yankees doubleheader, New York City had become an angry place. Justice for the eleven murdered women and children had been kicked like a can down the road—hell, it had been kicked into orbit and seemed like it might circle the globe indefinitely.

As I walked the streets, I could feel the hostility. It floated in the air like bad karma and was drawn in with every breath. The public wanted answers, and it didn't look like they were going to get them anytime soon. Between the high-level Mafioso hits and the DA going namby-pamby on its number-one murder suspect in the Palm Sunday Massacre…I mean, what did I expect?

I think everyone was just plain old pissed off and feeling as if they'd been played for fools. And that Reverend Pointer, he was getting so damn popular I half-expected him to challenge Mayor Irving for reelection. He certainly had the people's ear and played to it like a concert violinist, picking strings as if they were inflamed nerves. He staged daily protests, demanding justice, demanding an investigation into D. Wayne's mistreatment, demanding that heads roll, demanding, demanding, and more demanding. He made the police, the mayor, and the DA look like hacks, scheming, duplicitous hacks with nothing on their agendas but their own careers and well-being. Pointer somehow managed to leak a photo to the press depicting D. Wayne lying unconscious in a hospital bed. My feral friend had become the poster child for racial injustice and municipal corruption.

And all while he slept.

Pointer didn't know the half of it.

Not like I did.

Several days passed before NYPD allowed me to visit Mulligan in the hospital. The police department was on heightened alert. From what I read in the papers, every able-bodied cop was working around the clock and pulling overtime, investigating the massacre. For every Pointer protest, there was a corresponding NYPD police conference apprising the public of the latest developments and the initiatives being taken to get to the bottom of it all. But really, it was just the brass covering their collective rear ends—damage control.

The bottle Mulligan took to the noggin was no flimsy Hollywood stunt breakaway. It was a heavy champagne bottle, and it almost split the man's head in two. When I walked into his hospital room, he was lying in bed with his head bandaged like Boris Karloff's Mummy, the gauze stained with blood and serum.

I didn't figure a guy like Mulligan would appreciate flowers, but I stopped at the local OTB before getting to the hospital and placed a few cheap bets for the afternoon races. I handed him the tickets and the betting form.

"Thoughtful," he said with a glance at the stubs. "I trained you well. With all the Lofts and Barricini chocolates everyone is bringing, I'll probably develop diabetes before I get out of here. I'm glad you were smarter than that."

"I didn't think flowers were your thing but looking around…"

The room was filled with color, bouquets, and potted plants of every size and variety. "Stinks like the fucking botanical gardens in here." He held up the betting stubs. "Much appreciated. I hope you remembered all the things I taught you."

"Time will tell." I glanced at my Timex. "Actually, you might know before I leave. Depending, of course."

"Depending on what?"

"How soon you get tired of talking to me."

"I sent Patty and the girls home to rest, and the procession of NYPD muckety-mucks and brothers in blue is finally petering out. It's good to see a brother of another color." He laughed, then winced. "Hey, stop making me laugh."

"I'll keep it dry."

"Cop a squat."

"Do you feel as bad as you look?"

"Worse—my head hurts so bad it feels like someone's wailing away with a log splitter."

"That good, huh?"

"The only thing that makes me feel better is the news coming from the task force. I told you, Victor Tomlinson's a good egg. He dragged that sleazeball, Rico Bueno, in for questioning."

"About goddamn time."

"Must've sweated the bejesus out of him."

"Did he spill?"

Mulligan tried to smirk but couldn't. His face contorted into a painful grimace again. "Can't believe how much that hurt. Anyway, if you remember, one of the dead kids wasn't found in the living room but was found in bed under the covers in the adjoining room. And since the second gun was never recovered…Tomlinson told Bueno, 'We know you did your son.' He told him, 'We know you had a .45'—the caliber the boy was shot with. That big .45 slug went through the wall and killed the boy. Naturally, Bueno claims he didn't know."

"Is that possible?"

"Anything's possible, but if you ask me, the rat bastard was in denial. He knew his son was home in bed, sick. That's why he didn't go to church with the others. That fool, Bueno tried to cut a deal, a full confession in exchange for a reduced sentence, but of course, all his leverage had already gone down the drain when Felipe and his girlfriend got bumped off."

"But he confessed anyway, right?"

"The DA said she'd charge him with involuntary manslaughter—four years max, but when push comes to shove, there's no way Bueno is getting a paltry four years no matter how you slice it. I don't see how they can legally kick the charge up to voluntary manslaughter, but considering the heinous nature of the crime and the fact that he kept his mouth shut while worms ate his girlfriend and his unborn child…? I could see an outraged judge tacking on as many years as he could get away with."

"Are you going to tell me how the confession went down, or am I going to have to beat it out of you?"

"Ha, you can try. Even banged up like this, I'd wipe the floor with you."

Mulligan was a bull, but I had him in youth and overall size. For the moment, though, I'd let him think he could. "Well?"

"It was like we thought, Felipe was supplying Bueno, and Bueno was past due on his account. Felipe and his moll, this Joanna Nocaldo, stopped by Bueno's to collect, and an argument broke out because Bueno was short on what Felipe was due. So, Bueno pulled his .45, a shot went off, which presumably went through the wall into the bedroom and killed his son. Bueno dropped the .45 when he and Felipe were grappling, then took off before Felipe could waste him. And that's all she wrote. Felipe and Nocaldo had to have murdered everyone else. Why? We'll never know for certain."

"But we do know that Bueno's girlfriend, her sisters, and the kids went to church together. They might've walked in on Felipe and Nocaldo right after they discovered the dead boy in the bedroom, and ten witnesses to an alleged murder make bad odds for a reputed mob hitman. Felipe must've figured that dead men tell no tales, so he had Nocaldo hold everyone at gunpoint while he went from one to the next eliminating the liabilities. At some point when he was getting low on rounds, they switched guns, and he killed the others."

"Or she killed them," Mulligan said. "Maybe that's why they only found her prints on the .38 Special. Maybe that's why he held onto it. Nocaldo may have been a hot lay in the sack, but if push came to shove, he'd turn over the gun with her prints and cop a plea. He could say she was a crazy bitch. She panicked and insisted on killing them all. Accessory to murder ain't great, but it's not a life sentence—fifty percent of the sentence."

"Who in their right mind would believe that?"

"Maybe Felipe did. I mean, the asshole played Suzy Homemaker with skunks and rats and shit. He's probably certifiable."

"Sounds to me like Detti's fucked. He falsified every last ounce of evidence."

"Oh, yeah, he's finished. Hope he's got a good lawyer because he's going to need one. After this, he won't be able to get a job as a mall security guard."

"Don't you wonder why he did it? I know the brass wanted the case wrapped up in the worst way, but to throw an innocent man under the bus like that. That's *low, man*."

"You're naïve, Steady. Your pal Dennis Tyrone wasn't the first, and he sure as hell won't be the last to get flushed down the toilet. Innocent men get sent up the river all the time. And Altman, she's the friggin' queen of that shit. One day all of her evil deeds will come out, but she'll probably be long gone by then. Figures a parasite like her to get off easy."

I thought about the photos Tony had shown me, the ones of Altman's strung out, bi-polar daughter. *Get off easy*? Hell, any mother would trade slammer time for a healthy kid. I was tempted to tell him about Altman's daughter but decided that was a string I'd better not pull on. "Is that the best we're capable of?"

"Guess maybe it is, Steady. To tell you the truth, I think we're capable of much worse. Look at the goddamn Vietnam War. How many young men lost their lives to feed the military-industrial complex? That war was bullshit, and there's not a soul who'd deny it—just fat cats getting fatter. Street thugs like Dennis Tyrone…small potatoes, my friend. And no one gives a flying fuck about them."

A nurse walked in carrying a syringe on a tray. She was a mature black woman with bangs and a jutting rump. She wore those opaque institutional stockings guaranteed to kill a teenager's boner. She set the tray down on the nightstand and purged air bubbles from the syringe. "Guess what I've got for you?"

"Is it happy time, Agnes?" Mulligan asked.

"Sure is, handsome," she said. "Got you the primo stuff for you this time." She inserted the needle into the I.V. "Here comes La La Land. Who's your easy-on-the-eyes friend?"

"Steady, say hello to Agnes, the best nurse this side of the Hudson."

"*What*, you saying I don't have it all over those *Joise* hacks?" She depressed the plunger. "You're going to have to leave, Mr. Steady. Mr. Mulligan is about to go bye-bye."

"Yeah, get him out of here, Agnes. You can't trust these ghetto pretty boys."

The syringe empty, she withdrew it and placed it back on the tray. "Sweet dreams, Michael. Close those baby blues and drift off. And you, Mr. Steady…out!" She exited directly.

"Guess that's my cue," I said. "I'll be back when you're feeling more like yourself."

"Sure." His eyes were closed, his speech slurred. "You do that." His breathing grew heavy.

"Mike?"

It took a moment, but he answered. "Yeah?" It sounded as if he was coming from a far-off place.

"I hope Frankie Irish pulls through."

His response was weak. He was just about out, closer to sleep than consciousness. I had to put my ear near to his mouth to hear him say, "Yeah, me too."

Chapter Sixty

D. Wayne Tyrone was released, not from custody but from his earthly confines. With all he had suffered through, horrendous beatings, years of drug and alcohol abuse, and appalling mistreatment, it was an itty-bitty blood clot that took him from this world. He'd been exonerated, but he was never freed. He was one of those small potatoes no one cared about, dirt beneath the boots. Some say he was a victim of a broken system, a system of bureaucrats who chewed up the D. Waynes of the world and spit them out. And for what, another term in office and all the money they could stuff in their pockets with?

Yeah, that's for what—money and power.

No small potatoes.

He didn't get much of a turnout at his funeral, but the day was grand, nothing but blue skies and gentle breezes. I tried to convince myself that someone was smiling down on him—maybe not God, but somebody.

Sandy and I were there as well as a few city officials who had come to pay homage because their superiors insisted that they attend.

Vonda Gale, D. Wayne's on-again, off-again drug buddy with benefits, showed up and cried her veiny eyes out. A good actor that girl was. She cared so little for him that she was going to provide bullshit testimony to send him to prison, but she was now ready to benefit from his demise. She was suing the city for millions. Some young yuppie lawyer with a ponytail and wire-rimmed glasses said he could uphold her rights as D. Wayne's common-law wife. I couldn't imagine any twelve fool jurors awarding that turncoat hoe a red cent, but no matter—she'd blow every nickel on horse and crack and be dead within the year.

Maybe that was justice as well.

And maybe not.

Mulligan showed. He looked like shit, but I knew he was a happy camper. The doctors totaled him out like an auto wreck, a car that was beyond repair. He'd collect a full pension and disability without working another day for the rest of his life. For a guy like Mulligan that was some major league shit—a grand slam.

Or so you'd think.

I cornered him after the graveside service, and we walked off a ways.

"Sad," he said. "The system got him."

"Which system is that?"

"What, I have to spell it out for you?"

"I've got time."

"Come on, man. It was the powers on high, the fixers and the kingmakers. Irving, Altman, and Canton—the people wanted a monster. They gave them a monster. Got to admit, Tyrone was ripe for the role. He was one sleazy motherfucker, a piece of street shit no one cared about. Ain't nobody gonna miss him."

"You are aware they just lowered the man into the ground, not twenty feet from here."

He tapped me on the chest. "Fuck him. I came here for you, man, not for that drug-sucking waste of life."

"You don't feel you owe the man a debt?"

"Steady, for Christ's sake, what are you getting at?"

"How much you make off dead little Dennis Tyrone?"

"Fuck this. I thought you were my friend. I'm out of here."

"Look me in the eye and tell me you didn't have a part in this."

"Why you son of a bitch—after all the help I gave you. After I took you under my wing."

"Help? You manipulated my ass."

"Yeah, like I *really* handled you. Keep talking."

Keep talking meant shut the fuck up, but that wasn't going to happen. I'd been stewing over it for days and knew I was right. "All the shit you took when you reported D. Wayne stripping that car. Eighteen years on the job, and you never got written up before. And you knew who was behind it, Detti. The expensive suits, the fancy vacations, and the cars—you hated the son of a bitch."

"Yeah, that's it, you got me. I hated Detti. So what? Am I happy he's gonna get shit-canned? Yeah. Did I play some small part in exposing him? Yeah, I dropped those airport photos on IAD. Can you blame me? The man was a rat bastard and a dirty cop. He took mob money and used Cosa Nostra connections to make himself look good. Am I happy? I'm fucking ecstatic."

"How much did you get from Gromaggio?"

"What are you talking about, man? I think you're going soft in the head."

"This goes way beyond three lousy politicians and their hopes for reelection, and you damn well know it. Buratti's crew was selling drugs even though Gromaggio banned made men from dealing, under threat of death. Gene was arrested for dealing drugs a year ago. The feds bugged his house, and Gromaggio wanted the tapes, but big bro John refused to turn them over. It was everything Gromaggio hated and hoped wouldn't happen. Buratti hated Gromaggio. Gromaggio hated Buratti. It was only a matter of who made the first move."

"What's any of that got to do with me?"

"Buratti was the muscle behind Detti, and Felipe was part of Buratti's crew. And once a member of his Gambino crime family was exposed as the mass murderer of eleven women and kids…do the math. The police may not have known that Buratti was pulling strings to turn suspicion away from one of his soldiers, but Gromaggio sure as hell did, and the death of eleven innocent women and kids gave him all the ammunition he needed to pull the trigger."

"You're a smart spook, Steady, but I'm still standing here smelling pretty sweet. Make your point or move on."

"Gromaggio saw the handwriting on the wall. He needed the Burattis dead, but because of Cosa Nostra code couldn't do it without justification from the council of dons. He needed Buratti's soldier exposed as the murderer, and you got me to do it for him. Sure, I was grateful for all the info you shared, but when you introduced me to your Irish mob cousin…You told me the Westies signed on as torpedoes for Gromaggio. You had your cake and ate it too. Detti got the ax—you and Frankie Irish got a huge Gromaggio payday for dropping the bomb on 'Johnny Boy' and baby brother. Hits don't come cheap."

"It's a cute story, but you forgot one thing. You've got to prove it."

"No, I don't."

"And why's that?"

"Because there's no honor among thieves. Maybe you'd better see if Frankie Irish is still holed up in that Westside rat trap."

I could see the gears turning frantically in his head. "You're bluffing. He was wearing a mask."

That was all I needed to know I was right.

Would Frankie Irish get caught?

Maybe.

Would he rat his cousin if he got jammed up?

Anyone's guess.

But I'd planted a goddamn hungry seed in Mulligan's head and those roots…they can eat your motherfucking brain.

"Conspiracy to commit murder—a smart spook like me knows that a Class A-1 felony. You could get fifteen years, man. But being a peace officer, an outraged judge might stick his shiny black wingtip up your lily-white ass and sentence you to a hell of a lot more."

Chapter Sixty-One

e bury our dead and move on.

That's what Auntie had told me, not after we buried D. Wayne, but when my moms had passed away, and she became my second moms. Doors open and close. Whichever door D. Wayne went through took him to a better place than the one he left behind. I didn't see him being up in heaven, sipping bubbly and chowing down on prime steaks, living large in a mansion surrounded by rapper groupies. But maybe wherever he landed, he'd have a clean bed to rest when he was weary, free drugs, and all the KFC he could eat. Asking for anything more than that was just damn greedy.

A new door opened for Auntie. She and her girls got a gig at Ricardo's, a neighborhood restaurant with a regular crowd of folks who enjoyed the old tunes—I'd heard tell it was the place where Tony Bennett started out. They were booked for only one weekend, but that was about as much of a commitment as Auntie, and the gals wanted. After not performing publicly for so many years, they were unsure of themselves and needed a confidence booster. The pin money they would earn would be as good as gold. It would make them feel good about themselves and give them a new sense of purpose. Knowing Auntie the way I did, I figured she'd be back on top in no time, singing for all she was worth.

Sandy and I were enjoying large bowls of pasta and wine while Revitalize featuring Carrie Mae sang "At Last" so sweet and soulful Etta James would've been mesmerized. It had been Meyer's favorite song, and she couldn't get through it without shedding tears. She had a folded tissue tucked under the bracelet of her Rolex that she put to good use. I wasn't able to get the sham watch running again, but Auntie wore it to perform because she liked the way it sparkled under the stage lights.

She stopped at our table when the first set was done. "How'd we do?" she asked. "It's our first gig, and we're nervous as cats."

"You were great," Sandy said. "The way you sang Etta James…" She pressed her hands to her heart. "It was *so* touching."

"Thank you, darlin'. Used to sing that for my husband back in the day. After that, he'd grab me, and we'd dance around the apartment until our feet ached." She sighed deeply. "The good old days, you know?"

"Auntie, I always said you were better than Diana Ross. If you'd lived in Detroit, they'd be calling that Motown group Carrie Mae and The Supremes."

"Go on now," she gushed. "Steady Groove, when did you become such a polished ass-kisser?"

"I learned the boy good." The voice seemed to come out of nowhere. Uncle Barney seemed to just materialize. He looked every bit as scruffy as the last time I saw him, just before I got coldcocked and woke up in the hospital. "Carrie Mae, darlin', you're a sight for sore eyes." He hugged her, pressing his prickly stubble to her flawless cheek."

She pulled out of his grip. "Barney Booker, where the hell have you been?"

"Yeah, where *have* you been?" I stood and looked him in the eye. "You've got a lot of nerve showing up here after what you did."

"What *I* do?" he asked.

"What did you do? You sold out D. Wayne and for what, a favor from a dirty cop? Was he the one that dragged you out of Salty Monroe's place?" *The bastard that cracked me over the head.*

"Hell, Steady, that's water under the damn bridge. We're family, now—got to let bygones be bygones."

"I've still got the gash that Detti put in my head."

He examined the wound from a distance, taking his time to make it look as if it mattered to him. "Oh, come on now, Steady—*you're* fine."

"Why don't you take a hike," I said. "Stop raining on Auntie's parade."

"Take it easy on him, Steady," Sandy said. "Looks like he's seen some tough times."

"Listen to the snow bunny." His eyes went from Sandy to her dinner. "My-my, you got enough spaghetti there to feed an infantry. Mind if I—" He snatched a chair from the next table and dug in, sucking up Sandy's pasta. "Ain't et in days." He had red sauce all over his face as he wolfed down her food.

Auntie shuddered. "Disgusting, Barney, just disgusting."

"I guess the police don't need your bullshit testimony anymore," I said.

"Stop worrying," he said. "That fool friend of yours is gonna be just fine. I heard—"

Damn old fool doesn't know D. Wayne is dead and doesn't care. I erupted so fast I didn't realize what I was doing. I grabbed Sockeye by the scruff and hauled him out of his seat.

"The hell you doing, Steady? I'm—"

"You're not welcome here."

"Steady," Sandy plead," Don't—"

"Fish the garbage pails with the rest of the bottom feeders." I dragged him to the door and threw him out. It wasn't who he was but what he'd done that angered me so deeply. I could see the dirty cops and politicians using D. Wayne, but one of his own...? D. Wayne was from the street, the same as any of us, no better and maybe a hell of a lot worse. You may hate the hood, but we've got a code of our own—you don't sell out a brother.

Chapter Sixty-Two

Auntie's debut didn't end the way it started.

Sure, she went on to finish her second set, but Sockeye's appearance had fouled the mood and drained away most of her energy.

Revitalize did well enough to get booked for the rest of the month, but Auntie wasn't herself during the second set. She held back and let the other girls carry the performance. I knew she'd get over it. After all, being disappointed by Barney was nothing new to her, and she had always bounced back. It was just a shame the way that selfish bastard tarnished her big day.

Sandy was quiet the next couple of days. Can't say I blamed her. Tossing Barney out of the restaurant rubbed her the wrong way. I guess she didn't like seeing me in that light and needed time to decide if I was the man she wanted to spend more time with. I didn't know which way she'd lean, but I'd wait for her long as it took.

I'd returned to work. It was hard getting back into the flow of things after all the time I'd been off. And Sandy…she was cool.

A couple of weeks came and went before she opened up. "I didn't like what you did, Steady, but I understand why you did it. You did it to protect your Aunt, same as you stuck with your friend Dennis when everyone else turned their backs on him. You're loyal, Stedman Groove, and that's the kind of man I want to be with."

I'd been on the wrong end of a fishing line often enough to know that you never took anyone or anything for granted. The expression, hook, line, and sinker was a fallacy. There aren't any absolutes in life, and anyone who believes there are is a fool. No one is completely good or completely bad. Love comes, and love goes. That whole bit about the sea being a fickle mistress…yeah, man, that's true on the water and in life…Life is a fight, a fight for life and death sometimes, and you ain't always gonna win.

I may not wind up being the last man standing but standing I was.

For now, anyway.

And from what I've learned about life, that's pretty damn good.

Afterword

Hi, it looks like you made through to the end of the story. I hope you enjoyed sharing these pages with Steady. I enjoy that young man and hope he'll live in my imagination for as long as you like reading his deeds. Steady and I will go on to explore the unexplained and shed light over the darkness. You may find yourself shocked along the way.

Into the Groove is a work of fiction, but the Palm Sunday Massacre was all too real. The senseless murder of eleven women and children in 1984 will live on as one of the ugliest moments in New York City history and possibly one of the Big Apple's greatest miscarriages of justice. The story you read and the outcome have most certainly been altered, but I'm confident you'll be able to piece together the truth for yourself.

I thought you might find it interesting if I provided a smattering of the facts and observations surrounding the actual event. It might lead you to arrive at the same conclusions Steady did.

Hope to see you around.

Best regards,

Larry Kelter

The Palm Sunday Massacre

- Palm Sunday, April 15, 1984—Dubbed the *Palm Sunday Massacre* by the press, 1080 Liberty Avenue, Brooklyn became what was at the time the scene of the largest mass murder in New York City history. Christopher Thomas wasn't a saint. He wasn't much of anything—nothing more than a low-level street criminal with no guaranteed tomorrows. He had a substantial rap sheet and at the time of his arrest on mass murder charges was sitting in the Bronx House of Detention, dazed, confused, and unsure of what was happening to him. He's wasn't exactly the kind of guy you'd go to bat for, and no one did. The public wanted blood. They wanted a monster. And they were given a monster, a simple man incapable of advocating for himself, who'd been made to look like someone much worse than he was. Of greater significance—an embattled Mayor Koch was fighting to win reelection, Police Commissioner Benjamin Ward was about to be shown the door, and the mob sought to insulate itself against the long-echoing murders that followed the Lufthansa Heist. It was perhaps the most threatening convergence of evil ever assembled to railroad one simple man into jail.
- Not far from the scene of the crime, the Lucchese and Gambino crime families were still recovering from the aftermath of the infamous "Lufthansa Heist" at JFK Airport. The Gambino boss, "Big Paulie" Castellano, was struggling to hold onto control of the most powerful crime family in New York City and stay out of jail. Big Paulie, already concerned about the arrests of two members of John Gotti's Bergin Crew on major drug charges, had just come under Federal indictment himself.

- Big Paulie had been asking Gotti to obtain defense copies of incriminating FBI recordings made of members of his Bergin Crew for fear that this information might take him down as well. If Big Paulie got his hands on these tapes, Gotti would've had good reason to fear for his life and the life of his younger brother, Gene.
- Mayor Koch was vying for reelection in a city overwhelmed by racial tension.
- Newly appointed Police Commissioner Benjamin Ward was on shaky ground. He was desperate to hold onto his position and shore up his crumbling reputation.
- The massacre of eleven Puerto Rican women and children just upped the ante.
- Among those sadly forgotten victims was an unborn child. There was also one miraculous survivor who was subsequently adopted by a female police officer, who rose to become NYPD's highest-ranking female official.
- The Palm Sunday Massacre is the story of the brutal massacre of eleven women and children and of how the police, prosecutors, and the Italian mob came together in a sinister confluence of events to convict an innocent African American man.
- While under extreme emotional disturbance, Christopher Thomas stood accused and was found guilty of ten counts of first-degree manslaughter on July 19, 1985. He was finally released from prison on March 30, 2018, more than three decades later. He has always maintained his innocence.

Acknowledgements

It takes tons of work to generate a quality novel and I would be remiss if I didn't acknowledge the help I receive from my wife, Isabella, the unsung hero of my work who quietly reads late into the night to make sure that each and every one of my books is the best it can be.

At a time when good people are particularly hard to find, this author struck gold with Shawn Reilly Simmons and the LBB family. Happy to be aboard. A tip of the hat to a certain retired NYPD police officer for prying my eyes wide open.

About the Author

Lawrence Kelter hails from New York but now calls High Point, North Carolina his home. He is the bestselling author of more than twenty-five mystery and thriller novels including the Stephanie Chalice Mystery Series that has topped bestseller lists in the US, UK, and Australia. In 2017 he penned *Back to Brooklyn*, the studio-authorized sequel to the cult comedy classic "My Cousin Vinny."

Early in his writing career he received direction from literary icon, Nelson DeMille, who edited portions of his early work. Well before he said, "Lawrence Kelter is an exciting new novelist, who reminds me of an early Robert Ludlum," he said, "Kid, your work needs editing, but that's a hell of a lot better than not having talent. Keep it up!"

His novels are quickly paced and crammed full of twists, turns, and laughs.